CUNNINGHAM
SECURITY
SOLITUDE

A.K. EVANS

Solitude
Copyright 2019 by A.K. Evans
All rights reserved.

ISBN: 978-1-7328858-7-5

This is a work of fiction. Names, characters, places, and incidents are the product of the author's imagination or are used fictitiously. Any resemblance to actual events, locales, or persons, living or dead, is coincidental.

Cover Artist
cover artwork © Sarah Hansen, Okay Creations
www.okaycreations.com

Editing & Proofreading
Ellie McLove, My Brother's Editor
www.grayinkonline.com

Formatting
Stacey Blake at Champagne Book Design
www.champagnebookdesign.com

DEDICATION

To my ARC Team: Thank you for everything that you do.
I hope you love your cameos.

To my husband & my boys: Without you, I'd be in solitude.

PROLOGUE

Lorenzo

"DO YOU THINK I'LL EVER MAKE IT THERE?"

"Without a doubt. You're the hardest working, seven-year-old ice skater I know, Rocco. If you keep practicing, you'll end up in the NHL as a first-round draft pick."

"I'm going to be eight soon," Rocco reminded me.

I laughed. "I know. And then you'll be the best eight-year-old ice skater that ever lived."

Rocco turned sideways and started jumping up and down beside me. "Do you really mean that?"

"I'd never lie to you, Rocky."

My little brother and I were walking home as quickly as possible. It was Friday and the minute we got home from school we grabbed our skates, sticks, and a puck before we took off to the frozen pond not far from our house.

Mom didn't mind and mostly insisted that we get out of the house to play while we could. She trusted me to always look out for my younger brother. I had just turned thirteen and in two months, he'd be eight.

Given the opportunity, Rocco would spend all day, every day on the ice. It didn't matter that it wasn't my thing, I'd go and play hockey with my brother because he loved it that much. And when you lived the life we did, we'd needed something good that made us happy. My something good was making sure that Rocco was oblivious to anything else but hockey.

As we turned the corner onto our street, I looked down the block and saw the car in the driveway. I knew we weren't late; I'd kept track of the time. He was back early and that was rarely a good thing.

Not wanting to worry Rocco, but also wanting to make sure he wasn't going to witness anything bad, I came up with a plan.

"Hey, how about we have a campout tonight?" I suggested.

"A campout?" he wondered. "We're going to sleep outside?"

I shook my head as I picked up the pace. Rocco didn't miss a beat and kept right up with me. "It's January. We'd probably freeze if we did it outside, but we can pretend to have one inside. You can choose where we do it. My room or yours?"

"You mean we can turn my room into a campsite?" he bubbled with excitement.

"Sure."

"What about a fire?" he asked curiously.

Realizing I didn't have much time left, I explained, "We won't have a real fire, but we've got plenty of blankets to keep us warm. I have some ideas, but I'll need your help."

He looked up at me with wide eyes, waiting for additional instructions.

"We both know you're the best hockey player there is, Roc," I started, noticing the smile on his face growing by the second. "We need to see just how great of a camper you can be. I'll make sure I get our food for the campout. But when we get back, you need to go right to your room and get everything you can find to keep the bears out."

His eyes grew even wider. "The bears?"

"Yep," I answered. "Can you do that? Can you make sure you've got everything ready so the bears don't come eat our dinner or give us any trouble?"

He puffed up his chest and proudly announced, "I can do that. I'll make sure I keep us safe from the bears!"

We made it to the driveway and walked in through the open garage door. I turned toward Rocco, took the hockey stick from him, and put them away in the corner of the garage. He put his skates back where they belonged, right next to mine.

Just before we walked inside, I instructed, "Remember, bud, go right to your room and get everything you can find to keep the bears away."

He gave me a nod of determination.

Walking inside, I was surprised to find it silent. Rocco took off toward his room while I rounded the corner and walked into the kitchen. Mom was standing at the stove, plating dinner.

"Sorry, Mom. I didn't know he was coming back early," I apologized.

Her sad eyes came to mine. She spoke quietly, "It's not your fault, darling. I didn't know either. How about dinner in your room tonight? Can you keep your eye on Rocco for me?"

"Yeah," I promised. "Where is he?"

She jerked her head in the opposite direction. "In the shower."

I didn't respond. I gave my mom a look filled with worry. She saw it and immediately tried to reassure me, "Everything's fine, Lorenzo. Just make sure you watch out for Rocco, okay?"

"I will, Mom, but…" I trailed off.

"But what?"

"Is anyone ever going to watch out for you?"

Her lips trembled and her eyes started to get watery. "Don't worry about me," she whispered. "You just keep being the best big brother. Promise me you'll always do that."

"I promise."

She handed me two plates and ordered gently, "Go, darling."

I took the plates from my mom and watched as she started to give me the look. It was one she always gave me. Whenever I saw it, I knew she was proud of me.

"I love you, Mom."

She walked over, held my face in her hands, and moved her thumbs back and forth across my cheeks. "I love you, Lorenzo."

After she pressed a kiss to my cheek and one to the top of my head, she let me go. Even though I didn't want to leave her alone, I walked out of the kitchen toward Rocco's room. Once there, I found him prepared for our campout.

"I've got all of our stuff ready," he declared proudly.

"Good job, Rocco. I'm going to go grab a few things from my room and I'll be right back," I stated as I set the plates down on the floor in the middle of the room.

"Okay."

My room was right next to Rocco's, so I quickly ran out of his room to mine and got a few things I'd need to distract him. When I walked back in, he was sitting on the floor on the massive pile of blankets and pillows waiting for me.

I had finished most of my dinner and Rocco was about halfway through when he informed me, "I'm thirsty."

"I'll get you a drink," I said as I stood.

Suddenly, we heard the yelling.

Our father.

Rocco's frightened eyes came to mine.

He struggled to ask, "What if the bear gets you?"

"The bear won't get me, Rocky." I bent down and pulled one of the flashlights I'd gotten from my room out of the pile and handed it to him. "Here. Hide under the blanket with this until I get back."

He nodded slowly and took the flashlight from me.

Once he was underneath the covers, I went to get him a drink. As I walked down the hall, I could hear my mom crying.

My stomach started feeling funny. I hated this.

Hated it.

I made it to the doorway of the kitchen to hear my father scolding her. "You're nothing but a lazy, fat ass!"

Mom stayed quiet. She was sitting in the chair at the kitchen table while my father hovered over her.

He didn't stop. "I go to work every day to make the money that buys the food here and somehow you can't seem to ever make anything the way I like it. I'm beginning to think you do it on purpose."

I had no idea what he was talking about. I thought my mom made the best food.

She started to push the chair back away from the table so she could stand. She began apologizing, "I'm sorry, Vinny. I can make you something else—"

That's when he cut her off and did something I hadn't ever seen him do.

For the last five years, Dad had been getting angrier and angrier. He used to just yell. I noticed my mom crying more often. She was always happy when she was with Rocco and me. But when Dad was around, she never smiled. Over the years, his yelling turned to pushing. I eventually started seeing the bruises on her arms frequently and her legs occasionally. Sometimes, I'd stare at them, and if she noticed me looking, she'd quickly try to cover them up or distract me.

But never.

I'd never seen him strike her in the face.

Not until tonight.

I knew I'd never forget the sound of his hand as it connected with her cheek or the way it felt when I saw her head snap to the side. But most of all, I'll never forget the look in my father's eyes when my mom, with her hand covering the side of her face and tears filling her eyes, whispered, "Lorenzo."

I didn't know what the look meant, I just knew I'd never forget it.

"What are you doing out here?" he shouted.

I jumped back a step.

"Darling, go back to your room," my mom begged.

I tried to swallow, but it felt like something was stuck in my throat. "Rocco," I started, but my voice didn't sound like my own. My throat hurt. "Rocco needed a drink."

My mom quickly moved out from where she was and got a drink for my brother and me.

Handing them to me, she pleaded softly, "Please stay in your room."

Come with me. Because I'm so scared for you, Mom.

I wanted to say the words, but I didn't.

She put her hands to my shoulders and turned me in the opposite direction. After she gave me a gentle nudge, I walked back down to Rocco's room. When I entered the room, my brother's voice was trembling underneath the blanket. "Lorenzo?"

"It's me, bud."

I closed the door as he pulled the blanket from his face.

He looked so scared and I knew I felt enough fear for the both of us. I didn't want him experiencing it too, so I did my best to shake off how I was feeling and instructed, "Hurry up and finish your dinner. It's game time."

While Rocco finished eating his dinner, I went about building a tent for us to camp out in. It was really more of a fort, but he loved it regardless. Rocco and I then spent the next little while playing boards games under the fort. Most of them were meant for a kid his age, but I didn't care. I just wanted his mind focused on something fun and positive.

When he started yawning, I told him to go brush his teeth while I cleaned up the games. I joined him in our bathroom a minute later, brushed my teeth beside him, and followed him back into the bedroom.

"The bed or the tent?" I asked him.

"The tent."

We climbed under it together, put our pillows side-by-side, and settled ourselves under the blankets. As I laid there beside my brother in silence, I couldn't stop my mind from replaying what I saw my father do to my mother.

She was a girl.

And he was so much bigger than her.

She wouldn't ever be able to fight back and win.

But I was a boy.

I'd grown a lot in the last few months.

I was going to get bigger.

And once that happened, I was going to make sure he never hurt her again.

A long time had passed and just when I thought Rocco had fallen asleep, he surprised me when he called, "Enzo?"

"Yeah, bud?"

"Is it wrong for me to not like the bear?" he asked, his

voice worried and trembling.

I didn't know how to respond to his question. I never expected to hear him ask something like that.

Rocco went on, "He scares me. And he makes Mama sad."

He knew.

I hated that he knew.

"I don't like him either," I assured him. "But you don't have to be scared. I'll never let the bear get to you and hurt you, Rocky."

"We need to find a way to keep the bear away forever, Enzo. He hurts Mama."

"I know, bud," I sighed, not having any idea what to do. "I know."

A few minutes later, Rocco fell asleep.

It took me a lot longer to get there.

CHAPTER 1

Jolie

Eighteen Years Later

"HUDDLE UP, LADIES!"

That was me yelling out to the girls. I was at the bowling alley for Dom and Ekko's bachelor slash bachelorette party. Dom is my older brother, and Ekko is his pregnant fiancée.

We had split ourselves up into two teams, boys versus girls, and the girls and I were currently down by a lot of points. We'd already played one game and lost. I refused to see us lose again.

"Alright, here's the plan," I started, leaning into the huddle. "It's only the second frame, but if we keep this up, we've got no chance. They've got the strength to hurl the balls down the alley and take them down with sheer momentum. We've got to be smart. We need to distract them."

"What do you suggest we do?" Elle asked.

Elle was married to Dom's boss and the owner of Cunningham Security, Levi.

My eyes moved around the huddle before I answered, "Anything that'll work."

"When it's Dom's turn, I can pretend I'm having stomach

pains one round," Ekko suggested.

"Perfect," I praised. "Any other ideas?"

"I'll give Levi the look," Elle tossed out.

"The look?" Kendall, my older sister, asked.

Elle nodded and explained, "Yep, the look. After he sees it, he'll be too distracted thinking about doing naughty things to me that he isn't going to be able to focus."

"Kate and I will work on distracting Colton and Memphis," Ekko declared.

Kate is Ekko's maid-of-honor and co-worker from the Windsor Public Library. Colton and Memphis are my eldest brothers.

"That's good because not only can I not do that since they're my brothers, but Dom's going to lose his mind if you're being extra friendly to our brothers," Kendall noted.

Elle added, "That leaves Lorenzo for Jojo and Kendall."

I lifted my head from the group, looked over in the direction of the guys, and made eye contact with Lorenzo before I looked to the girls and declared, "Kendall might get the night off because that man is one I will have no problem attempting to distract."

Lorenzo De Luca was one of Dom's co-workers and he was heartbreakingly beautiful. It was rare that the size of a man impressed me because all three of my brothers were really tall and Dom, in particular, had a lot of bulk on him. Lorenzo may have been an inch or two taller than my brothers and he had a slight bit more muscle than Dom did.

Dark hair.

Dark eyes.

A neatly groomed, close-trimmed beard framing his perfect lips.

He was perfect.

And I liked the way he looked at me.

"Uh oh," Ekko said, snapping me out of my thoughts. "Ladies, I think Jojo has finally found her guy."

I grinned at the girls and confirmed, "Everybody ready?"

They smiled back at me before we all turned our attention to the guys.

"I don't like this one bit," Levi announced. "Those looks. They're up to something."

"This feels a little scary," Colton added nervously.

Dom tried to act unaffected. As Ekko walked over to pick up her ball, he got his. She walked slowly up to our lane while Dom kept his focus on his lane. Ekko sent her ball down the lane and knocked down eight pins. She was doing the best of the girls because she and Dom came bowling on a semi-regular basis. After her pins were down, she stood there watching and waiting for Dom to go.

Just as he started taking a few steps and swinging his arm back, she prepared herself. With near perfect timing, she doubled over and Dom's ball went flying into the gutter and he rushed over to her.

Still bent over, she turned her head to the side to look at us. She gave us a devilish grin before she lifted her head to him and burst out laughing.

"I've never seen you get a gutter ball!!" she cried through her hysterics. "That was great!"

"Sugar, that was not cool at all."

She acquiesced, or so it seemed. "You're right. I'm sorry. I'll make it up to you later."

Ekko finished her turn, knocked down one more pin, and Dom's mind was clearly on her making it up to him later.

Just as we had planned, Elle managed to do a great job distracting Levi with just one look. Colton and Memphis were easily distracted by Kate and Ekko. Of course, Dom was growing more and more frustrated seeing Ekko trying to distract his older brothers.

Unfortunately, when I tried distracting Lorenzo, I wasn't as successful. I had discreetly readjusted my top to show a bit more cleavage just before I walked over to get a ball. There was no doubt that Lorenzo noticed my ample breasts as I leaned over to grab a ball at the same time he did. His eyes heated, but beyond that, his game was not ruined.

"Not so easily distracted, big guy?" I wondered when we both came back to get our balls.

He cocked an eyebrow at me.

"Stop looking at her like that, De Luca," Dom ordered from behind us.

Lorenzo and I both looked at my brother.

"You've got nothing to worry about," Lorenzo assured him. "This one is nothing but a boatload of trouble, though."

Then, he lifted his ball, turned, and knocked down his remaining pins. Once they were down, he looked at me and smirked.

Damn.

I finished my turn, only knocking down a total of six pins, and flopped down in the seat between Kendall and Kate.

"Maybe one of you should try," I huffed. "He's clearly not attracted to me."

"Are you kidding?" Kate laughed.

"No."

Kendall put her hand on my leg and assured me, "He is absolutely attracted to you. Trust us. That man's eyes spoke for him. We just need to come up with another tactic."

I shrugged my shoulders. "What can I do?"

"Maybe he's too easily able to appreciate the visual aspect

of your game," Kate suggested. "What if you try getting physical?"

I sat up a little straighter and leaned in. "I'm listening."

"Girl, you've got boobs and an ass. We know he's not completely immune to the sight of your curves, but given what he does for a living as a private investigator, he has practiced the art of self-control and focus. You need to up the distraction."

"Hmm," I hummed.

I could do that.

As the rest of the girls and guys took their turns and we were slowly closing the gap in the score, I tried to come up with a plan.

When it was my turn, I walked up, but accidentally lost my footing. Inches before I went face first into the bowling balls, Lorenzo's arm caught me from the opposite side. His hand was at my belly, my breasts against his forearm. Tingles shot through my body and the only reason I put my hands out to push up off the balls and out of his hold was because I needed to see if Lorenzo felt the same thing I did.

Looking at him, I found his face littered with concern, but he mostly looked unaffected from a sexual tension standpoint. When he spoke, his voice was gruff. "Are you okay?"

I nodded and clarified, "That wasn't intentional."

"I didn't think it was."

Finding myself thrown slightly off-kilter, I picked up the ball and walked away to my lane. I managed to get down a measly four pins, but I figured it was better than a gutter. When I turned around to walk back to the ball return, I glanced over to see Lorenzo eyeing me. He quickly looked away and took his turn. I watched as his ball skimmed the edge of the lane all the way down, only managing to knock over a single pin.

The girls cheered from behind me while the boys groaned.

I could only barely register the sounds coming from behind me because my gaze was focused on the man in front of me. Lorenzo's eyes were narrowed and his brows furrowed, as he looked down at the ground a few feet in front of him.

Maybe I had been wrong. Maybe Lorenzo was the tiniest bit affected by me.

My ball came back, so I picked it up and moved to the lane. I did my best to focus, rolled it, and managed to knock down the remaining six pins.

A spare!

I spun around, locked gazes with Lorenzo, and sauntered right over to him. Pressing my hand to his chest, I felt him tense up before I taunted, "How do you like me now, big guy?"

He let out a laugh.

After I gave him a wink, I walked back over to where the girls were celebrating. They all congratulated me, and when I looked back at Lorenzo, I found he only got another two pins down.

Once he was back over by the guys, he glanced over at me. I couldn't read the look on his face. He wasn't angry, but he wasn't happy. If nothing else, he seemed contemplative.

My sister sat down next to me and whispered, "I think we found Lorenzo's weakness." When I directed my attention to her, she went on, "Physical contact with you."

I bit the corner of my lip and felt the giddiness overtake me. Maybe I wasn't a total turnoff and there was still a chance he might be into me.

We'd made it through several more rounds, the girls managing to get within a few points. When we were on the tenth frame, I knew I had to give it all I had. I took my time to concentrate on my lane, threw the ball, and got my first strike. I was so excited I began jumping up and down. Lorenzo was the closest to me since he was preparing to take his turn, so I closed the short distance between us and wrapped my arms around him to hug him.

The second I was there, I knew I didn't want to let him go, but I felt his body tense against mine. It took a moment, but one of his arms came around my back and gave me a gentle squeeze.

"Congratulations, Jolie," he said softly.

I beamed up at him, "Thank you, Lorenzo."

His head jerked back and his fingertips pressed into my skin a little harder. I loved it, but Lorenzo almost immediately dropped his arm from around me and stepped back.

Just like that, the warm feeling that had washed over me was gone. I moved back to celebrate my strike with the girls while Lorenzo matched my strike with one of his own.

The boys ended up winning.

After bowling, Dom and Ekko wanted everyone to join them back at their place. A bunch of Dom's co-workers met us there and the rest of the night was spent just hanging, chatting, and having a good time.

Sadly, as much as I had hoped to talk with Lorenzo, it never happened. We stole glances at each other throughout the night, but he never approached me.

To say I was disappointed when he left would be an understatement. The truth is, I wasn't exactly having much luck in the dating scene. It had been a long time since I'd had an official boyfriend, but dates weren't exactly easy to come by either. While I was overjoyed that my brother had found Ekko, there was a part of me that was feeling sorry for myself. I had seriously missed having not only physical intimacy but also companionship.

Two weeks later, I saw Lorenzo at Dom and Ekko's

outdoor wedding rehearsal. I would have been lying if I said that I wasn't secretly thanking them for pairing me with him. As we walked down the aisle, I took full advantage of being able to curl my fingers around his bicep and inhale the scent of him.

Following the rehearsal, the bridal party and a few close friends and family had dinner together. Elle was seated next to me on one side, Lorenzo on the other. Pre-wedding festivities had taken over and there wasn't an opportunity for me to have a conversation with Lorenzo. What I got instead might have been slightly better. Every so often, my arm brushed up against his or he'd send an intense stare in my direction. Those things made me feel far more than any conversation could have at that moment anyway.

At the end of the night, I made my way home to my condo and got ready for bed. While I left the rehearsal dinner feeling slightly disappointed, there was no denying that I had a serious crush on Lorenzo. Of course, a huge part of that crush was a result of his looks, but I was intrigued by the mystery of him. Unlike most of my family, an outgoing bunch, Lorenzo was quiet, reserved, and maybe even a little detached.

For that reason, and so much more, I found I wanted to know more about him.

The wedding reception wasn't far away and I was very much looking forward to having an opportunity to dance with Lorenzo. Something told me he wasn't much of a dancer, but I knew I'd have, at a minimum, the bridal party dance. Truthfully, I wouldn't care if he had two left feet. The sexual tension between the two of us was high and I just wanted to have my body pressed against his while he held me in his arms. On those thoughts, feeling very giddy, I fell asleep.

The next morning I was up early and out the door. All the

girls were meeting at the venue to get ready together. Once we'd made sure that our bride was looking stunning for her groom, we ushered her off for her first-look session with him. After Ekko had left to get some pre-wedding photos done with Dom, I pulled my sister aside.

"I'm freaking out, sissy."

She blinked her eyes at me. "Because Dom's getting married?"

I shook my head. "No. I'm freaking out because I can't seem to get a grip. Ever since we went bowling, my brain won't stop thinking about Lorenzo. I think I really like him."

"Jojo, you barely know him," she noted.

"I know," I agreed. "It doesn't make any sense. I'd like to get to know him, but we are the definition of opposites attract. I mean, I hope there's an attraction on his end."

"So why don't you try talking to him?"

I swallowed hard at the thought. "I want to, but he's so serious. What if he's just off-put by my outgoing nature?"

She shrugged her shoulders. "Then he doesn't deserve you. I know that's not what you want to hear, but if any man doesn't like you for who you are, you have to move right along. That said, I saw the way he looked at you when we went bowling a few weeks ago. That alone told me he is attracted to you. But yesterday? If I hadn't already thought so, yesterday would have solidified that for me."

I blinked my eyes and jerked my head back. "What do you mean? What happened yesterday?"

"During the rehearsal dinner, I glanced over at him a few times when you were rambling on about something to the entire table and he was looking at you."

"Okay," I began. "Considering I was talking, I'm guessing he was just looking at me because that's what you do when someone is speaking."

She shook her head. "No," she stated firmly. "He was *looking* at you. Trust me, there was a distinct look he had in his eyes. That man had just finished the whole plate of food in front of him, but Jojo, he looked at you like he was starving."

My breath caught in my throat.

"Do you think he's just shy?" I wondered after several seconds of silence had passed. "I don't mind making the first move if that's what it is, but I don't want to have my heart crushed if he's not interested."

"I'm honestly not sure. He's certainly quiet, but he also seems confident. Looking like he does and seeing how you've been around him, I'm guessing he knows you're attracted to him. It won't hurt for you to talk to him. I don't think he'd purposely try to hurt you. Keep in mind that he's one of Dom's closest friends. That alone is reason enough to assume he won't be a jerk to you."

I took in a deep breath. "You're right. Okay, I have to work up the nerve to say something to him at some point today."

Kendall smiled at me. "Good luck. You know I'm here for you if you need me."

"Always, sissy."

A few minutes later, Ekko was back and the wedding was about to start. We took our places and the next thing I knew I was standing at the end of the aisle in the gorgeous champagne-colored, plunging neckline, A-line bridesmaid dress Ekko had picked out.

As I walked down the aisle, my eyes first went to Dom. He gave me a look of adoration. I couldn't have been more proud than I was at that moment to be part of his special day. My eyes left Dom and slid to his left, where they moved past

Colton, Memphis, and Levi before finally settled on Lorenzo.

His eyes were glued to me and the intensity of his stare sent shivers down my spine.

I made it to the end of the aisle and took my spot. While I waited for the rest of the bridesmaids, and ultimately the bride, to join me, I couldn't help but look at the man standing in the same spot opposite of me.

Once the ceremony began, I redirected my attention and focused on the real reason we were all there. To witness two people commit themselves to each other. Two people I absolutely loved and adored. I felt myself getting emotional as Dom and Ekko said their vows to one another and had to fight to hold back the tears.

The next thing I knew, Dom was being told he could kiss his bride. After they turned and made their way down the aisle, I started feeling nerves in my belly. I took steps toward the aisle as each bridesmaid paired up with her respective groomsman. Just as Elle and Levi started walking away, Lorenzo came into my line of vision.

I was so distracted by him that I missed stepping over the aisle runner and tripped instead. Lorenzo's eyes widened briefly, but he acted quick and caught me before I fell. It happened so fast, but oddly, the second he wrapped his arm around my waist and caught me, he turned so that his back was to the guests.

"Sorry," I lamented as I moved to stand up straight.

He cleared his throat and got out a husky, "Your dress."

"What?"

"You're nearly exposed," he stated, his voice sounding strained.

I looked down and gasped. The cut of the dress was not conducive to nearly face-planting. That's why Lorenzo turned so quickly. He was using his body to cover me so that I didn't flash everyone at my brother's wedding. I hadn't completely fallen out of my dress, but I was certainly close.

I readjusted myself and looked back up at him. He wasn't looking at me. Instead, he had his head up and turned to the side.

Was he trying to be a gentleman?

I took a small step back. Lorenzo dropped his gaze to me and confirmed, "All good?"

Giving him a quick nod, I replied, "Thank you."

He didn't respond. Instead, he turned and held his arm out. I wrapped my fingers around his bicep and walked along-side him down the aisle.

After spending some time taking photos with the bridal party, we made our way to the reception. Introductions were made before Dom and Ekko shared their first dance. Immediately following their dance, the bridal party joined them on the dance floor.

Lorenzo put one arm around my waist and held me close while he wrapped his hand around mine. As we moved slowly with the music, I stared up at him and the rest of the world melted away. For the first half of the song, I did nothing but hold his intense gaze and enjoy being there with him. I eventually realized that if I was going to make a move, I needed to do it before the song ended.

"Thanks again for making sure I didn't completely embarrass myself earlier," I broke the silence between us.

"You're welcome. Are you always so clumsy?"

My eyes widened. "What?"

"That's the second time I've saved you from getting your face busted open," he clarified. "I'm just wondering if that's a normal thing for you."

I shook my head. "No, it seems to only happen around you."

He offered one slow nod but said nothing in response. His eyes left mine and he scanned the room.

"Lorenzo?" I called.

He dropped his stare to me and answered, "Yeah?"

"What's happening?"

He pulled his brows together. "Come again?"

"It's just..." I stammered. "I feel like there's something more going on here between us."

"Fuck," he muttered quietly, looking away from me. He took several moments to live inside his own head. When he looked at me again, his eyes were haunted. "Do you want this one day?" he asked.

"I'm sorry?"

"A wedding? Marriage? Commitment?"

I felt my body get tight. "Sure, yeah, I mean, one day I want to get married. But not now."

"Right. Then you need to understand now that I'm not that man and I never will be," he stated firmly.

"Okay," I replied, stretching out the word hoping to indicate my confusion at his statement.

He didn't offer an explanation, but I was still curious. Was he saying that he was okay with a one-night fling, but nothing long-term?

"So, if I had said that I was just looking for a hookup, would you have had a different response?" I wondered.

His eyes flared. "Is that your thing? Having a random hookup?"

I shook my head slowly. "No, but that doesn't answer my question."

He shrugged his shoulders. "If you were anyone else,

sure. But you're not just anyone else. And that means nothing will ever happen between us. Ever," he stated firmly and with such conviction.

My whole body went rigid as my eyes darted back and forth trying to figure out how I could have so easily mistaken the glances from him and the attraction I thought was mutual.

"I don't understand. Are you not attracted to me?"

Something flashed in his eyes. Regret maybe? Frustration perhaps? I couldn't tell, but it didn't matter because he answered, "Doesn't matter, you and I won't ever happen, Jolie."

Thankfully, at that moment, the song ended.

I pulled out of his hold and walked away. I went to the bathroom so I could pull myself together. When I stepped out a few minutes later and returned to the reception hall for the dinner, I stopped at the bar and grabbed myself a drink.

If Lorenzo didn't want me, that was his loss. Clearly, he believed I wasn't good enough for him. That was fine; I was going to enjoy myself tonight. I kept my attention focused on anyone and anything other than Lorenzo. As the night went on, I had more drinks and did a lot of dancing.

Putting him out of my mind, or at least telling myself that that is what I was doing, was the best decision I could have made. Because if I hadn't, I would have realized that he spent the rest of the night with his eyes on me.

CHAPTER 2

Jolie

Five months later

"**W**HAT DO YOU THINK ABOUT THIS ONE?"

I was standing in the dressing room at my favorite department store in the Windsor Mall with one of my closest friends, Ava Oliver. Ava and I work together at Serenity Salon and Spa where I am a massage therapist and Ava works as an esthetician.

It was Wednesday afternoon and we decided to take a trip to the Windsor Mall to buy new dresses for this weekend. Ava and I were meeting up with all of our co-workers for a night out. I wanted a new dress for this weekend's festivities, and being my partner-in-crime for these outings, Ava had driven us both here so she could also snag herself something fancy as well.

I was currently wearing a short, form-fitting, ultra-violet cami dress while asking for Ava's opinion. I figured one last purchase of a dress like this would be all I'd have left for this year because it was early October. It was still in the sixties, but within the next week or two, the temperatures would start dropping and tiny dresses would no longer be an option.

"If I had your body," she sighed. "You look incredible."

"Thanks, Ava. And I don't want to hear any of that. You are gorgeous, girlie," I shot back as I turned and assessed myself in the mirror one last time. "Alright, I'm going to get this one."

While she waited for me to change out of the dress and back into my clothes, she wondered, "Why are we still single, Jojo?"

I rolled my eyes. "I wish I had that answer. I mean, we're cute and fun. We have good jobs and we like people. I can't figure it out, but something's got to give soon. I'm going on the world's longest dry spell."

"I hear that. Let's hope we can meet someone this weekend because I'm getting desperate," she said.

After getting my clothes back on, Ava and I went to the cashier to pay for our dresses. As she was ringing up my purchase, my phone rang. I fished my phone out of my purse and saw Kendall's name on the display.

"Hey sissy, what's going on?"

"The babies are coming," she cried. "Dom and Ekko just got here a little bit ago and she's already halfway to the finish line."

I gasped. "Oh my goodness. Okay, I'm coming right now. Tell her to wait!!"

Disconnecting the call, I tossed my phone back in my purse and looked to Ava. "Dom and Ekko are at the hospital. The twins are on their way. Can you drop me off at Rising Sun Medical Center?"

"Absolutely."

I paid for my dress before Ava and I hustled through the mall to the opposite end where we had parked. We hopped in her car and sped off.

Once we pulled into the hospital parking lot, Ava pulled

right up to the front door. I grabbed my bag out of the back seat and yelled, "Thanks so much. I'll call you later."

"Send me pictures!" she shouted just before I closed the door.

I took off running through the door and right up to the information desk.

"Hi, um, my sister-in-law is here. She's in labor with twins. Ekko Moore."

"Okay, hang tight a minute while I look her up," the woman behind the desk said.

"Jolie," I heard the familiar deep voice come from behind me.

My body went tight, and I slowly craned my neck toward the sound that made me weak in the knees.

Just as I suspected, Lorenzo was there. I hadn't seen him since the wedding five months ago. He still looked as good as ever.

"They're on the fourth floor," he offered. "I'm heading up there now to wait."

I gave him a quick nod and glanced back at the woman. "Thank you."

Lorenzo and I walked to the elevators and I was beyond uncomfortable. He was one of my brother's closest friends, so it wasn't like I could just tell him to go. All I could do was hope that Ekko's labor progressed quickly and that she had the babies soon. I wasn't sure I'd be able to wait in the same room with Lorenzo for hours.

The elevator chimed and the doors opened. Nobody was inside, which made everything that much worse. I stepped inside and moved to the back corner. When I turned around, Lorenzo was looking at me with disappointment written all over his face.

"I'm not going to bite you," he muttered as he turned around and pushed the button for the fourth floor.

I gave his back an assured look. "I know that," I returned sarcastically.

His body didn't move, but he snapped his neck to the side so he could look back at me. "Still angry with me, I see," he pointed out.

"I'm not angry," I insisted.

"You've been angry from the minute that song ended at your brother's wedding."

It wasn't anger.

It was hurt.

Frustration.

Embarrassment.

I wasn't going to tell him that, though.

I shook my head and corrected him, "I wasn't angry with you. I was pissed at myself for thinking I was someone worthy of getting to know before being judged once again, especially by someone my brother holds in such high regard."

His brows pulled together. It was evident to me he must have been really good at his job as a private investigator because if I didn't know any better, I might have actually believed he had no idea what I was talking about.

"Jolie—" he started, but was cut off by the doors opening.

I didn't wait around to listen to what he had to say and walked past him off the elevator. Thankfully, I caught sight of Kendall within seconds. Kendall was a nurse at the hospital.

She saw me and started walking toward me when her gaze went behind me, stopping her in her tracks. I felt his heat at my back. Kendall knew what happened the night of the wedding because by the end of the night, I was hammered and spilled my guts to her.

Since she stopped walking toward me and Lorenzo was too close, I started putting one foot in front of the other and went to my sister.

"How is she?" I asked.

"In a lot of pain," Kendall began. "And tired. But she's already at eight."

"How's Dom?"

Kendall smiled. "He's so excited right now. He hates seeing her in so much pain, but he can't wait to meet those two precious babies."

"Who else is here?" I continued questioning her.

"Mom, Dad, Levi, and Elle are in the waiting room. Colton and Memphis are on duty, but they will be coming over as soon as they're off. Ekko called Kate to let her know. She's still at work and said she'd stop by as soon as she finished and closed up."

"Can I go see her?"

Kendall jerked her head to the side and answered, "Yeah." She looked behind me to Lorenzo and hesitantly asked, "Are you coming?"

I didn't turn around to see his response, but I heard him reply, "I'll be in the waiting room."

A couple seconds had passed when Kendall put her hand to my elbow and questioned, "What's going on?"

"Is he gone?" I whispered.

She nodded.

I let out a breath and my shoulders slumped. "I didn't know what floor Ekko was on. When I ran in and asked them at the information desk, he came up behind me and told me she was on the fourth floor. We had a hostile elevator ride and now I'm here."

"Hostile?" she repeated curiously.

I gave Kendall a rundown of our elevator ride.

Her brows furrowed. "It doesn't make any sense to me. I've seen the way he looks at you, Jojo. I saw it when we went bowling. I saw it at the wedding. And I saw it just now."

"Now?"

"Yes," she said softly. "Before he walked away, he looked at you like it physically hurt to have to walk in the opposite direction without you. Jojo, he definitely likes you. There's something else going on."

Kendall started walking and I fell into step beside her.

"I don't know. Unless...do you think it's Dom? Would Dom tell him to not pursue anything with me?"

"Not unless he had a good reason to do that. I know Dom was teasing him when we were bowling and you were pulling out all the stops to distract Lorenzo, but I really don't think that's it."

We stopped in front of a closed door. Kendall knocked before she opened it and walked in. I followed behind her. Ekko was sitting up in the bed, her legs hanging over the edge, while Dom stood in front of her. Her forehead was resting on his abdomen as she took slow deep breaths.

"Ekko, sugar, Jojo's here," Dom told her.

She turned her head to the side and let out a pained, "Hey."

"How's it going?"

"She's feeling it in her back," Dom explained. "It's marginally better when she's sitting up, but it's still not good."

I walked over to the opposite side of the bed. "What part of your back?" I asked her.

"From the middle and down," she answered.

I looked over to Kendall and held my hands up. "If she's okay with it, can I?"

Kendall gave me a nod.

I put a knee to the bed and leaned over toward Ekko. Putting a hand on her shoulder, I lowered my head next to hers and offered, "I've got magic hands, babe. Do you want me to try to help you out?"

"Dom tried already," she practically cried. "It didn't work."

I laughed and moved my hands to the middle of her back. "Yeah, I'm not surprised. I'm a professional; he is not."

"I'll do anything for some relief."

I got to work. Within seconds, she moaned, "Oh, Dom. After this is over, you owe me a year of Jojo-provided massages."

He chuckled and promised, "I can give you that."

"And you need to tip her well," Ekko added.

I grinned up at him and shared, "I knew I always liked her."

Dom shook his head in disbelief at me. He did it with a smile on his face, so I knew he was just happy that Ekko was feeling some relief.

For the next hour, I did what I could to help Ekko get through the most brutal part of her laboring. When she finally got to the point where she started feeling enough pressure to want to start pushing, her doctor came in to examine her.

I moved to the door to excuse myself when she called out to me. "Jojo?"

"Yeah, babe?"

"Thank you for being here for me."

I gave her a big smile and shared, "I wouldn't have missed this for anything. Good luck with your pushing. I'm not going anywhere until I know if I'm going to have two little girls or two little boys to spoil."

At that, I walked out and made my way down to the

waiting room. I knew Lorenzo was going to be there, but there was no way I was leaving. My nieces or nephews were about to be born and I was feeling like a big ball of love.

When I stepped into the waiting room, five sets of eyes came my way. Only one of them caused a tingle to run up and down my spine, though.

"Your sister was just in here," my mom informed me. "She said you were helping Ekko with her labor pains."

I held my hands up in front of me and joked, "Magic hands."

"How is she doing?" Elle asked.

"She's feeling the urge to push, so they're checking her now. I think our family is going to be a little bit bigger very shortly," I announced.

"Oh, the suspense is killing me," my mom cried. "I can't believe they didn't want to know if they were having boys or girls."

"Well, it shouldn't be much longer now."

As I looked around the waiting room, I realized I wasn't going to have a choice. The only seat vacant within the same vicinity as my family was the one next to Lorenzo. There were other chairs in the waiting room, but I wasn't going to cause a scene or be dramatic. This wasn't the time or place.

I took a seat next to him and watched my mom and dad direct their attention back to the television.

"I'm going to see if I can find some hot tea," Elle declared as she stood from her chair.

I was about to jump up and offer to go with her when Levi stood. "We could be here a little bit. I'll come with you and grab a coffee. Anybody want anything?"

I shook my head.

"I'm good," Lorenzo answered.

My dad declined, but my mom asked if they'd bring her back a hot tea.

Once Elle and Levi were out of the room, I realized that my parents were talking to each other, but I could barely hear them. I figured if I was having a hard time making out their conversation, they wouldn't hear me if I spoke quietly.

I turned my head in Lorenzo's direction and spoke softly, "I'm sorry about what happened on the elevator. I didn't need to be a bitch to you."

He shook his head. "Don't call yourself a bitch," he demanded.

"Okay, fine. But I'm sorry. I don't like to hold grudges and I'd be lying if I said I haven't been holding on to one. I'm going to be an aunt soon. I don't want to hold on to anger right now."

Something moved over his face, but he remained silent.

"Do you accept my apology?" I wondered.

Lorenzo offered a gentle nod and replied, "Yeah. I'm sorry, too."

He had nothing to be sorry for, but I didn't think it was worth getting into another argument with him. Instead, I asked, "Can we be friends? At least for today?"

"I can do that for you, Jolie."

I loved the way my name sounded as it rolled off the tip of his tongue. "Thank you, Lorenzo."

He dipped his chin. "So…magic hands?"

I wiggled my fingertips in front of his face and admitted, "People are willing to pay a lot of money for what these hands can do."

Lorenzo's jaw clenched as he stared at my hands.

"I'm a massage therapist. When I went in to see Ekko, she was having a lot of back pain. So, I did what I could to help her through it."

"That was nice of you," he remarked.

I let out a laugh. "Yeah, but then she told Dom he had to buy her a year's worth of massages with me and that he had to tip me well, so I made out."

For the first time since I'd met him, Lorenzo laughed.

Seeing that made my belly twist. He was such a beautiful man as is, but when he laughed, he was stunning. When he stopped laughing, his eyes came to mine and they were shining for a moment. The air left my lungs at the sight of them. It was short-lived and the dark intensity replaced the look within seconds. Even still, I knew I'd never forget seeing that light in his eyes for as long as I lived.

A few minutes later, Elle and Levi returned and the intimate moment I had with Lorenzo was gone. We all chatted about inconsequential things for a bit until the door to the waiting room opened and Dom stepped in.

The grin on his face grew and he announced, "I'm a dad!"

"Boys or girls?" Mom demanded to know.

I didn't know how it was possible, but he smiled even bigger when he answered, "One of each."

I jumped up out of the chair and ran over to him. Throwing my arms around his neck, I cried, "Congratulations, bro. I'm so happy for you." He thanked me and gave me a hug. My parents moved in to congratulate him, followed by Levi, Elle, and Lorenzo. Once everyone had the opportunity to congratulate him, I asked, "How's Ekko?"

"Perfect. Exhausted, but perfect."

"What are their names?" I pushed for more.

He jerked his head to the door and stated, "I'll let her tell you that. Why don't you all come down and meet my babies?"

We followed Dom down the hall and walked into the

room to find Ekko sitting there holding one of her babies in each arm. Kendall was sitting in a chair beside the bed gazing down at the precious little souls.

"I told them we have a boy and a girl, but I thought you could tell them their names," Dom said as he walked over to her.

The smile on her face grew before she announced, "Meet our son, Hendrix, and his little sister, Grace. We've already started calling them Hank and Gracie."

"Can I hold one?" Mom asked.

Dom looked to his wife and she gave him a nod. He took the baby closest to him and said, "Grandma, this is your grandson."

Mom immediately broke down into tears as Dad kept his arm wrapped around her back and looked at his new grandchild.

"Jojo?" Ekko called.

My eyes left Hank and went to my sister-in-law. "Would you like to hold Gracie?"

With the tears filling my eyes and the tightness in my throat, I couldn't speak. So, I nodded as I walked over to the bed.

The second I had my niece in my arms, my entire world changed. She was the most beautiful little girl I'd ever laid my eyes on. The love I felt for her was something I couldn't even begin to describe. I took my moment with her before I walked over to Elle, Levi, and Lorenzo. Elle and Levi were focused on Gracie; Lorenzo was looking at me intently.

"Isn't she just precious?" I finally asked the group.

Lorenzo still hadn't looked at her when he answered, "She is."

I swallowed hard and looked back down at the baby in my

arms. I managed to get another minute or two of snuggling in when my dad walked over and declared, "I think I'd like to hold my granddaughter."

I kissed the top of her head, handed her over to him, and immediately felt the loss. Thankfully, Mom filled the void by bringing Hank over to me and settling him in my arms. I looked down at the little boy and felt my heart swell.

"You're the big brother, Hank," I told him. "That means you've got an important job ahead of you. When you're older, you'll have to make sure you always protect your little sister. That's what your daddy and your uncles did for me and your auntie Kendall and that's what you'll need to do for Gracie. There's no other job more important than being the world's best big brother."

Hank didn't respond. He didn't even open his eyes.

I was so caught up in memorizing every feature on my nephew's face that I didn't instantly notice Lorenzo had walked out of the room. In fact, it wasn't until Kendall suggested that the first breastfeeding lesson start and Levi and Elle took that as their cue to leave that I realized Lorenzo wasn't there.

After Elle and Levi left, I congratulated Dom and Ekko again and handed Hank over. I promised them I'd be back the next day to visit. Once again, they thanked me for being there. I pressed a kiss to the top of Hank's and Gracie's head before I walked out.

Once I stepped out into the hall, I moved down the hall to the elevators. Lorenzo was there, waiting.

"You snuck out," I stated the obvious.

"I had to take a call," he explained the reason for his disappearance. "Congratulations on becoming an aunt."

"Thanks. Are you planning to head back down there?" I

wondered. "Ekko's learning the art of breastfeeding right now."

He shook his head. "Levi and Elle said. I'll let them have their time. I can visit them when they get home and get settled."

"I'm sure they'll like that."

Lorenzo gave me a nod before he shared, "When you arrived earlier, I saw you were dropped off. I thought you might need a ride home."

"Right," I muttered putting my palm to my forehead. "I completely forgot I didn't drive myself here. Are you sure you don't mind? I can get an Uber if it's out of your way."

"It wouldn't matter if it was. It's not a problem."

I offered him a friendly smile, feeling ashamed that I'd acted so poorly to him before. Clearly, he was a decent guy. If I wasn't his type, as hurt as I was about it, I couldn't be angry with him.

"I appreciate it."

At that, Lorenzo and I rode the elevator down to the ground level and walked side-by-side out to the parking garage. When we got to his truck, he opened the door for me. It was sweet and chivalrous, but I tried not to think too much about it.

After he got in, I gave him my address and he backed his truck out of the parking spot. Five minutes into our silent drive, I rested my head back on the headrest, turned toward Lorenzo, and sighed, "I think I'm in love."

It was a good thing we were stopped at a red light because his body went visibly tight and his eyes cut to mine.

I smiled and clarified, "With the babies."

The tension left his body as the corner of his mouth twitched. He turned his attention back to the light and I went on, "I know it down to my bones. In a matter of seconds, my whole life changed seeing those innocent little faces."

"I think that's a normal reaction," he assured me as he began driving again.

"Yeah, but I don't know if the rest of what I'm feeling is normal," I mumbled.

He glanced at me and asked, "What?"

"I don't know," I started. "I've never in my life been a violent person, but the second I held Gracie in my arms, I knew I would do anything to keep her and her brother safe. I'd kill someone just to protect them, or die trying."

It was silent in the truck for such a long time, I began wondering if I should have kept that thought to myself.

"Sorry," I lamented. "Maybe I shouldn't have said that."

Lorenzo pulled up outside of my condo. When he put the truck in park, he turned to me and said, "It's fine, Jolie. What you said is real. Some people don't have anyone strong enough to stand up for them. Nothing is ever going to come to harm those babies. Your brother alone will see to that, but it's good that they've got more than just him to look out for them. They're lucky to have you."

"So you don't think I'm a crazed lunatic for feeling that way?" I asked, though I wasn't sure why his opinion mattered so much to me.

His voice was deep and filled with emotion when he replied, "I find peace in it."

I held his eyes a moment, allowing his unique choice of words to settle inside me. I put my hand on his forearm resting on the center console and said, "Thanks for the ride home, Lorenzo. I'm glad we could move past the awkwardness of the wedding."

His eyes dropped to my hand on my arm. When he

brought them back to my face, he responded, "You're welcome, Jolie. Take care of yourself."

I didn't know why, but something about the way he said it made me feel like this friendship we forged was temporary. I had a feeling that Lorenzo had no intentions of continuing it after I got out of his truck. As much as it pained me to know that, I gave him a gentle squeeze on the arm and returned, "You too."

Then, I opened the door, grabbed my bag with my dress, and got out. It wasn't until I was safe inside the condo and looking out the window that I realized something bigger was going on. It was easily a good ten minutes after I'd walked out of the truck and closed the door before he pulled away and drove off.

CHAPTER 3

Jolie

IT WAS FINALLY SATURDAY, LATE AFTERNOON, AND I WAS STANDING outside the room I'd just finished an eighty-minute massage in, waiting for my final client of the day to emerge. Following any of my massages, it seemed like my clients took a bit longer to come out from the room.

I always took that as a good sign that I'd accomplished what most of them were there paying for…relaxation.

So, I didn't mind that I ended up standing there longer holding a small cup of water in my hand. And I typically found that the longer they stayed in there, the larger their tip was.

When the door finally opened and my client stepped out, I asked, "How are you feeling, Mrs. Mitchell?"

"Divine," she sighed.

I held the cup of water out to her, "Happy to hear it. Be sure to stay hydrated today and I'll see you in a month."

"I will, thank you. Have a great weekend," she replied before she walked down the hall and through the door to the front reception area.

"You too!" I called out.

I went into my massage room and started cleaning up. I had to remove the table linens and round up the used towels from the hot towel foot treatment into my arms before taking them down the hall toward the back of the spa where we washed everything. Afterward, I went back and made up the table so that it'd be ready for tomorrow. Once I'd completed all of my job-related tasks, I went to the employees' lounge in the back. Ava was standing there texting on her phone.

"Hey, Jo. All finished?"

"Yeah, I just got my room all taken care of, so I'm ready to head out."

"I'm still picking you up tonight, right?"

I nodded. "What time is everyone meeting up?"

Ava took in a deep breath and started, "Well, Niki, Michaela, Jennifer, and Tara are bringing their shenanigans to the party by no later than ten-thirty. Brandee, Susana, and Jenny said that that time would work for them, too. Amy, Joanne, Trudi, and Victoria are traveling the longest distance, so they'll probably be a little later, closer to eleven."

"The boys are coming, aren't they?"

"Yep, but I have no idea if they're arriving together or separately. They just said they'd be there. And considering they decided to take one for the team and stay close so all the ladies could leave early to get ready, I figured it was best to let them show up whenever is good for them."

"That's probably a wise idea. So, when is my chariot arriving then?"

Ava laughed. "Planning to meet your Prince Charming tonight?"

Lifting my arms to the side as I shrugged my shoulders, I answered, "I don't know, but if I had to guess, I'd say it's not likely."

"Our luck is going to turn around, girl. I know it's coming soon."

"How can you be so sure?"

"I'm not," she confessed. "It's just that I'm sick of buying batteries for my vibrator. It's been entirely too long."

I tilted my head to the side and wondered, "How is it that we spend our days getting paid to make people feel so good, yet we're left hanging night after night? This feels like some sick, twisted joke."

Ava threw her head back and burst out laughing. "We aren't delivering daily orgasms, Jojo!"

"Yeah, maybe not to our clients," I huffed. "I'm just saying I need some physical intimacy soon or I might combust. People can tell me I've got magic hands all they want. They aren't feeling very magical to me lately. I think it's because I've become too well acquainted with them!"

Ava continued to laugh. She walked toward me and threw her arm around my back to rest her hand on the opposite shoulder. "Let's get out of here so I can pick you up early and you can get a head start tonight," she suggested. "We'll get there before the rest of the crew arrives, scope out the place."

With that, Ava and I made our way down the hall to the reception area. Antonio, or Neo as we called him, was the only one out front. Neo was one of our massage therapists.

"We're heading out," I announced. "We'll see you tonight, right?"

"For the millionth time, yes," he replied sarcastically.

"Jojo and I are going to be there early to find her a guy. Her hands are tired from delivering too many self-induced orgasms."

I hit Ava's arm with the back of my hand. "Seriously?"

"What's this about orgasms?" Ethan wondered as he walked out from the back.

Ethan was our most highly sought-after male massage

therapist. Some of our clients preferred a male therapist and he was always in high demand.

I dropped my head back as I looked to the ceiling. "I love my friend, I love my friend, I love my friend," I chanted in an effort to calm myself.

"It's been a while," Ava went on. "Tonight, I'm her wing woman. Getting Jojo a guy is the goal, but if I've got to hang with the friend or something, I'll do it for my girl."

"How many guys do you really think we're going to find there by going early?" I scoffed. "Most people aren't heading out at nine o'clock. And if they are, it's certainly not the single ones."

Just then, the door that Ethan had walked through opened again and Samuel walked in. Samuel had always been a source of contention in the workplace. The other guys didn't seem to mind him, but he made the girls crazy, especially Jennifer. Mostly, she was perturbed by the fact that he refused to answer to anything but Samuel. If you tried getting his attention by calling him Sam, he'd flat-out ignore you.

I'll never forget the time she went on a rant about his insistence of being called Samuel at our first team-building night out after he started working with us. Luckily, he wasn't in the vicinity when she went off the deep end. "My name is Jennifer. Do you think people haven't ever called me Jen or Jenny before? It's not a big fucking deal. I mean, it's not like his parents paid for the use of the U, E, and L that he needs to get their money's worth. Your name is Samuel, dude. And Sam is a completely acceptable nickname!"

Ever since then, a valiant effort had been made to make sure Jennifer and Samuel didn't work together very often.

"This conversation is done," I announced, not needing to add Samuel to the list of people who knew about my lackluster or, more precisely, nonexistent sex life. "We'll see you tonight."

Before she could get another word out, I grabbed Ava by the hand and dragged her out of the spa.

"Go home and get ready," I instructed. "While you're doing that, try to figure out how you're going to be a good wing woman. You can't make me look desperate!"

"I've got you, girl. Don't worry."

At that, we both got in our cars and left.

Three hours later, I was finally ready. I had my new cami dress on with a fabulous pair of shoes. I'd done up my makeup and put some big curls in my hair. Fifteen minutes after I finished getting ready, Ava arrived.

She walked in and marveled, "I don't think you're going to need a wing woman tonight, Jojo. Holy crap you look phenomenal!"

"Thanks, babe. You're looking pretty hot yourself."

"Yeah, yeah, but I don't have the curves you do. Wow, your boobs look amazing," she exclaimed.

I rolled my eyes and laughed at her.

"You sure you don't mind driving tonight?" I confirmed. "We could call for a ride instead so that you can have a few drinks tonight, too."

"I don't mind," she assured me. "But I want to go now, so I hope you're ready to leave."

I grabbed my clutch, grinned at her, and marched over to the door.

The next thing I knew, we were walking into Carter's, a nightclub in downtown Windsor. It wasn't yet bursting with people, but it was well on its way.

Ava and I walked in and managed to snag two seats at the bar since nobody from work had arrived yet. She ordered a non-alcoholic beverage while I started with a vodka and cranberry.

"Food to go with your drinks?" she wondered.

"Probably not a bad idea," I agreed. "Tortilla chips with some spinach and artichoke dip."

"Want to split that with some mozzarella sticks?"

I grinned. "Mmm. Nothing better than bar food," I replied sarcastically.

We gave our food order to the bartender after she set our drinks down in front of us. Picking up her drink, Ava searched the area around us.

"What about that guy?" She jerked her chin in the opposite direction. "The one with the blonde hair. He's cute."

"Blondes aren't really my thing," I replied.

She continued searching the room and asked, "Alright, well, what about the guy standing over there? He's hot."

"Ava, he's perfect for you. He's too short for me," I pointed out.

She rolled her eyes at me. "You're being picky now."

I wasn't being picky. Aside from a guy needing to be a decent person, I believed you had to be physically attracted to any person you were going to be with. At five feet ten inches tall, and with the need to wear heels on a regular basis, I wanted a guy who was a bit taller than me. If he was any less than six feet two inches tall, it would never work for me.

"I would tower over that guy," I stressed. "He's definitely cute, but there's no way I could do it. A short guy is a hard limit for me."

She groaned her frustration at me.

Our food arrived a few minutes later and we dove in. I knew it wouldn't be smart for me to drink too much without having something in my stomach. As we ate, Ava kept her eyes peeled to the door, scouting for any possible suitors.

While she was unsuccessful in this, I noticed when she lifted her hand and started waving. I turned to see some of the girls from work had arrived.

"You finished?" she asked, nodding to the nearly empty basket of chips.

I nodded.

Feeling full and having had two drinks, I declared, "I need to use the ladies' room. Can you take care of the bill? I'll tell them to go get our seats and I'll meet you over there then?"

She nodded, so I pulled some cash out of my clutch and handed it to her.

Carter's always got crowded and we knew that if we hadn't reserved an area, it wouldn't have made for a very effective team-building event.

Hopping down from my stool, I took off toward the restroom. As was not uncommon for the ladies' room, there was a line. After waiting for a solid five minutes, it was my turn. I did my business and walked out of the stall to wash my hands. With my clutch tucked up under my arm, I felt it vibrate. I quickly dried my hands and stepped outside the restroom.

Pulling my phone out, I saw Ava had sent several texts.

OMG. I found the perfect guy for you. He's not blonde and he's really, really tall.

A second text followed that.

Jojo, this man.

I started laughing until I continued on to her third text.

I just approached him.

Oh no. I was going to kill her. I knew this once I read her fourth and fifth text.

He's single. I've confirmed it. He seems like he could be interested in a good time.

And he's nice.

I finally responded.

What is wrong with you?

She replied almost instantly.

Nothing. Get over here. I'm still over by the bar. I'll just make a quick introduction and skedaddle to our reserved area.

I let out a sigh. As I walked over, I came up with a game plan. I figured if the guy was hot and seemed nice enough, I could have a drink with him. If not, I'd blame my inability to chat on needing to not ditch my co-workers.

When the area of the bar where Ava and I had been sitting earlier came into view, I thought my eyes had to be deceiving me. Ava's back was to me as she was rambling on about something, likely me, to the man next to her. I had to give her credit. The guy was gorgeous. He wasn't blonde and he was tall. There was one small problem, though.

The man was Lorenzo.

I took in a deep breath, let it out, and moved over to her.

"...and it's been a while for her. I just want her to have a good time tonight," Ava said until she stopped speaking because Lorenzo was no longer paying attention to her.

He caught sight of me, ran his eyes over the length of my body until they settled on my face, and never returned his attention to my outspoken friend.

Ava noticed he was distracted and turned around to find me standing there.

"Here she is," she declared. "Jojo, this is...I'm sorry, what's your name?"

"Lorenzo."

"Right, sorry," she muttered. "Jojo, this is Lorenzo. And Lorenzo, this is my friend, Jolie. Everyone calls her Jojo."

I looked to Lorenzo and asked, "Would you excuse us one second?"

He gave me a nod.

I grabbed Ava's hand and dragged her a few feet away as she called out to him, "Save her seat!"

When we'd moved out of earshot of Lorenzo, I leaned in and seethed, "What did you say to him?"

Oblivious to what she'd just done, she was grinning from ear to ear. "First, I confirmed that he wasn't here with anyone and that he wasn't meeting anyone. Once I established that he was single and available, I told him, in not so many words, that I had a friend who needed some companionship before we had to buy stock in batteries."

I closed my eyes and stood up straight to pinch the bridge of my nose. "Please tell me you did not do that."

"Jo, have you seen him?" she cried. "That guy is gorgeous. I know you'd prefer to have a relationship, but if that guy can give your hands a break for the night, why not?!"

"I know him!" I nearly exploded.

She jerked her head back in surprise. "You know that guy and you haven't hooked up with him?"

Just then, a few more of our co-workers had arrived and walked up to us. I took in another deep breath and advised, "I'm going to go deal with the colossal mess you've just put me in. I'll meet up with you in a few minutes."

Ava took off with the girls from work and I turned back to Lorenzo.

I was in big trouble.

Lorenzo

That dress.

Why was she wearing that dress?

When I showed up at Carter's tonight, I honestly had no idea what I was doing. This wasn't my scene.

But for five months, I'd struggled not to think about her.

And then a few days ago, I saw her again. Ever since I dropped her off at home that night, I hadn't been able to get her off my mind.

Coming out tonight, I thought I might be able to find a way to distract myself from her.

Evidently, I was wrong.

Because now she was here and her friend had just shared some very personal information with me. Information that, if I was being honest, I didn't mind knowing when I didn't know who her friend was. Of course, now knowing that information, knowing it was Jolie who hadn't been with a man in a long time and seeing her in that dress, I couldn't get the images of her pleasuring herself out of my brain.

She stood there scolding her friend, I assumed, for approaching me without her prior knowledge. And I couldn't do anything but watch her and fight the urge to go over, scoop her up in my arms, and carry her out of here.

Her friend and a few other girls who arrived walked off and she looked over at me. She wanted to come over and talk, but I knew she was struggling to move. I jerked my head to the stool next to me, and she finally walked over and sat down next to me.

"I'm sorry," she lamented. "My friend's heart was in the right place, but she doesn't know when it's too much sometimes."

She was talking and I could just barely pay attention to what she was saying. Jolie's scent overpowered me, and she looked amazing. If there was ever a girl perfect for me, it was her. She was tall, with legs that went on for days. Long dark hair, a gorgeous ass, and full round breasts were some of her greatest assets. A man would consider himself lucky to have a woman with just one of her physical features, but she had all that and something else.

Something even better.

A smile, marked with one beautiful dimple, that when she blessed you with the sight of it, you couldn't help but be mesmerized by it. Her personality was the opposite of mine. I'd been around her a few times now, and it was not lost on me that she wore her heart on her sleeve.

Snapping myself out of my thoughts, I assured her, "No need for an apology. Your friend said you were here for a work thing?"

I figured it was best to redirect the conversation to something else.

She nodded. "Yeah, we do this once every couple of months. All of us get together outside of work for a bonding experience, if you will. Half of them have already arrived, I expect the rest will be here soon."

Jolie got dressed up like she was now at least once every couple of months and came out to a place like this to bond with co-workers?

When too much time had passed and I hadn't responded, she asked, "What are you doing here?"

Trying to distract myself from you, I thought.

"I haven't been out in a long time. Figured I'd get out for a bit," I answered.

Her eyes moved back and forth like she was trying to

figure something out. "Well, I hope you have a good time then. And please ignore whatever my friend told you."

I wish I could.

Jolie continued, "She didn't know that we already knew each other or that...well, just ignore whatever she said. I already know where I stand."

She uncrossed her legs and stood from the stool. I didn't like what she said. It was the second time she indicated to me that she had a clear misunderstanding of things.

"Jolie," I called before she could walk away.

"Yeah?"

I wanted to tell her.

Instead, I shook my head and ended, "Nothing. Just...take care of yourself."

She lifted her chin slightly, curiosity washing over her face. If she had a question, she never asked it.

Then, she turned and walked over to her co-workers, and I watched her legs and ass the entire way.

I might have made decisions about how I'd live my life, but that didn't mean I couldn't appreciate beauty when I saw it.

And Jolie Moore was sheer beauty.

CHAPTER 4

Jolie

"**J**UST GREAT," JENNIFER SNEERED. "THE DOUCHE CANOE has arrived."

We all turned our heads to look and, sure enough, Samuel was walking over to the group.

"Time to dance," Michaela announced, attempting to diffuse the situation before it even had the opportunity to get out of control. She knew that Jennifer mixed with a bit of alcohol would result in a bit more than her usual amount of snark.

At that, about half of the girls got up to dance.

I was one of them.

Samuel was the last of our group to arrive and in the time that I joined my co-workers after my conversation with Lorenzo and now, I'd successfully downed another two drinks. As a result, I was feeling good.

Truthfully, I was feeling as good as anyone who had four drinks in them would feel. It was my only option, though. Taking the time to ponder the millions of thoughts I had about Lorenzo would not have likely ended well, so dancing was a nice distraction.

When I first joined the group after my talk with Lorenzo, Ava tried to get the scoop from me. Next to my sister, Ava was my closest friend. I'd give her the details, but I wasn't going to do it tonight. To set her mind at ease, though, I explained that Lorenzo worked with Dom at Cunningham Security and that he wasn't some psychotic ex-lover or anything like that.

Over the next few hours, I thoroughly enjoyed my time with my co-workers. We danced, we sang, we drank, and we had a whole lot of laughs. Throughout the night, I did steal glances at Lorenzo. Occasionally, I'd catch him looking in my direction. That made me feel good, but also very frustrated. I couldn't begin to understand why someone would give off the vibes that he did and not want to pursue anything, especially considering I'd made it very clear that I was interested in him.

At one point during the evening, I'd looked over and saw a woman had walked up and sat next to him. She started talking to him and I felt a wave of jealousy run through me. That feeling made me angry because while I'd grown accustomed to guys not liking my outgoing personality or my willingness to always just say what's on my mind, I didn't like how it felt knowing that Lorenzo was one of those guys. I didn't like that I felt such a strong attraction to him and he, without ever really getting to know me, had written me off.

I saw the woman that was talking to him lean in a little closer and put her hand on his arm. I couldn't take it anymore. I turned away and looked at Ava.

"I think I'm ready to head out," I told her.

"Really?" she asked. "We're having such a good time, though."

"I know, but I'm just not feeling it anymore. I think I'm destined to live the rest of my life alone," I pouted.

Yes, I was pouting.

Just then, Ava's eyes looked behind me and grew wide as I felt a hand settle low on my back. I tensed briefly as I turned to the side.

Standing beside me was a very handsome man. He was tall. Tall enough to meet my height requirements. And he had dark hair. He wasn't nearly as built as Lorenzo, but he was certainly in great shape.

"I just wanted to tell you that I think you look really pretty," he started. "I know that probably makes me sound like I'm totally hitting on you, which if I said I wasn't, I'd be lying. But in all honesty, this color looks amazing on you. I thought you should know."

At least he cut to the chase and didn't try to cover up his motives.

I offered a friendly smile and returned, "Thank you."

He held his hand out to me. "I'm Colin."

"Jolie," I replied, putting my hand in his.

"It's nice to meet you, Jolie."

He was silent a beat before he asked, "If I asked you to dance with me, would you turn me down?"

My eyes moved to the side where I had a clear shot to where Lorenzo was sitting. I found that he was no longer at the bar. Neither was the woman that had been talking to him.

I glanced back at Ava, a few of the girls from work, and all of the guys. They all had encouraging looks on their faces.

"I'd love to dance," I finally answered.

Colin grinned and escorted me away from my friends and out onto the dance floor. I had a great time and he wasn't a total creep. He kept a reasonable distance and allowed me to be the one to close the gap between us. It was nice to have a guy be respectful.

As the night began to wind down and some of my co-workers left, Colin pulled me off to the side.

He had moved us toward a dark corner of the room and

I suddenly didn't have good feelings about it. Initially, his back was against the wall and he had pulled me close to him with his arm around my waist.

Using my hands to push against his chest, I said, "Let me go. I'd like to go back over with my friends."

"Oh, come on," he began, a smirk spreading across his face before he turned and pressed my back against the wall. "We're just getting started."

"No," I stated firmly, pushing harder against him again. "Please move and let me go."

Colin shifted and pushed his forearm into my throat, pinning me tighter to the wall, forcing me to struggle to breathe. He lowered his head and just before he put his mouth on my chest, I lifted one leg off the floor and sent my knee up, right between his legs.

Instantly, he removed his arm from my neck as he doubled over in pain. It took me a second to catch my breath. I got about two steps past him when my head jerked back and I heard him yell, "You bitch!"

He was pulling my hair, yanking me backward toward him when suddenly he stopped and released my hair. I turned around and saw Lorenzo with his hand at Colin's throat, squeezing.

"If you *ever* put your hands on her or any other woman again, I will make it my life's mission to see to it that you spend the rest of your life breathing through a tube," he clipped. "Do I make myself clear?"

Lorenzo's hold on Colin had to be tight because Colin's face had started turning red. He held his hands up and croaked out, "Yeah, man."

A second later, Colin dropped to the floor like a ragdoll. Lorenzo turned to me and asked, "Are you okay?"

I nodded. "Yeah, thank you for helping me."

"Did you drive here?"

I shook my head. "No, my friend did."

"Good. I'm taking you home now, Jolie," he advised.

I blinked my eyes in surprise. "What?"

Lorenzo didn't respond with words. His face got angry, but he stayed silent. Even in his silence, I realized he meant business. Considering he'd just helped me out of a scary situation, I figured it was best to let him take me home.

So, I spun on my heels and found my friends. When they saw me and, more accurately, Lorenzo standing beside me, conversations came to a halt and they stared at us.

"Hey, guys, I'm calling it a night," I announced through the awkward silence.

Ava immediately walked over to me and pulled me into a hug. With her mouth at my ear, she whispered, "Are you alright?"

"I'm fine, I promise. I'll call you tomorrow."

She gave me a squeeze before she let me go. I said goodbye to the rest of the group before I turned and walked toward the front door. Once we were outside, Lorenzo put his hand to the middle of my back and guided me through the lot to his truck. He opened the passenger side door for me and helped me in.

The entire ride back to my condo was filled with silence. The anger rolling off the man next to me was so palpable. I was going to say something but thought it would be best to give him some time to cool off instead.

When he pulled up outside my place and put the truck in park, I turned toward him and said, "Thank you for the ride."

"No," he stated before he got out of the truck, leaving me stunned and in shock.

What was going on with him?

He came around to my side and opened my door. After I stepped out of the vehicle, he closed the door, beeped the locks, and walked alongside me to my front door.

As soon as I had my key in my hand, I tried again. "Thanks for walking me to the door."

"In," he ordered.

I raised my eyebrows and replied, "Yes, boss."

I heard him growl as I unlocked and opened the door, disabled the alarm my brother had installed a few years ago when I moved in and turned on the lights. Lorenzo had come in behind me but stood just inside the door. I hadn't invited him in, so if he had something he wanted to discuss he was going to have to start talking.

"Did you know that guy?"

"I just met him tonight," I answered.

Lorenzo's hands were balled in fists at his sides. Evidently, the silent drive did little to help with the rage he was feeling.

"I thought you were supposed to be bonding with your co-workers," he pointed out.

"I was, we were," I huffed.

"So why was that guy anywhere near you?"

I jerked my head back. "What do you care?"

"If I pick up the phone right now and call your brother, I can guarantee you that he'll not be happy hearing what I just witnessed."

"You wouldn't do that," I dared him.

"No?" he countered. "Then how about you tell me why the hell a woman as smart and beautiful as you, who's been getting herself off with a vibrator or her own damn hands for more than a year now, suddenly decides to find a man tonight? What were you thinking?"

He thought I was smart and beautiful?

I tried to ignore the fact that he'd paid me those compliments.

I also made a mental note to kill Ava for sharing such personal information with him.

"What was I thinking?" I shouted. "I was thinking I went out tonight to have a good time. I was thinking that for the first time in a long time a guy actually had something nice to say about me. I was thinking it felt good to not be judged. And I was thinking I needed to find a way to distract myself from the fact that you want absolutely nothing to do with me, but you had no problem leaving Carter's with that woman who sat next to you, talked to you, and touched your arm."

I gasped.

I hadn't meant for that last part to come out.

Lorenzo's face changed, but I only had a second to register the look before he was moving toward me. He framed my face with his hands.

"I didn't leave with anyone," he whispered. "And you're wrong about me wanting nothing to do with you, Jolie. I want you so bad I haven't been able to think straight for the last five months."

My eyes rounded at his admission. "What?" I rasped.

Lorenzo didn't answer.

At least, not with words.

He leaned forward and crushed his lips to mine. I was stunned, so I opened my mouth to ask him what he was doing and he took the opportunity to slip his tongue inside. The moment I tasted him, I let go of the shock. It was replaced by burning hot desire for him.

The minute I moaned into his mouth, Lorenzo's control slipped a bit. One of his hands wrapped around the back of my head while the other went around my back and shifted me forward, closer to him. My tongue tangled with his as we took the kiss deeper.

Then, we were in a frenzy. My hands were at his shoulders, my fingernails digging in. His hands moved again, one at my hip and the other at my neck. Lorenzo's mouth left mine and his lips began trailing desperate kisses along my jaw and down the side of my throat.

I dropped my hands to his waist, bunched his shirt up, and finally touched my fingers to warm skin. His body was solid and powerful, but the warmth coming from him made him feel inviting. I pushed the shirt up his body until I could go no higher and Lorenzo disconnected his mouth from me to pull the shirt over his head.

I barely had a moment to take in the beautiful sight of his bare chest and abdomen when he distracted me.

"This fucking dress," he muttered, bringing his mouth to mine again while his hands went to the dress at my legs.

His fingers touched my thighs, pressing in only briefly, just before he began sliding my dress up. He got it up over my ass and my breasts, pulled his mouth from mine and tore the dress off over my head.

Wasting not a single second, he lifted me off the ground, one hand catching me under my bottom, the other at my thigh. My legs instinctively wrapped around his waist as my shoes fell from my feet to the floor. I lowered my head and pressed my lips to his neck, my tongue darting out to taste him. I couldn't get enough.

"Bedroom, Jolie. Which way?"

"Upstairs," I panted. "Second door on the right."

I felt him moving but didn't pay attention to where he was going. All I could concentrate on was the utter pleasure I already felt having my skin touching his and how I knew it was about to get a whole lot better. As he climbed the stairs, I continued to taste him while I ran my hands along his shoulders.

Seconds later, he lowered me to my back in the bed and stepped back to look at me. Never taking his intense eyes from me, he worked to kick off his shoes as he pulled his wallet from his back pocket. He tossed the wallet to my nightstand before removing his jeans.

The moment they were off, his body was over mine, his hands were everywhere, and his mouth roamed to cover every inch of my exposed body. The palms of Lorenzo's hands were rough, and I loved the way they felt against my skin. One hand came up, tugged down the material covering one of my breasts, and his mouth clamped down over my nipple. My back arched as I moaned in response.

"Lorenzo," I rasped.

He shifted his body to the side and took me with him. With his back to the bed, his hands came up behind me, unhooked my bra, and tossed it to the side. Then he rolled us so I was on my back again.

He had turned his body toward mine but didn't come to settle over me. Instead, propped up on his elbow, he lowered his mouth to mine again and let his free hand trail down my abdomen until it reached the edge of my panties. He slid his fingers under the fabric and instantly moved them through my wetness.

My hips bucked.

He slid a finger inside.

The moan that escaped from the back of my throat was captured in another kiss.

He slid a second finger in.

His hands were big, his fingers long.

I felt every inch as those two fingers moved in and out. And I needed more. I needed it harder, faster. I rode his fingers hard, desperately seeking to relieve the ache.

His mouth left mine and he muttered, "Fuck, baby."

Baby.

"Lorenzo," I breathed, unable to get out anything else, feeling myself so close.

And in that moment, I lost his fingers.

"Panties," he asserted as he lifted up and moved off the bed.

I wasted no time. Slipping my fingers under the fabric at my hips, I tugged them down my legs. He watched as he removed his boxer briefs and pulled a condom out of his wallet. As he tore it open with his mouth, I used that time to check him out. Everything I'd felt leading up to this moment was true.

Lorenzo was a large man...everywhere.

"Spread for me," he ordered as he began rolling on the condom.

From the minute we were in his truck outside my place, he'd given me several commands, mostly one word, and I never expected it'd turn me on as much as it was at this precise moment.

I felt the flush hit my cheeks, but I parted my thighs.

The next second, he was positioned between my legs. He inched forward.

"Take me," I begged.

"You're tight." His voice was thick, strained.

He pulled back and inched forward again, this time only a bit more than he previously had gone.

"Lorenzo, please," I pleaded. "I need more."

"I'm not going to hurt you, Jolie," he shared, pulling back

and pushing back in, but not completely.

"You won't, boss. Take me," I encouraged him.

"Slow," he replied on another outward glide.

I could feel the tension in his body, the loose hold he had on it.

I brought my hands up to frame his face. "Please, Lorenzo," I stressed. "Fuck me now please."

Any restraint he had left vanished and he entered me completely. I moaned in delight, my back leaving the bed, at the pleasure I felt from the fullness of him inside me.

As he began moving slowly, he whispered a strained, "Most beautiful woman I've ever seen."

If the utter delight I'd already been feeling from just having his body joined with mine wasn't enough to get me there, those words would have done it. I could have cried at how good they made me feel and how deeply I felt them.

"Boss," I exhaled, unable to say anything else.

He picked up his pace and I couldn't hold back anymore. "Baby, give it to me," he urged.

So, I gave it to him.

And it was phenomenal.

My limbs convulsed around him, my thighs pressing tight to his side as my back arched and I pressed the back of my head farther into the pillow beneath me. In the middle of it, I felt a rough, calloused hand cover one of my breasts.

He thrust a few more times before he drove in deep and buried himself, an intense growl escaping him as he came.

Lorenzo collapsed on top of me briefly, but quickly pulled out and rolled to the side.

"Bathroom?" he wondered.

"The next room," I answered.

"Be right back."

At that, he got up and walked out of the room. He was gone a long time and I started to worry. When he walked back in, I learned I had every reason to be concerned because he said four words in a tone that was low and foreboding.

"We need to talk."

CHAPTER 5

Lorenzo

ONE DECISION.
One choice.
And then, life changes.

I made a promise to myself a long time ago that I'd never turn into him. I'd never allow it to even become a possibility. So, while I'd certainly had an appreciation for the female form over the years, I decided to never get involved beyond the point of a one-night stand. Any woman I was with knew this and if she wasn't okay with it, nothing happened.

Five months ago, I told Jolie there'd never be anything between us. I did this because I knew she wasn't a girl who'd want just a one-night stand. I was close with her brother; I knew she came from a good family. She was everything I wasn't. She deserved to live free to be happy without fear.

And tonight, I took that away from her.

Because now I was in her bathroom disposing of a condom after having her for the first time and I knew it wasn't enough. I needed more of her.

Her body, her mouth, her dimple. Her larger-than-life personality.

But I needed to be fair to her. She needed to know what

she just signed up for.

I pulled myself together, walked out of the bathroom, and stepped back into her bedroom. In the time that I was gone, she had flipped on the bedside lamp.

"We need to talk," I advised.

Jolie had moved under the blankets, but at my words, she sat up in the bed and tugged the cover up higher. She nervously bit her lip.

I hated seeing her worrying like that.

"Do you want to do it here?" I asked.

She shrugged. "I...I don't know. This feels like it's going to be bad."

I sat on the edge of the bed and twisted my body to look back at her gorgeous face.

It could be bad. I knew it would be bad for me if she decided she couldn't handle what I was about to tell her. And if she decided she could, I knew it had the potential to be bad for her down the road. That, without a doubt, was far worse.

She swallowed hard. "What is it?"

"I lied to you."

Her eyes widened and she wrapped her arms tight around her body, already visibly uncomfortable with where she thought this was headed.

"At the hospital," I clarified.

Her face changed and she grew curious.

"I walked out when you were holding Hank, but it wasn't because I had to take a phone call," I explained.

"Oh. Well, why did you leave then?"

I let out a sigh. "It was because of what you said to him."

"Me? What did I say?"

"You told him that the most important job he'd ever have was being the best big brother he could and that he needed to always protect his little sister."

I stayed quiet a minute, trying to figure out how to tell her what I hadn't told any other woman.

"Lorenzo, I don't understand."

"That's because you're a Moore and your parents are who they are," I noted after some silence had passed between us. "I spent the better part of my childhood doing everything I could to protect my younger brother from a monster."

Her lips parted in shock.

I continued, "I did everything I could think of to shield him from that."

Jolie was silent for a long time. Eventually, she whispered, "What happened?"

I closed my eyes.

She wanted to know. She wanted the ugly truth.

I heard the movement before I felt her touch. Her warm, soft body curled up behind me and instantly brought me peace. Peace that, anytime I recalled this awful part of my life, eluded me. Her arms wrapped around me from behind.

She waited.

"It started when I was eight. My brother was three," I said.

Jolie's arms tightened.

I went on and told her everything that happened over the years. She stayed close, her body tight against mine and somehow pressing in farther with each word I spoke. I explained how the abuse against my mother started and how it got progressively worse over the years. Then, I told Jolie about the day I saw my father hit my mother in the face and how I decided that day to put an end to it.

I paused a moment and felt a drop of wetness land on my back.

She was crying.

I brought my hands to hers, disconnected them from in front of me, and turned toward her. Picking Jolie up, I settled her in the bed and curled up next to her. After I pulled the blanket up over our hips, I ran my hand gently up and down her back.

"It's too much," I muttered, angry at myself for having upset her.

Her hand was pressed against my chest. "No, I want to hear it. It's just…I'm so sorry. This makes me sad."

I didn't tell her anything else. I didn't say another word.

"Lorenzo?" she called.

"Yeah, baby?"

"Did he ever hurt you?"

My hand stopped trailing up and down her back. "He tried to," I shared. "Once."

"What happened?"

"After I made my decision to put a stop to it, I did what I had to do to make sure he wouldn't be able to get the best of me. I was a teenage boy, so I started working out a lot, eating a lot. Within three years, I'd added a considerable amount of strength and some size. Add raging hormones to the mix and I was a force. During those three years, I did my best not to leave Mom alone, but I was in school. And as soon as I could start working at fifteen, I knew I needed to so that when we got out of there, we'd have money. I came home from work one day and found Rocco hiding outside in the garage. He was scared and didn't know what to do so he went outside to wait, knowing I'd be home soon. My parents were inside and I could hear my father yelling at her."

Jolie's body tensed as she braced for what was coming.

"Are you sure you want to hear this?" I confirmed.

She nodded and cuddled closer to me.

"Rocco told me our father had come home from work and immediately started calling her names and complaining about dinner. That was typically how it always started with him. There wasn't any name he didn't call her. Stupid bitch, worthless cunt, and lazy, fat ass were his favorites. Dinner was almost always a problem for him. She was a great cook, but he'd find something to bitch about. And then he'd take it out on her."

"That's awful, Lorenzo. What did you do that day?"

I took a minute to collect myself. "I told Rocco to wait until I came out to get him. Then, I walked in. Nothing could have prepared me for what I saw. My mom was pinned against the wall, my father's arm up at her throat, her eye swollen shut, and his free hand groping her as he screamed things at her I don't want to repeat. I slammed the door shut and yelled at him to get his hands off her."

"Did he?"

"He dropped his arm from her throat and turned toward me. He was shocked because I hadn't ever spoken to him like that. I'd never gotten involved in their fights before then. I told him that it was stopping and that he was never going to put his hands on her again. He came at me slowly and thought he'd catch me off guard, but I'd been preparing for that day for three years. He took a swing at me, I ducked, and then I let my strength, adrenaline, and rage over what he'd been doing for years take over. I eventually had him pinned to the ground, gasping for air. My mom called out to me, telling me I was going to kill him. I told her that if she wanted to be sure I didn't murder him that she needed to call the police. She hesitated for about two seconds before she called them. I held him down until they arrived."

"Lorenzo," Jolie cried.

"Even though there were our accounts of what happened and my mother's clearly-visible injuries, my father had no prior convictions. This was the first report of any domestic violence, so he was able to get deferred sentencing. Essentially, he had to pay fines, do a bunch of community service, not leave the state, stay employed, and have no further arrests. We slept in the house that night, but it was our last night there. I told my mom I had been working and saving all my money. We got out the next day, Mom got a job, and we never saw him again."

Jolie and I stayed there for a long time, neither of us saying anything. When I could no longer stand the silence, something that I'd grown to love over the years, I spoke. "It's killing me not to know what's going through your mind right now."

"I'm honored that you chose to share this with me, but I'm not sure I understand why you did," she answered honestly.

"Five months ago, you made it clear that you were interested in me. As attracted as I was to you, I insisted that nothing would happen between us. When I saw you at the hospital a few days ago, I was thrown right back into having to fight your pull. It was like a magnet. Tonight, you showed up in that dress and I fought against everything in me not to go back on what I said months ago."

"I didn't think you liked me at all," she shared. "Well, I originally thought you might be attracted to me, but then the wedding happened and I realized I'd read you wrong. Or, I thought I had."

I needed to set something straight. "This is something we've got to talk about in a bit more detail, Jolie. I don't know what's happened before now, but let it be known that there's not a single thing about you that I find unattractive."

She tipped her head back and looked up at me.

"You're the most beautiful woman I've ever laid my eyes on."

Wetness hit her eyes.

I continued, "And I'm not just referring to your face and your body, both of which deserve some serious compliments. Deep down, the woman I see, Jolie, you're beautiful."

"How did we end up here now?"

"Seeing you looking like that, dancing, after your friend told me you hadn't been with a man in over a year, I couldn't tear my eyes away from you. Until I did. And that asshole put his hands on you. The woman at the bar, she was the friend of a girl who'd been involved in a bad case I was investigating a while back. She saw me and recognized me from that. Her friend is doing well, and she wanted just to thank me for the role I played in that case. I saw her safely out to her car. When I came back inside, I saw you dancing with that guy. I went and used the bathroom and when I walked out, I couldn't find you. Once I finally located you, you were across the room with his arm at your throat, the same way my father's was against my mother. I couldn't move fast enough to get to you. Then, you jammed your knee into his balls and I was so proud of you. I got there about two seconds after he pulled you back by your hair."

"I know all of that…well, most of it. What I don't under-stand is why you finally gave in to what you were fighting and why you kissed me? Or, maybe more importantly, why did you not do it months ago?"

As much as I didn't want to, I knew I needed to answer her second question. It was the one that would allow her to make the choice she needed to be free to make.

"I don't want to become him," I cautioned her. "And I feel

it occasionally."

"What do you feel?"

"Working the cases I do sometimes, I get angry. The anger I feel is so strong in those moments, I want to lash out the way he used to toward my mom."

Jolie's hand trailed up my chest and rested on the side of my neck. Her thumb stroked over the skin at my throat. "Are you angry at people who've done bad things or innocent people?"

I nodded. "I'm angry at people who've done *really* bad things," I clarified.

"You wouldn't hurt me, Lorenzo," she insisted.

"What if I do? They didn't start that way, Jolie. They were in love once."

"You're not your father. I'm not afraid of you either."

I had to give this to her. "It's been fifteen years since he last put his hands on her," I began. "He crushed her spirit and I don't think she'll ever get that back. I see it every time I visit her. Baby, I'd never forgive myself if I did that to any woman, but especially if I did it to you."

Jolie shifted in the bed and sat up. She pulled the sheet up to cover her chest and looked down at me. "Listen to me, boss," she ordered.

I couldn't help but grin at her. I thought she was the most adorable human being in the world.

"You can't live your life in solitude because you're worried about becoming someone you could never be. I can see the kind of man you are, Lorenzo. You are not an abuser and you proved tonight that it's not even a possibility that you could ever be one. You came to my rescue earlier tonight at Carter's, which should be evidence enough. But if it's not, the way you were with me in this bed a little bit ago should get rid of any lingering doubts you have about it."

I fell to my back and reached my arm out behind her. I nudged her toward me. A second later, she was curled into my body, her head on my chest and her arm draped over my body. The peace I felt in that moment was something I couldn't begin to describe.

"I think you're someone I could really feel something strongly about," I shared. "I don't want to ever hurt you, though."

She lifted her cheek from my chest to look at me. "You won't, big guy."

We stared at each other for several long moments before I admitted, "I can't believe it."

Jolie tilted her head to the side and asked, "What?"

"For five months, I couldn't stop the images of your beautiful face and that single dimple from consuming my mind, and now I'm here in your bed."

A coy smile spread across her face before she confessed, "I really like you in my bed."

"Are you sure you're up for seeing where this could go?"

Without hesitation, she responded, "Yes."

"It's late," I noted. "Are you tired? Or do you think you've got it in you to lie back while I put my face between your legs?"

Her eyes heated before she rolled to her back. "I think I can muster up the strength for one more round."

Happiness at her playful tone speared through me. I turned to my side, brought my mouth to hers, and kissed her lips before I worked my way down her body. Once I had a single taste of her on my tongue, I knew I'd never be able to give her up. So, I did what I had to do to make sure she thoroughly enjoyed what I had to offer.

After delivering a second orgasm with my mouth and a third with my cock, I fell asleep with the most precious woman in the world tucked tight to my body. And I hoped, with everything in me, that I'd never forget just how much of a treasure she was.

CHAPTER 6

Jolie

I WAS LEANING UP AGAINST THE COUNTER IN MY KITCHEN, A CUP OF coffee in my hands, my thoughts running wild.

I'd woken up this morning with Lorenzo beside me in bed, holding me close. I looked up at him, still asleep, and wondered how it was possible that a man who looked so peaceful could be so tortured on the inside. Last night, I'd gotten a whole lot more than I bargained for. I never expected to learn what I did, but I knew I wanted to do something about it.

My heart hurt hearing about Lorenzo's childhood. But what made it shatter was hearing him tell me that was afraid he could end up being just like his father. From the day I met him months ago, I knew he wasn't that kind of man. In fact, he'd saved me from injury and embarrassment due to my own clumsiness on two occasions. And then there was everything that happened last night with Colin.

He wouldn't hurt me.

I knew it.

I just needed to make sure he knew it.

So, before I could formulate any plan of action for accomplishing this task, I knew I needed to get up and get some coffee in me. I managed to sneak out from under his arm and now I was here, drinking my coffee while trying to figure out what to do.

My thoughts were interrupted when I heard Lorenzo descending the stairs. He found me in the kitchen, let his eyes rake over my body, which was covered only by a t-shirt, and I saw the smile tug at the corners of his mouth.

Lorenzo walked over to me, put his hands on the counter on either side of me, and nuzzled his face in my neck.

After kissing me there, he pulled back and rasped, "Good morning, Jolie."

"Morning, boss. Coffee?"

He gave me a nod and took a step back so I could get him a cup. After I handed it over, along with the cream and sugar, he stated, "You looked like you were deep in thought when I walked in."

"I do my best thinking in the morning," I replied.

"Do you want to share any of those thoughts?" he wondered.

I shook my head.

The look on his face changed, indicating he was worried.

I wanted to ease his mind. "It's nothing bad, just some stuff I'm working out in my head."

He relaxed a little just before he gave me another nod.

"How is he?" I asked after a few moments of silence had passed.

His eyes shot up. "Who?"

"Your brother. I know you told me about your mom last night, but you never said how your brother was doing."

Lorenzo's face broke out in a full-blown grin. "He made it," he declared and even though I had no idea what that meant, I could tell he was filled with pride.

"Made it?" I asked.

"First round draft pick for the NHL when he was eighteen," he explained.

My eyes rounded in surprise. "He plays hockey?"

"Yep."

I wracked my brain for about two seconds trying to figure it out. "Oh my God. Rocco De Luca. Rocky's your brother??" I bubbled.

Lorenzo jerked his head back. "You've heard of him?" he asked.

I set my coffee cup down and started pacing. "I can't believe I never made the connection. I mean, I realize I met you when it wasn't hockey season, but I don't know how I didn't put it together or at least consider it. Of course, what are the chances that you'd be related?"

I stopped pacing and looked up at him. Lorenzo was smiling, the biggest I'd seen yet.

"What's that look for?"

"You like hockey?"

"I am a *huge* hockey fan!" I cried. "And I love the Wyoming Summits. They are my team!"

Lorenzo set his cup down on the counter, sauntered over to me, and wrapped his arms around my waist. After he tugged me close, he questioned me. "Are you planning to watch the game tonight?"

"Um, yeah," I shot back sarcastically because it was the most ridiculous question he could have asked.

"Want company?"

I nodded slowly.

Lorenzo stopped the movement when he dropped his mouth to mine and kissed me. He lifted me up under my arms and set me on the counter, situating himself between my parted thighs. When he pulled his mouth away, he asked, "What are your plans for today?"

"I have to call Ava," I started. "She's probably been freaking out since last night. I wouldn't be surprised to see that she's texted or called my phone a million times already. After I call her, I think a call to Kendall is necessary. I thought about going to visit Hank and Gracie sometime this afternoon, after I go shopping for them, of course. And then I'm coming home early enough to be settled in to watch the game."

"Full day then," he noted. "Can I ask you a question?"

"Sure."

"The call to your girl and your sister...will those conversations involve you discussing things happening between me and you?"

"That's a safe assumption," I answered. Then, I thought about it and figured he might be worried about me sharing. "I'm only sharing me and you," I assured him. "Not what you told me about last night."

"Doesn't matter to me either way, Jolie. I'm just wondering if you telling them means I've got to be prepared for the conversation that's going to result from your family knowing, which specifically refers to your brother, Dom."

I shook my head. "Not yet. Kendall and Ava won't tell anyone and I'm not ready for that situation with Dom, Memphis, or Colton. So, you've got time."

"He knows," Lorenzo blurted.

"What?"

"Dom knows about everything I told you last night. He knows that and he knows how I've lived my life until now. If you want him to know there's an *us* now, I'm fine with it. I'm just not sure he'll handle it well."

I honestly didn't know how Dom would handle it either. Colton and Memphis would have their own thoughts on it, but Dom was different considering he worked with Lorenzo. They were close and Dom was not one to stay quiet when he had an opinion about something.

"Let's just be us for a while," I suggested. "If he's going to react negatively, I don't want to do it now when the babies are still so new. We'll give it some time, and when we know we're solid, we'll share it."

"Baby?" he called, giving my thigh a gentle squeeze.

My eyes, which had dropped to my lap, came to his.

"What do you like to eat for breakfast?"

"Donuts."

He chuckled. "You eat donuts for breakfast?"

"Well, no, not usually. That's what I'd like to have for breakfast every morning, but I usually wake up too late and don't have time to stop and get fresh donuts. So I typically just have coffee and whatever I can find here that's easy to eat on the drive to work."

"You usually wake up too late for a proper breakfast during the week, but on a Sunday morning after I've given you three orgasms and you've gone to bed well past a reasonable bedtime you wake up at the crack of dawn?"

"I had a lot of things I was thinking about," I retorted. "One of those, I'll share now, was the fact that I'd had the pleasure of experiencing three orgasms that weren't self-induced."

Lorenzo laughed. "Okay, so what are the chances you'll let me take you out for donuts this morning? I'll bring you back afterward so you can get on with the rest of your plans for the day. Then, I'll meet you back here with dinner so we can eat and watch the game together."

"I'm trying to find the downside," I teased.

"Good. And after the game, we'll talk."

My brows shot up. "Talk?"

He nodded.

"About what?"

"We'll talk about it tonight after the game," he repeated.

"Why not now?"

His mouth dropped to my neck. I tilted my head to the opposite side to give him better access. Lorenzo's hands trailed up my thighs and under the hem of my shirt, where he cupped my breasts in his hands. He pulled his mouth from my throat, stroked his thumbs over my nipples, and claimed, "Because if we have that conversation now, it'll delay me being able to bring it home for you at least two more times this morning, which will ultimately end in you not getting donuts for breakfast, but donuts for lunch instead."

I felt a spasm between my legs.

"We can talk later," I acquiesced.

Lorenzo grinned and let go of my breasts, but only so he could whip my shirt over my head and put his mouth on them instead.

"Most beautiful woman," he muttered just before he sucked a nipple into his mouth.

Then, he brought it home for me.

Twice.

After, I ended up having donuts for brunch.

"Wait, are you serious?"

That was Kendall.

After Lorenzo took me out for donuts, he brought me home so I could get on with my plans for the day. The minute he left, I called Ava.

She had sent about a thousand text messages to me by the time I called her back, too. Even though I hadn't responded to her sooner, she completely understood why when I filled her in. And she couldn't have been happier for me. She admitted to being slightly jealous, but incredibly happy.

We were both working overlapping hours tomorrow, so I told her I'd give her the juicy details of our hockey-game-watching date night then.

After I got off the phone with Ava, I called my sister.

"Hey, Jojo!" she greeted me.

"I need to tell you something, sissy," I replied.

She braced herself for it and I told her. I'd just finished explaining how Lorenzo brought me home and started interrogating me. Then, I divulged how I answered one of those questions and he just attacked.

Hearing it, she was shocked and that's precisely why she was questioning me now.

"It was hot," I swooned. "He complimented my dress. His exact words were 'this fucking dress,' and then he lifted it up over my head."

"I'm so jealous," she confessed. "Unless, of course, he wasn't good. Was it good?"

"The best ever, bar none," I answered. "Seriously, Kendall, he made me come three times last night and another two times this morning. He's incredible."

"So unfair!" she shouted.

I giggled.

"In all seriousness, though, I'm so happy for you Jojo. But I have one question. Why did he suddenly decide that he was into you after telling you it was never going to happen between the two of you?"

I knew Lorenzo said he didn't mind if I shared that

information, but it just didn't feel right to me. Clearly, he was still dealing with his own issues with the whole situation and I didn't think it was my place to blab it to anyone who would listen.

"It was something serious," I started. "I don't want to share it, Kendall, because I told him I wouldn't, even though he said it wouldn't bother him if I did. But I will just leave it at telling you he had a very valid concern because of something he went through when he was younger. I don't necessarily agree with his logic, but I understand where he's coming from. I think it's just going to take him some time to work through."

I could hear the smile in her voice. "I really hope it works out for the both of you," she said. "You deserve to be happy."

"Thanks, sissy. I hope it stays good, too. Which kind of leads me to my next thing."

There was a pause before she asked nervously, "What?"

"Please don't mention this to Dom. I don't want him freaking out. Ekko needs him focused on the kids right now and I don't want to do anything to distract them from their most important priority. I'll tell him soon, but I want to give Lorenzo and myself some time to figure us out. When we're both feeling good about it, then we'll share it with Dom."

"I think that's a really great idea, but did you honestly believe you needed to ask me not to share it with him? I'm no fool and that, my dear sister, would be a foolish move."

I couldn't help but laugh at her. "I know, I'm just being extra cautious right now because I think I really like him, Kendall. A lot. I don't want anything happening to ruin it before we even have the chance to start."

"Well, I'm rooting for the two of you," she assured me.

"Speaking of rooting," I began. "I should go so I can do

some shopping for Hank and Gracie. I want to visit with them today for a while and then I'm heading home to watch the hockey game. Guess what!"

"What?"

"Lorenzo's brother is Rocco De Luca, the center man for the Summits. We're watching the game together tonight," I shared.

"Oh, you two are perfect for each other," she gushed. "I'm so glad there's going to be someone there to rant at the television with you, especially if they make it to the playoffs again this season."

"I am so excited, Kendall. You have *no* idea."

Kendall chuckled and ended, "Alright, I'll let you go. Kiss my niece and nephew for me. And call me later this week to let me know how things are going."

"I will. Love you, sissy."

"Love you too, Jojo."

I disconnected my call with Kendall, grabbed my purse and keys, and left. I had some babies to cuddle and I didn't want to waste another minute.

I'd stopped at the mall on the way to Dom and Ekko's place because I simply couldn't show up empty-handed. I was determined to win over those adorable faces by any means necessary. Of course, I knew that they wouldn't even know that I was buying them stylish outfits right now, but I didn't care. I wanted to spoil them rotten.

When I arrived at their place, I saw just how exhausted my brother and sister-in-law were. Since I was there to see the babies, I insisted they both go take a nap. Ekko initially fought it, worried that leaving them without one of their parents made her a horrible mother, but luckily, Dom managed to get her to see reason.

"We're still going to be in the house, sugar," he told her. "Jojo won't let anything happen to them. You're exhausted; I'm exhausted. They both just ate. We'll take a break for a half hour and close our eyes. Jojo will come get us if anything goes wrong."

Ekko looked to me and confirmed, "Promise you'll wake us if they need us."

"I promise."

I spent the next hour and forty-five minutes watching my niece and nephew sleep. I watched as their chests rose and fell with each breath they took and I memorized the outline of their perfectly shaped lips. They were, without a doubt, the most beautiful babies I'd ever seen.

Hank was the first to stir. I hadn't wanted to wake them before, but once it had been nearly two hours, I couldn't hold back any longer. I scooped Hank up in my arms and cuddled him close. Ten minutes later, Gracie woke up. A minute after she started crying, Dom walked back into the room to pick up his daughter. She was so tiny in his arms.

"Did you get some rest?" I asked.

"You're a lifesaver, Jojo. I feel like a million bucks now," he shared before looking at his daughter. "Did you behave for Auntie Jojo?"

"She was an angel," I confirmed. "Ekko's still asleep?" I wondered.

He nodded. "I know they're going to be ready to eat any minute now, but if we can keep them happy for just a bit longer, I'd like to give her a few more minutes to rest."

I looked down at Hank and declared, "We can do that. Right, buddy? We need your mama getting some sleep so she can take care of you. You can give her a few more minutes, can't you?"

Hank just yawned at me in response.

A few minutes later, he started getting fussy. After I changed his diaper, Dom took him from me, gave me Gracie, and walked out of the room to take Hank to his mama. My niece lasted about ten minutes in my arms before she was done waiting. I changed her diaper, stood with her, and took her to Ekko.

Walking into the bedroom, I said, "She's ready to eat, Mommy."

The grin on Ekko's face grew. She wasn't even a week in and she was already such a wonderful mother. Dom took the now-sleeping Hank from his mom.

Once Gracie had latched on to eat, Ekko looked at me and sighed, "Thank you so much for coming here today. You have no idea how grateful I am."

"We are," Dom corrected her.

"I love them," I announced. "And I love you guys. Whenever you need me, I'm here for you."

"Thanks, Jojo."

"You're welcome."

I sat and chatted with them for a little while longer, but once both babies were fed and sleeping again, I left. I got my time in with them and managed to give Dom and Ekko a bit of a break, but they were still a new little family and I wanted them to have their time to figure out what worked for them.

On my way back home, I made a quick stop at the grocery store. Lorenzo said he was going to be bringing dinner, so I thought it was only fair that I pick up dessert. I zipped through the store, picked up a few options, and dashed out.

I wasn't typically one for rushing, but I had a guy I'd been crushing on for several months coming over to eat dinner and watch hockey with me. There was no way I was missing that.

CHAPTER 7

Jolie

MY DOORBELL RANG.

I'd had just enough time when I got home, following my grocery store run, to take a quick shower and get myself ready without making it look like I was trying too hard. Even though Lorenzo and I were only going to be watching a hockey game, I still thought it was important to put in some effort.

Opening the door, I found Lorenzo standing there holding up a box of pizza. "Someone called for delivery?"

I laughed as I stepped back to let him in. "Please tell me there's either plain cheese or pepperoni in there," I implored.

"Half and half."

"Goal!" I cheered.

Lorenzo's body shook with laughter. "You're a goof," he teased before he pressed a quick kiss to my cheek. "An adorable one, but a goof nonetheless."

"Why don't you take that into the living room and have a seat?" I suggested, nodding toward the pizza box. "I'll grab the plates and napkins."

After grabbing them and drinks, I met Lorenzo in the next room. Walking in, I started rambling, "I made a stop at the store on my way back home. I wasn't sure what you'd like, but I picked up beer and dessert."

"Looks like we've got it all covered," he said, standing beside the couch.

He wasn't sitting.

"Is something wrong? Do you not drink beer?" I worried.

"I do."

"Oh, why aren't you sitting?"

He grinned and took the remaining two steps toward me. "Because I wanted to give you a kiss first."

"But you gave me one when you walked in," I reminded him.

"Is there a limit?" His voice was low as he slowly bent at his neck.

My breath stuck in my throat. "No," I answered, my voice husky.

With his mouth at my ear, he whispered, "Good, because that was not the kind of kiss I wanted to give you right now anyway."

I swallowed hard as a shiver ran through me.

Lorenzo gave me a different kind of kiss.

Then, we sat and ate pizza while I explained, "I'm not sure if we'll be able to do this again."

He turned his head to me and asked, "What?"

"Distracting me like that before a game is not nice. I need to be focused and that kissing bit was a major distraction."

He shook his head at me as the corners of his mouth tipped up and he turned his attention back to the pizza. "I'll promise not to do that again. I've seen what happens when you're distracted."

I blinked my eyes in surprise. "What's that supposed to mean?" I wondered through a mouth full of food.

Lorenzo continued to laugh and explained, "Jolie, did you already forget nearly face-planting at bowling or nearly exposing yourself to everyone but me at the wedding?"

I rolled my eyes at him. He was right, but that still didn't mean I was going to let him get away with it.

"I didn't expose myself to you," I scoffed.

He shot me a disbelieving look. "Baby, you did."

"You weren't even looking at me!" I cried. "After I readjusted myself, I looked up at you and you were looking everywhere but at me."

"I was trying to be a gentleman, but trust me, I saw what I needed to see."

I had nothing else, so I returned an angry scowl.

Lorenzo got back to eating. So did I. Five minutes later, he remarked, "In my whole life, it was the best thing I'd ever seen."

"Was?"

He looked back at me, did a full body scan, and confirmed, "Was. I've seen a bit more since then."

I smiled inwardly but made no response.

Then, we settled in to watch the game.

The moment the first period ended, I shot up off the couch and announced, "I need dessert. I can't believe we're down two."

The Summits were not winning. I had been known to get pretty animated during a game. Lorenzo had just witnessed my ability to do that throughout the entire first period. It was a wonder he hadn't left.

Storming into the kitchen, I pulled the containers filled with desserts from the grocery bag and set them on the counter. Baked pumpkin churros. And chocolate chip muffins. I hoped Lorenzo would like at least one of them and I'd be able to make up for my antics.

I turned around to get dessert plates when I heard Lorenzo walk into the kitchen and set our dinner plates down. Reaching up into the cabinet, I stated, "I got two different desserts. I know some people despise everything pumpkin spice, so I figured chocolate chip was a safe bet."

There was no response as I pulled the plates out. Before I had the chance to turn around, Lorenzo's solid body pressed against mine from behind. He brushed my hair to one side and dropped his lips to my neck. Working his way up to my ear, he whispered, "There are still two periods left."

"I know. I'm sorry if I ruined watching the game for you. I just don't like seeing them down two," I sighed.

"You didn't ruin anything," he assured me, trailing his hands gently up my sides. "And they'll come back."

I arched my back, pushing my bottom into him. He groaned as I asked, "What if they don't?"

"It's a bit of a turn-on seeing you like this," he admitted. "If they don't win, I'll come up with a way to help you work out your frustration."

I turned and wrapped my arms around his neck. "Don't you think it'd be much more fun to celebrate their win?"

He laughed and shrugged his shoulders, "Either one works for me."

When he put it that way, I couldn't say I disagreed.

I took a deep breath in and sighed, "So, baked pumpkin churros or chocolate chip muffins?"

"Churros."

Grinning, I asked, "Can you grab them and I'll bring the plates?"

Lorenzo stepped back, grabbed the churros, and followed me back into the living room. After the second period ended, our team was up by one. During that intermission, I told

Lorenzo all about my day, minus the specifics of the conversations I had with Ava and Kendall. He asked how Hank and Gracie were doing and, of course, I couldn't help but gush over them. They were the lights of my life.

When the third period started, I was sitting on the opposite end of the couch. Lorenzo reached out for me and tugged me toward him.

It was abrupt and I was caught off guard.

My chest collided with his.

Our mouths were inches apart.

Instead of kissing me, though, Lorenzo gently turned me so I could rest my head on the armrest, my booty in his lap, and his arm curled around me.

That did it for me. The two of us just cuddling together on the couch, watching a hockey game. I knew this thing between us was new, but having that with him right then I knew it was something I wanted forever.

And it got me worried.

Because I suddenly remembered he wanted to talk after the game.

As much as I tried to focus on the game, I couldn't. At least, not with the same intensity that I did the first two periods. When there was less than ten minutes and they cut to a commercial break, Lorenzo interrupted the thoughts swirling in my mind.

"Everything okay?"

"Yeah," I lied.

He cocked an eyebrow, clearly not believing me.

"So, it's during the third period when the game is tied that you settle down?" he asked, though it wasn't a question for which he needed an answer.

I bit my lip nervously.

"I'm trying to have faith in my team," I said.

"Right," he answered, but I knew he wasn't buying my reasoning. Even still, he didn't press me further. The game was back on, so we abandoned our conversation and directed our attention to the television.

With a minute and ten seconds left in the game and the Summits on the penalty kill, there was a definite feel of tension in the room. But Rocco blocked a pass and took off on a breakaway. Rocco was one of the quickest guys in the NHL and, with the closest opposing player nowhere close to him, was unmanned heading toward the net. He came in hard, was quick with his hands, and fired a shot. It landed in the back of the net.

I glanced up at Lorenzo.

He was grinning at the television, watching his brother celebrate, and he had a look filled with such pride.

"He's so good," I shared.

"Yeah, he is."

The game ended and our team won. Dom picked up the remote and turned off the television.

He dropped his eyes to me, but they were following his hand that was running through my hair.

"Tell me what happened that made you go quiet, Jolie," he pleaded.

I had to laugh.

"Most people would be thanking their lucky stars that I got quiet," I retorted.

His eyes shot to mine and his hand stilled in my hair. "I'm not most people," he returned. "Now tell me why."

"I was enjoying being here with you like this," I started. "But then I remembered that you wanted to talk after the game. Since you never shared what we were talking about, I got worried."

"Don't ever stay silent, Jolie," he instructed. "No matter what, never stay silent. Not when you want to say something, and especially not when something isn't right for you."

"But—"

"No," he interrupted. "Because if you go quiet when you want to speak up or when you know you should, you change who you are. I saw it happen to my mom; I don't want to see it happen to you. Promise me. Promise you won't choose silence when you need to make noise."

I held his gaze for a few beats before I agreed, "I promise, boss."

"What I wanted to talk to you about was just that," he said. "There have been several times now that I've heard you say things that don't sit well with me."

My mind was scrambling trying to recall what I could have said that would have bothered him.

"What?" I finally asked.

"The first time I heard it was on the elevator at the hospital," he began. "You said something that made it seem like you believed you were unworthy of others getting to know you. You hinted that people make judgments about you before they take the time to see who you really are."

I couldn't deny it because it was the truth.

He went on, "Last night, you ended up in a bad situation because some guy said something nice to you."

"You think what happened last night was my fault?" I asked, shocked at his accusation.

The look on his face turned serious. "Not. At. All."

"I'm confused then."

"What I'm saying is that after hearing your friend tell me that it's been so long since you've been with anyone and hearing you say what you did in the elevator, I'm not surprised that you reacted to a positive compliment. That guy played you, that's on him. But you've made it clear to me that you don't believe that who you are is enough."

"Quite the contrary, big guy," I started to correct him. "The issue isn't that I don't think I'm enough. It's that I'm too much."

"What the hell does that mean?"

Now it was my turn to cock an eyebrow. I pressed my head back into the arm of the couch and questioned, "Did you watch the first two periods of the game with me?"

"Yes."

"Did you see me during those two periods?"

"Yeah, and then you disappeared in the third," he noted.

"Which is what you should be grateful for. I mean, I finally shut up and wasn't ranting anymore."

"You do recall that I asked what was wrong, don't you?"

I nodded.

"Did it occur to you that maybe I enjoyed seeing you exactly like you were throughout the first two periods? That maybe I missed that girl and wanted her back?"

Hope surged through me. My lips parted to reply, but nothing came out. I closed my mouth and still had the urge to speak, but I was so caught off guard by what he said.

Lorenzo patiently waited for me to pull myself together.

"You…you like that I disrupted the game?"

He shook his head in disappointment. "Your problem is that you think you were a disruption. Jolie, baby, you're not a disruption. You're a distraction."

The wind left my sails.

"Distractions can be good, you know," he advised. "Seeing you so riled up over something like a hockey game is a huge turn-on. But it's not just that. I admire your ability to just put yourself out there the way that you do. Or, at least, the way I've seen you do sometimes when you aren't inside your own head. You walked into the waiting room at the hospital and didn't have a problem telling everyone about your magic hands. You found a way to be creative with your girls at bowling just so you could get an advantage. You're competitive; I like that. You can ramble on about nonsense, but you also say some of the most profound things when you just blurt them out. It's when you stop yourself from being you and start thinking about it too much that you take away that girl that I'm most attracted to."

"You...I...you don't think I'm too social?"

He shook his head.

I felt the tears prick the backs of my eyes.

Lorenzo noticed and asked, "Why would I?"

"That's why I'm alone. All of the guys I've dated told me that I'm too much. Too talkative, too forward, too...just too much. I've been trying to tame myself a little bit, but I've been like this my whole life. After twenty-nine years of being one way, it's not exactly easy to change overnight."

"They weren't the right guys for you if they expected you to change," he insisted. "Don't lose who you are for anyone else, Jolie."

"But what happens when I don't want to lose someone?"

"If they love you, they'll love everything about you."

My body froze.

"Relax, baby. I'm not saying we're there yet. I will say that I really like you, though. And I love the way you live your life when you're confident in who you are. As gorgeous as your body is, there's nothing sexier than seeing you happy and laughing."

"I'm going to cry," I squeaked.

"Then I'll dry your tears."

I slid my arms around his neck and pulled my body toward

his. Lorenzo wrapped his arms around my back and hugged me tight. I allowed the good feeling that he gave me to settle over me, and when I'd finally given myself enough time to do that, I pulled back and kissed his cheek.

Bringing my palm up to the side of his face, I said, "You're the sweetest man I've ever met. I don't know how it's possible that you believe you could ever hurt someone when you won't even stand for seeing me hurt myself."

His face softened with a look I couldn't read. I just knew that whatever the look was had to be a result of him ridding himself of any negative thoughts.

"So, you've got to follow through on your promise," I reminded him.

"My promise?"

"To help me find a way to celebrate the win."

Lorenzo's eyes got intense as his arms tightened around me. "They were fools," he muttered.

"Who?"

"The assholes who wanted to tame you. If a man gets creative enough, he can use that to his advantage. When you get wild, that's beyond sexy. A man wanting to tame that is an idiot."

Pressing my face close to his, I smiled against his lips.

"Their loss," I breathed.

One of his hands traveled up my shirt and cupped my breast. "Damn right," he proudly agreed.

Then, he crushed his mouth to mine and we celebrated the win.

Lorenzo appreciated me being a little wild and I found that I liked him using that to his advantage.

CHAPTER 8

Jolie

"DO YOU HAVE ANY TALENT FOR DRAWING?"

It had been just shy of two weeks since Lorenzo brought me home from Carter's. Things had been going great for us. We had only seen each other on three occasions in that time, but we'd spoken to each other nearly every day. He came over twice to watch hockey games, once just to see me, and we spent a few nights talking on the phone for long periods of time. There were a couple days I didn't get to talk to him because I was working the later shift at the spa and he had something keeping him tied up at work.

I was currently at work, on my lunch break, and I decided to give him a call.

"Drawing?" he repeated. "What exactly am I drawing?"

"A face. Actually, several faces. Maybe five or six. I guess it depends on what we decide to do."

"We? Baby, if you'd give me a little bit more information than you are, I might be able to answer your question."

I finished chewing the food in my mouth, swallowed, and explained, "Well, I was planning to get some pumpkins this weekend since Halloween is less than a week away. I wanted to carve them, but I have no artistic talent."

"Where are you getting pumpkins from?"

"I was just going to go to the grocery store and buy a couple from the ones they have in the bins there."

"When are you planning to buy these pumpkins?" he asked.

"Saturday afternoon," I answered.

"Hang tight one second for me," he said.

"Sure."

I heard his muffled voice talking to someone. A few seconds later he returned to the phone and explained, "I'm sorry, Jolie. I've got to go help Pierce and Holden with a case they're working on."

"That's okay. I can talk to you later," I assured him.

"Definitely, but instead of you buying your pumpkins at the store on Saturday I'd like to take you to the pumpkin patch to get them if you're up for it."

He was so sweet. "I'd love to do that with you."

"Good. I'll bring donuts for breakfast on Saturday morning and then we can go hunting for pumpkins whenever you want."

"You're the best," I declared.

He laughed. "I'm trying."

A moment of silence stretched on until he broke it, "I've got to go now, but I'll call you later today."

"Okay."

"Have a good day, baby."

"Thanks, big guy. You too."

We disconnected and I got back to my lunch. My mood must have been displayed prominently on my face because when Ava walked into the break room a minute later, she stated, "Well that look can only mean one thing."

I turned my gaze in her direction and gave her the

goofiest grin. "He makes me so happy, Ava. It's so effortless for him."

"What did he do now?"

"I planned to pick up pumpkins this weekend to carve. I only wanted him to help me with the artsy part of pumpkin carving and he told me he'd take me to the pumpkin patch instead."

"Aw, that's so cute."

"Want to know the best part?"

Her eyes nearly popped out of her head as she sat across from me at the table. "You mean, that wasn't it?"

I shook my head slowly as I smiled. "He's bringing me donuts for breakfast. Are you jealous?"

"Uh, I'm so jealous, but I'm so happy for you. Does he have any brothers?"

Now it was my turn to give her wide eyes. "Oh, I almost forgot. Yes! As it turns out, he does have a brother."

"Is he single?"

I scrunched up my nose. "I'm not sure if he's single, but I can tell you he's pretty freaking handsome."

"I was only half-kidding, but I'd be up for a good time. You need to find out if he's single and hook a girl up," she ordered.

"Noted, but you aren't much of a hockey fan, are you?"

She shook her head. "Not exactly. Isn't it violent?"

I laughed. Hockey wasn't like it used to be and it was clear Ava didn't watch. "It's not that bad. The guys who play are tough and sometimes they'll throw down their gloves, but it's all good. And it's kind of hot, to be honest."

"Why are you even talking to me about hockey?"

I shook my head, ridding the unnecessary thoughts from my head. "Gosh, it's so easy for me to get sidetracked. I was mentioning hockey because Lorenzo's brother plays for the Wyoming Summits. His name is Rocco, but the fans call him Rocky."

"Oh, that's kind of hot."

"I'll look into it and see what I can find out. I'm sure a simple internet search might tell us what we need to know, but it's not always trustworthy. I'll talk to Lorenzo," I said as I started picking up my mess. "I've got to get back out there. I've got four more clients lined up for today."

"Yeah, I was in later this morning, so I'm here until closing tonight. I'll see you before you leave, though."

At that, I walked out of the break room and made my way to my room to prepare for my next client.

Five hours later, I was on my way home.

When I got back, I changed into my workout gear and did a quick workout of some squats and light stretching before I hopped in the shower. After I made myself some dinner, I climbed into bed and flipped on the television.

There wasn't a hockey game on, but I found reruns of one of my favorite sitcoms on, so I watched that. Twenty minutes later, my phone rang.

"Hey, boss," I greeted him.

"You sound like you're a mix of sleepy and happy," he returned.

I giggled and confirmed, "That's because I am. I'm snuggled up in my bed watching sitcom reruns. You sound alert and focused."

"I'm working a case with the guys still, but wanted to take a minute to call you before you drifted."

I didn't respond. I loved all of the sweet, little gestures he did. And on one hand, it pained me to think that he'd been holding himself back from having a relationship with someone because he thought he could be like his father. Of course, on the other hand, I was comforted by the fact that when he finally decided to take a chance, he chose to take it with me. I knew it worried him that things could go sour down the road, but I truly believed he was a gentleman.

"You there?" he cut into my thoughts.

"Yeah, I'm here. Sorry, I was just thinking about how great you are," I replied.

He laughed at me and wondered, "And you're apologizing for thinking that about me?"

"Well, I'm sorry for ignoring you to do it," I clarified. After a beat of silence, I shared, "I miss you."

"Miss you too, baby."

Pulling the blanket around me tighter, I smiled. "Wish you were here," I added.

"Me too. Unfortunately, Pierce and Holden just heard me tell you I missed you and now they want to know who I'm talking to."

"Oh no," I worried. "Dom introduced me to Pierce once a long time ago, but I've never officially met Holden. I know all the guys came to the wedding, but I didn't get to meet everyone. If you tell them it's me on the phone, won't they have some moral obligation to uphold and tell Dom?"

He burst out laughing, "No, they don't. Even still, I'm not giving them your name until you're ready for that. Of course, in saying that they'll know you're connected here somehow."

"Crap."

"Don't worry," he tried reassuring me. "I promise it's fine."

I took in a deep breath. When I let it out, I gave in. "Okay, I'm putting my faith in you on this one."

"Good."

"Is your brother single?" I blurted.

"Come again?"

"Is Rocco dating anyone?"

He stayed quiet a minute. Then, he asked, "Can you tell me why you're asking that?"

"After I got off the phone with you this afternoon, Ava walked into the break room. I was telling her how great you are and she jokingly asked if you had a brother. It dawned on me that I didn't know if he was with anyone, so I thought I'd find out."

"He's got a girl he's been with for quite a while now."

"Bummer for Ava, but it's okay. I'm glad he's got somebody, and she really isn't looking for a serious thing right now anyway. I figured if they were both single and looking for some fun, why not, right?"

Lorenzo chuckled. "I guess so."

"Yeah, okay, I'm coming," Lorenzo called out to someone. "Baby?" he returned his attention to me.

"You have to go?"

"Sorry," he lamented. "I'll make it up to you on Saturday morning, okay?"

"Donuts and orgasms before pumpkin picking," I advised.

"I can do that," he assured me. Then, his voice got quiet when he whispered, "Good night, Jolie."

"Good night, Lorenzo."

We disconnected, and ten minutes later, I fell asleep smiling.

My doorbell rang.

I was so tired and when I peeled one eye open, I saw that

SOLITUDE | 91

it was still dark outside. Reaching out to my nightstand, I lifted up my phone and saw that it was a quarter after six in the morning.

I rolled out of bed and made my way downstairs.

"Who is it?" I called out.

"Me," a familiar voice said.

I quickly disarmed my alarm and opened the door.

Lorenzo held out a box of donuts. "These are for later," he stated as he gave me a closed-mouth kiss on the lips. "Go put them in the kitchen while I lock up."

I went out into the kitchen and put the donuts on the counter. Just as I turned to go back and meet him, I collided with his solid body. Lorenzo managed to lock up and remove his jacket and shoes in the time it took me to walk to the kitchen.

He wrapped an arm around my waist and put a hand to my bottom as he lifted me clean off the floor. My ankles crossed behind his back while my arms did the same around his neck.

Lorenzo moved to the stairs and carried me up. Seconds later, we were in the bed and he wasn't wasting any more time. We hadn't seen each other since last Sunday, so it had been a while.

Lorenzo and I were tearing at each other's clothing, desperate for the skin-to-skin contact. His shirt was tossed aside before mine floated through the air. He brought his mouth to my breasts and instantly sucked, pulling one nipple in. As he lavished one breast and then the other, he brought his hands to the waistband of my panties. Lorenzo tore his mouth from me only so he could watch as he pulled my panties down my legs.

My hands shot out to his jeans and I worked to open the

fly. I couldn't get them off him fast enough. Lorenzo noted my frustration and took over. As he removed his pants, I sat up in the bed, shifted to my knees, and began kissing his torso. He managed to get his pants pushed down to his knees when I had the sudden urge to take him in my mouth.

"Can I be in charge this time?" I asked as I moved my mouth up over his chest and began sliding my hand down his abdomen.

"Kiss me first," he ordered.

I kissed him as my hand reached the prize. While I stroked his length, Lorenzo groaned into my mouth and squeezed my ass. He effortlessly turned our bodies and lowered his back to the bed, taking me with him.

Disconnecting my mouth from his, I lifted my body from his, removed his boxer briefs, and crawled back up along his outer thigh. With my body positioned beside his hip, I leaned over and went to work. As I worked his length with my lips and tongue, I used both hands to pump along the base.

"Jolie," he growled. "So wild."

I wasn't one to brag, but I had to agree. And Lorenzo made me that much more enthusiastic. I craved being able to make him feel good. Lucky for me, he never seemed to want to let me go at it alone. So, while I eagerly sucked him into my mouth, his hand drifted from my hip and over my ass.

"Shift toward me," he got out through his groans.

Never allowing him to leave my mouth, I shifted myself in the bed, giving him a better angle.

Within seconds, my mouth full of him, I had to drop my hands from his length. One shot to his hip, the other to his thigh. He'd plunged two fingers inside me, leaving his thumb free to tease and torture my clit.

As he used his hand to pleasure me, I sucked him harder

into my mouth.

Lorenzo's fingers were relentless, and it didn't take long for him to build me up. Knowing it was about to hit, I released his cock from my mouth and breathed, "Lorenzo...babe... don't stop."

He moved faster.

I kept myself steady with one hand on his hip and wrapped the other around his hardened length. The closer I got to my orgasm, the faster my fist pumped. Lorenzo's thumb pressed hard, circled, and I exploded.

My orgasm tore through me, the pleasure searing through my limbs as I rode his fingers through it.

I'd barely just come down when his hand left my body, wrapped around my wrist, and he began sheathing himself. Seconds later, he hauled me up his body, where I straddled his hips and positioned him. I slid down over him and threw my head back on a moan.

When my head dropped forward, Lorenzo rasped, "Missed you so much, baby."

"Same, boss."

"I need you to move, Jolie."

I did as he requested and began moving. His hands were everywhere—at my thighs, my ass, and my breasts. My palms were planted on his chest as I moved my hips over him.

The buildup began, coming quick. I leaned forward, arched my back a bit, and moved faster. I was on the verge again and just before I shattered, Lorenzo urged, "Bring it home."

I tried.

And just as it began feeling the pleasure splinter across my body, I could no longer move my hips. I dropped my chest to his. Lorenzo wrapped his arm around my waist and drove the other into my hair, clamping his mouth tight to mine, as he took over and thrust his hips up.

Lorenzo brought it home, drawing out my pleasure as he sought and found his own.

Collapsed on his chest like a ragdoll, I sighed, "I was not expecting a wakeup call like that today. It was totally worth being woken up for."

Lorenzo laughed and claimed, "It's funny how that works."

"What?"

"You're talking about a wakeup call. I'm feeling like I've just been hit with a tranquilizer shot and hoping for an hour or two of sleep beside you."

I lifted my head from his chest and shared, "I'm completely alright with that, too."

"Let me take care of this condom and we'll get to it."

"Okay."

Once we were in the bed together again, Lorenzo curled up behind me, pressed a kiss to my shoulder, and draped his arm over my side, where he held my breast in his hand possessively. It felt so good having him next to me, and combining that with the fact that I was utterly spent from our morning romp, I quickly drifted.

It was just before nine when Lorenzo and I woke up.

"So, what made you ring my bell, both literally and figuratively, at six fifteen this morning?" I wondered.

"My options were to stay awake, alone in my bed, where I couldn't sleep because all I wanted to do was be next to you or get up, get your donuts, and come here. I chose option two."

"You made a good choice," I assured him.

He gave me a squeeze in response.

"You know, you never answered my question yesterday," I pointed out.

"What question?"

"Can you draw?"

He shook his head. "Not exactly."

"So our pumpkins will look hideous?"

"I can't draw, but I'm good with a drill, baby."

I lifted my head and cocked an eyebrow. "A drill? For pumpkins?"

"Trust me."

My reply to that came from my stomach, which had rumbled so loudly I shoved my face into the pillow, completely embarrassed.

Lorenzo curled his body over my back. "Hungry?"

"Nope," I lied.

I felt movement in the bed but refused to lift my head to see what was going on. The next thing I knew, I was being lifted in Lorenzo's arms.

I screeched, "What are you doing?"

"Taking you downstairs to feed you."

"I'm naked!"

"The shirt over my shoulder is for you," he declared.

I looked to his shoulder and saw the shirt he was wearing when he walked in early this morning resting there.

"Yes!" I cheered.

We made it to the kitchen a moment later. Lorenzo got me steady on my feet, handed me his shirt, and asked, "What are you so excited about?"

After slipping my hands through the armholes and pulling the shirt down over my head, I explained, "We've just reached a crucial point in our relationship, boss. I'm wearing my man's shirt."

His eyes shot to mine and a serious look washed over his face.

Seeing it, I second-guessed my choice of words. Perhaps we hadn't reached a crucial point in our relationship.

"Apparently, that was the wrong thing to say," I murmured.

He still said nothing.

"Lorenzo, I'm sorry. I wasn't thinking. I didn't mean anything by it," I insisted.

"You did."

My eyes dropped to the ground. "Well, yeah. I mean, I think things have been going great between us. I realize it hasn't been that long, but I just assumed that we were on the same page regarding exclusivity. If you don't want that—"

"We're exclusive," Lorenzo stressed with a low tone, cutting me off.

That was a relief. I didn't think he was with anyone else and he had been very attentive. He'd call just to check in or he'd buy me donuts at six in the morning so he could come over early and cuddle with me.

"I don't understand what's wrong then?"

He shook his head. "Nothing. You caught me off guard by saying that."

"Oh. I wasn't trying to make you uncomfortable. If you aren't looking to make it official between us yet, I understand. It was a silly comment," I tried brushing it off as I tore my eyes from him and looked to the side.

I tried taking a few settling breaths to stop myself from losing it. The truth is, I had assumed, considering the conversation we'd had previously about the two of us seeing where this could go, that we already made it official.

Lorenzo's palm cupped my cheek and gently turned it toward him. "Jolie, I'm not upset. And it wasn't just a silly comment. It caught me off guard; I wasn't expecting it. That doesn't mean that I didn't like hearing you say it."

My head dropped to his bare chest as my hands went to his hips. His arms came around me and he got out a strained, "It's okay. I'm really not upset."

I tipped my head back and looked up at him. My eyes were filled with unshed tears and his face changed. He looked genuinely troubled. Unfortunately, I couldn't stop the tears from escaping and rolling down my cheeks.

"Baby, you're killing me here. Please don't cry," he pleaded with me as he wiped away the tears.

"Feed me donuts and I promise to turn it around."

On that, he lifted me up and set me on the counter where he opened the box of donuts and let me go crazy.

A few hours later, we went searching for pumpkins.

CHAPTER 9

Jolie

"**W**AIT!" I CRIED. "I'M NOT READY YET!"

"Jolie," Lorenzo huffed, his dwindling patience evident in his tone.

"I promise this is it," I began. "Look how cute they are. I just need two of them."

His eyes looked about ready to pop out of his head. "You already have four pumpkins picked out. Why do you need more?"

I batted my eyes at him and declared, "For Hank and Gracie. They're too small yet to really get into the fun of Halloween, but that doesn't mean they shouldn't each have their very own pumpkin."

Lorenzo's face softened and I knew I had him. I directed my attention back to the baby pumpkins and spent the next five minutes trying to find the perfect ones for my two favorite kids. Truthfully, I could have spent another ten minutes looking at them, but Lorenzo had evidently had enough.

"Alright, I'm ready," I finally said, pulling myself away from the bin.

"Are you sure? I mean, they've got so much other stuff

here you could buy."

I squinted up at him and asked, "Are you giving me a hard time?"

"Baby, I had two donuts for breakfast about a million hours ago. We came here and the second you saw all they had to offer, this became something other than just a pumpkin-picking event. We had to go put quarters in a machine so you could get food to feed the goats. Then, you insisted on going in that corn maze. I'd have had us in and out of that in five minutes, but you swore you knew the way to go. We were lost in there for an extra hour because of it. After that, you finally agreed to go get the pumpkins, but I'm inclined to believe it was only because they gave you a hayride out to the patch. At this point, it's been hours and I need to eat."

I gave him a curt nod. "Right, boss. You're a *hangry* private investigator. Let me just pay for my pumpkins and we'll go."

Lorenzo picked up the three large pumpkins while I grabbed the fourth and smallest of them along with the two for my niece and nephew. We set the large pumpkins down on the scale and I placed the two smaller ones on the counter.

"Forty-seven twenty-five," the girl behind the counter declared.

I pulled my wallet out of my purse and fished through for a fifty. Just as I held my hand out with the bill in it, the girl was putting change in Lorenzo's hand.

"What are you doing?" I asked him.

He looked at me, shoved the money in his pocket, bent to pick up the pumpkins, and began walking. I grabbed the small ones and caught up to him.

"Lorenzo, I can pay for pumpkins," I said.

"I know you can, but I wanted to buy them for you."

I blinked my eyes. "Just like that? You couldn't ask me first?"

We continued walking toward his truck, but he looked over at me. "I need permission to be able to buy my woman a pumpkin?"

His woman.

He called me his woman for the first time.

I finally understood his reaction from earlier that morning. I couldn't get out any words, so I simply shook my head at him. A minute later, we made it to the truck, where he loaded the pumpkins while insisting I get in.

A couple of hours later, Lorenzo and I had gotten some food and were nearly finished with carving the first two pumpkins. Well, he was nearly finished carving. I had my hand stuck in the third pumpkin and was pulling out the seeds. Lorenzo refused to take any part in pumpkin-guts removal.

"You weren't lying. You really are great with a drill!"

Lorenzo cocked an eyebrow at me and smirked. "Was there ever really a doubt in your mind about that?"

I shrugged my shoulders. "I don't know. I just didn't know if you were the creative type. Handyman I could see, but I didn't know what to expect when it came to creativity."

"I'm very handy and while I might not be an artist, I can certainly be creative when I need to be," he assured me.

I narrowed my eyes at him. "Are we still talking about power tools and pumpkin carving?"

He burst out laughing.

I watched.

I loved seeing him like that.

Happy, carefree.

When his bright, shining eyes came to mine, I asked,

"Will you kiss me?"

He stepped closer and leaned into me. Once his lips hit mine, it didn't take long for him to become consumed. As much as I enjoyed it, I knew I'd enjoy what I was about to do just a tad bit more.

Clamping my fist around a pile of seeds and pumpkin goo, I pulled it out of the pumpkin's cavity and opened my fist at the last second to press all of it on Lorenzo's neck.

His mouth moved a fraction of an inch away from mine and he warned, "Please tell me you did not just put pumpkin shit all over me."

I smiled against his mouth. "If I did, I'd be lying. And I'm not a liar."

"Jolie, that is so damn disgusting," he cringed.

Now I was doubled over in a fit of laughter.

It was my crucial mistake because Lorenzo seemed to no longer have an aversion to pumpkin goo, as evidenced by the fact that I suddenly had it in my hair. He gripped my hair at the back of my head, lifted me so I was upright, and walked me backward until my back was against the wall.

Pressing his body into mine, his voice was low when he asked, "How does it feel?"

I stared at the intensity in his eyes, swallowed hard, and rasped, "I'm scared."

Lorenzo's entire body went rock solid as nothing but shock registered on his face. He immediately took his hand from my hair and stepped back from me. "What?" he croaked. "Jolie...I—"

"No, I mean—" I got out before he cut me off.

The look on his face changed, but he looked completely devastated. "Are you afraid of me?"

I took a step toward him, reaching my hand out to him,

and he took one backward. "Lorenzo, I didn't mean that I was afraid you were going to hurt me. I shouldn't have said that the way that I did."

"What did you mean?" he whispered.

I looked up at him, his eyes begging me to explain why I said what I did.

"I'm scared at how much I feel for you. It terrifies me that I already feel like this just two weeks in," I explained.

He dropped his head to one side. "How do you feel?"

I pulled my bottom lip in between my teeth before I answered, "I feel like it's happening really fast. The physical attraction has been there since day one for me. Emotionally, though, I didn't expect to feel this much this quickly."

"How do you feel?" he repeated his question.

I swallowed hard. "Like I really, really like you."

The muscle in his cheek twitched, but he said nothing.

"A lot," I added on a whisper.

"Are you alright with taking a break from pumpkins for now?" he asked, his voice thick with emotion.

I nodded.

"Good. Time to get cleaned up," he said as he picked me up over his shoulder and moved to the stairs. He walked us straight to the bathroom where we got in the shower.

While Lorenzo didn't ever respond directly to my admission of my feelings for him, he made it very clear to me in the shower that he appreciated hearing what I had said. I was only slightly disappointed he never verbally returned the sentiments.

Lorenzo

I pulled out my phone, found the number I needed, tapped on the screen, and held it to my ear.

After two rings, I heard, "Enzo."

"Nice win last night, Rocco."

"Thanks," he responded. "I'm glad you got to watch it."

It was late Monday morning, and after the weekend I'd had with Jolie, I decided to call my brother.

"As long as I'm not on a case where it's physically impossible to watch, you know I always do."

There was a moment of silence before he responded, "I know you do. So, how's it going? Am I going to see you anytime soon?"

"I think that depends on you," I began. "You're the one with the crazy schedule right now. Things aren't too out of hand for me at the office, so I've had some downtime."

"November is full," he started. "There are only four times throughout the month where we've got two days off between games. Other than that, it's either one day off or none."

"I saw that. I actually took a look at the schedule and was thinking about coming to your home game against the Pens that Friday at the beginning of November."

"That would be awesome. You want a box? I can get you one or, at the very least, really good seats."

I laughed. "I'm good either way. Just looking forward to seeing a live game. It's always so much better than watching it on television."

"I'll take care of it. How many seats do you want?"

He was going to know as soon as I said it.

"Just two."

"Two?"

I wasn't going to play the game with him, so I just let it out.

"I've got someone I want you to meet," I blurted.

Rocco didn't respond for a long time. Eventually, he asked, "Would you mind repeating that again?"

"I met a girl, a little over five months ago, and I want you to meet her," I said.

"You've been dating a girl for five months and you're just now telling me about her for the first time?" he questioned me.

"We've only been officially together for just over two weeks. I met her for the first time several months ago," I clarified.

"So you've been hooking up for five months and just recently decided to make it official?" he wondered.

I laughed. I wished. "No. I've been fighting a war with myself to not hook up with her since late April. She was interested and I was not willing to go there with her."

"Is she hot?"

"Seriously, Rocco?" I scolded him.

He laughed. "What? I'm trying to figure out why you'd turn down a willing participant. If there was no attraction, I could understand it."

Attraction didn't seem like the right word to describe the pull I felt toward Jolie. It was something else entirely.

"Your silence tells me what I need to know. She's hot."

"Stop," I grunted.

He was my brother, but that didn't mean I wanted him thinking about or referring to Jolie being hot. He hadn't even met her, and I was already feeling this way. Maybe introducing them after I had the opportunity to let a few more weeks with her completely consume me wouldn't be a good idea.

"You like her," he remarked.

It wasn't a question.

"What?"

"She was willing, and you were attracted, so there are only one of a few explanations. The fact that you're getting irritated I'm commenting on her looks tells me what I need to know. You liked her and didn't want to have just a one-night stand with her."

The asshole knew me too well. Even still, I wasn't going to give in. "When did you give up hockey and become a P.I.?"

Rocco began laughing. When he got himself under control, he stated, "I don't need to be a P.I. to know when my brother is *finally* giving himself something he deserves."

It seemed my brother's ability to render me speechless was in full force this morning.

"I'm happy for you, Enzo. All these years have gone by and you've never asked me to meet a girl. This one's got to be special," he surmised.

I could have denied it and told him it wasn't the truth, but that's not who I was and he'd see right through it anyway.

"She is," I admitted. "In fact, she's my complete opposite, Rocky, but I can't get over what I feel for her. She's really special to me and I think you'll like her."

His voice was an octave lower when he replied, "Then I'll make sure I get you two a box. That way, if she comes to the game and is completely bored, she'll at least be bored in comfort."

"She won't be bored," I returned.

"You sure about that?"

I had to laugh. I couldn't wait for him to meet Jolie. "Positive. Especially considering she loses her shit when you guys are down."

"She's a hockey fan?"

"Yep."

"Okay, I already like her."

I smiled into the phone and agreed, "Me too. She's perfect."

My mind drifted to thoughts of my girl. There wasn't anything I didn't like about her. Even though I may have made it seem to her like I was annoyed on Saturday at the pumpkin patch after we'd been there for hours, deep down I really didn't mind. She was so happy, brightening up my world with her infectious laughter and that dimple. I didn't know what I'd do if something ever happened to take that away from me.

Something such as myself.

"I'm afraid I'm going to fuck it up, Roc."

"What? How?"

I shook my head back and forth. "I don't know, but this weekend she told me she was scared. Initially, it completely stunned me because I didn't think I'd done anything to make her fearful of me. She explained that she's scared by how much she feels for me. I get it because it's how I feel about her, but what if that changes? What if I hurt her?"

Rocco was silent a minute and I knew he was preparing to launch into a full-scale tirade like he'd done on so many previous occasions. "You're not him, Enzo. Never have been, never will be."

"I could have killed him that day," I reminded Rocco. He didn't know the day it went down, but years later, I told him the truth of what happened when I walked into the house and left him in the garage.

"Yeah, you could have, but you stayed in control and didn't go that far. Even if you had, that wouldn't mean you were like him and you know it."

I waited because I knew he wasn't finished.

"You're a protector and always have been. I can remember that fear I felt living in that house with him like it happened yesterday, but even in that fear, I never once doubted that I'd be safe. I knew you'd never let anything happen to me."

"Stop," I demanded.

I couldn't handle this.

"No, I'm not going to stop, Enzo. You need to hear it. And I'll say it as many times as I need to say it for you to realize that it's true. You spent our childhood looking out for me; now I can return the favor. If you feel something for this girl, don't let him get in the way of that. You'd never lay a hand on her, and if you dig deep, you know that's the truth."

My throat was tight, thick with the weight of emotion Rocco's words left in me. I needed a minute to regain my composure.

"Does she know?" he asked.

"Yeah," I managed to get out.

"She's not afraid?"

"She said the same thing you did, insists that I couldn't ever be that person. It doesn't change the fact that I'll still worry for her sake."

Rocco let out a grunt. "That's a good thing. The fact that you worry about her like that should tell you all you need to know. And years after we got out of there and Mom finally had the means to seek help for all of us, you know what the therapist told us. Kids who go through what we went through typically respond one of two ways. They either mimic that behavior or they put an end to it. We're the latter, Enzo. I think it's good that you're mindful of the fact that, especially as a big dude, you've got the power to put a serious hurting on anyone.

For a woman, it could be detrimental. That said, given the fact that you are who you are, any woman who's with you couldn't find herself safer in anyone else's arms."

"Alright," I replied, needing this to stop.

He recognized it and decided to let it go.

"Look, I'll just say this. If you need to talk, you know I'm here for you. But you know I'm not the only one that sees the kind of person you are. I'm sure if you talk to any of the guys at work, they'll tell you the same thing I am."

"I can't."

"What?"

I sighed. "They don't know about her."

There was a long pause before he asked, "You haven't said anything to them?"

"She's Dom's sister."

Rocco had met most of the guys I worked with before. He'd hung with Dom on several occasions.

"Oh, bro," he started. "That's tough. How do you think he's going to respond?"

"Not a clue," I answered honestly.

Rocco pointed out the obvious. "He's a crazy motherfucker that runs into burning buildings, so it could go one of two ways. Either he'll be pissed at you for hooking up with his sister or he'll know the kind of guy you are and give you a handshake while welcoming you to the family."

It was no secret what Dom did when Ekko's life was on the line. And what Rocco said was the truth. Dom was crazy. He could go either way, but I was relatively certain he wouldn't be welcoming me to the family anytime soon.

"Yeah, I'll deal with that when the time comes and she's ready to tell her family."

"She wants to hide your relationship?"

Even though he couldn't see me, I shook my head and answered, "No. She just wants to make sure we're solid first."

He stayed quiet a moment. "Good luck. Let me know how it goes when you get to that point."

"Will do. Thanks for the talk, Rocco."

"It's nothing, Enzo. You know it."

Rocco and I disconnected. I sat back in my chair and thought about his words for a few minutes. As difficult as I found it to hear Rocco say the things he always said to me when he thought I needed to hear them, I never let one of those conversations go without a second thought. Sometimes, I'd think about it right after we spoke. Other times, his words would hit me hard when I was alone somewhere and had the headspace to really consider them. I had a feeling, though, that this particular conversation was going to be one I'd replay several times.

I needed to start believing in what others saw in me.

Because now, there was a woman I cared about a lot. And I didn't want the faith she had in me to be misplaced.

CHAPTER 10

Jolie

"**H**OW ARE YOU FEELING NOW, ROSA?"

"Unbelievable," my client answered. "But I should have made this appointment for later in the evening. I just want to go home and nap now."

I let out a laugh. "Well, if it makes you feel any better, it's not the first I've heard that. If it works for you, just schedule your next appointment for one of my later shifts. Then you'll be able to go home and go right to bed."

Rosa sighed, "I think I might do that."

"Perfect," I returned. "I'll step out so you can get dressed. Take your time and be careful getting up off the table. I'll meet you outside your room when you're ready."

"Thank you."

I left Rosa to do her thing while I made my way to the front reception area. After I filled up a small cup of water for her, I looked to Joanne and Niki sitting behind the desk.

"Hey, ladies. My client, Rosa, should be heading out any minute. She's looking to schedule her next appointment for the evening hours. Can you make sure she gets that?"

Joanne gave me a nod as Niki replied, "Absolutely."

I walked out of the reception area and down the hall

toward the room Rosa was in. As I leaned against the wall waiting for her, I gave myself a minute to think about what I had in store for tonight.

Nearly two weeks had passed since my trip to the pumpkin patch with Lorenzo. It was now Friday, one week after Halloween, and Lorenzo told me he had planned a surprise for me. I tried to get it out of him, but he refused to tell me anything. No matter what tactics I tried to engage just to get a tiny hint, he never gave in. All I knew was that he wanted me to come home from work and get ready to go out on a date. The only instructions I had were to dress casually in jeans and sneakers.

I had one more client after Rosa and then I'd be off until Monday.

At that moment, my thoughts were interrupted when the door opened and Rosa walked out.

"Got everything?" I asked as I held the cup of water out to her.

"Yeah, I think so," she replied.

I jerked my head toward the front and shared, "I told Joanne and Niki that you're interested in possibly setting up an evening appointment with me for next time. Just let them know what works for you and I'm sure they'll find something that fits well with your schedule."

"Great. Thank you."

"You're welcome. Have a good one."

Rosa took off while I walked back into the room to change the linens and get everything prepared for my last client. Once I had everything ready, I walked out to check and see who was on the schedule and if they'd added any of the massage enhancements we offered.

When I stepped out into the front reception area, I felt

him there. I looked over to the seating area and saw Lorenzo waiting in a chair.

After I walked over to him, I asked, "Is everything okay?"

"Yeah."

"What are you doing here?"

He grinned at me. "I'm your last appointment today," he explained.

My eyes rounded. "Really?"

It had been such a busy day today that I hadn't had the opportunity to check the schedule when I first arrived at work.

Lorenzo nodded and reached over to the seat next to him. He'd completed his intake form and handed it to me. "Are you ready for me?"

"Yeah," I breathed. "Come with me."

"Planned on it."

I rolled my eyes at him and turned to walk away. I was going to be professional about this, so I treated him the same way I did all my other clients. I opened the door and held it for him.

"We're down the hall in room number four. It's on the left," I explained.

He walked by me and that's when I saw Tara and Brandee standing there with Joanne and Niki. They were all staring at me. Well, they were all staring at the space where Lorenzo had just been.

"Go ahead, girl," Tara encouraged me. "You've got a client waiting."

"Yeah, go," Niki added. "You don't leave a man like that waiting."

I giggled and walked down the hall toward room four. When I stepped inside, I closed the door and barely took two steps before Lorenzo bent and touched his lips to mine.

I stepped back and held my hand up. "You, my friend, are here for a massage. A regular Swedish massage. Unless, of course, you decided to go for the hot stone or deep tissue instead."

He shook his head and admitted, "No, but I did spring for the extra thirty minutes with you."

"Right. Fine. So that means, you will get your massage the same way any other client would and you will not try to distract me from doing my job as the professional that I am. This is a highly-respected salon and there are no happy endings given here. I trust that you'll respect that."

The corners of his mouth tipped up and he wondered, "Do you give this lecture to all of your clients?"

"Nope. You're the only one who's been bold enough to kiss me the second I walked through the door and closed it."

"That makes me feel better."

I smiled and shook my head at him in disbelief. I looked down at his form and checked it over. "Have you ever had a massage before?"

"Nope."

"Any areas of concern?"

He cocked an eyebrow.

"Before you even think about saying it," I began. "I'm the boss in here. If I don't like your answer, this will end before it begins. And, I'll have you know, I give good massages. You'll regret not ever having the opportunity to experience one."

He held his hands up in defeat. "You're the boss. What do I do?"

"I'll step outside while you undress. Most people strip down to your underwear, you can take off or leave on whatever you are comfortable with."

"Jolie, you've seen me naked. Do you really think it's

necessary to step outside the room?" he asked.

"Yes, I do. Because I'm a professional and this is my job. We do it my way or not at all," I insisted.

"Okay. You're in charge."

"We'll start with you face down on the table. I'll be back in a couple minutes."

He gave me a nod and I stepped outside. I took a few deep breaths. I was going to do this, and I was going to remain a professional.

A few minutes later, I knocked on the door.

"Yeah, come in," he responded.

I stepped inside the room, closed the door, and dimmed the light. I didn't need to be distracted by him more than I already was. Lorenzo was face down on the table, the blanket pulled up to his waist.

"Did you have a preference for pressure? Light, medium, firm?"

"Firm," he returned.

"Okay. If it's too much or you'd like me to focus on any one area, please let me know. Otherwise, just relax and enjoy it."

He stayed quiet, so I took that as an indication he was settling in to enjoy his first massage. That was my cue. After rubbing my hands back and forth to put some heat into them, I squirted a generous amount of oil into my palm and got to work.

I stood up by his head and looked down at his body. My hands started at his neck before I ran them down the length of his back. Within just a few minutes, the initial stiffness I felt in his muscles dissipated and I easily managed to work through any lingering tension. After working his neck, shoulders, arms, hands, and upper back, I moved to his lower back. I shifted the blanket farther down and was about to tuck it into the waist-band of his boxer briefs, but I found he didn't have any on.

Great.

Keep it together, Jojo.

Filling my palms with oil again, I put them on either side of his body so that the heels of my palms were against the top curve of his ass. It wasn't normally something I saw as anything other than my job, but this was Lorenzo. He was technically my boyfriend and he had a great ass. I remained focused on the task at hand and gave Lorenzo what I hoped he'd think was an incredible lower back massage. When I finished it several minutes later, I used a hot towel to clean the oil from his upper body.

I covered Lorenzo's torso with the blanket and moved to his legs. In all my years as a massage therapist, I'd given a lot of massages. There hadn't ever been anyone who ever matched Lorenzo in size. His muscles were solid, and he looked amazing, but he had, by far, the tightest leg muscles I'd ever massaged.

Typically, I didn't talk while I was giving someone a massage, so I made a mental note to make sure I discussed what he'd need to do moving forward. I didn't know if he'd listen to me, but I wouldn't be doing my job properly if I ignored it.

Shortly after I finished his legs, I lifted the blanket and had Lorenzo flip over to his back. I moved to the foot of the bed and took care of his feet before I worked my way up his legs and focused on his quads. When I finished them, I came back up to the head of the bed and worked his pectoral muscles.

Most clients kept their eyes closed during their massages, but every time I glanced at his face while I was working, I found him watching me. There was a look of pure adoration in his eyes.

I loved how seeing it made me feel.

When his time was up and I'd finished the massage, I asked, "How are you feeling?"

"I don't know," he started, and I felt my body grow tense. "I have so many thoughts running through my mind right now, but I'm not sure you'll want me to share all of them with you."

"Oh," I sighed, feeling disappointed that he either didn't enjoy or he enjoyed it only for what he likely took as intimacy.

"You're incredible," his voice cut into my thoughts. "Honestly, I never realized just how hard you work and assumed a massage was something that anyone could do. There's no way I could come close to giving you a massage that would be anything like what you just gave me."

"So you enjoyed it?"

"Immensely," he replied.

My mood instantly changed. It felt so good to hear him say that he appreciated the work that I did and that it was actually a pleasant experience for him.

"Can I make a recommendation?" I asked.

His brows pulled together as he answered, "Yeah."

"You need to stretch," I asserted. "I've given a lot of massages, Lorenzo, but your legs have some of the tightest muscles I've ever worked with. It doesn't have to be a lot, but I strongly recommend doing it, even if it's only for ten or fifteen minutes a day."

"Really?"

I nodded. "I'm serious. It would be a really good idea for you to try and get into the habit of it. I'll warn you now that you need to make sure you warm the muscles up first and then stretch. I can show you some good stretches later if you'd like."

"Okay."

I jerked my head back. "Seriously?"

"You're the professional and you're good at what you do. I value what you've got to say," he remarked without a second thought.

"What are you planning to do when you leave here?" I wondered, knowing I needed the opportunity to show him just how much it meant to me to hear him say that.

"Can I answer you honestly?" he challenged.

I gave him a nod.

"I'm planning to wait outside until you leave so that I can forget about the fact you need it to be professional in here and I can tell you exactly what I thought about your massage."

I licked my lips. Lorenzo's eyes dropped to my mouth.

"I'll let you get dressed then," I advised, my voice husky.

I walked out of the room and let out a breath. Lorenzo and I had obviously gotten ourselves very well acquainted with each other a lot over the last several weeks, but something about what just happened in that room was more intimate than any sexual act.

I did my very best to shake it off and walked down the hall to the reception area so that I could get him a cup of water. Thankfully, none of the girls from earlier were there except for Joanne. She happened to be on the phone at the time, so I quickly grabbed Lorenzo's drink and walked back down the hall to wait for him. It was much more than a minute later when the door opened and he stepped out.

I held the cup out to him. "This isn't going to do a whole lot for you, so make sure you drink a lot of water after you leave. I'm not sure what you've got planned tonight, but whatever it is let's hope you'll be able to increase your fluid intake."

He grinned. "I can manage that."

"Great. You can head back down the hall out to the front. One of the girls will help you out. I'm going to get the table linens changed and finish up everything I need to do before I leave. I'll meet you outside?"

"Yep. Thank you for such a fantastic first experience, Jolie."

"You're welcome, Lorenzo."

At that, he turned and walked down the hall while I went back into the room. As quickly as I could, I did what I needed to do. It wasn't more than fifteen minutes later when I found myself standing at the front desk.

"I'm heading out now," I announced as I turned toward the front door.

"Wait!" Niki called out. "You almost forgot your tips for the day and your paystub."

That could have all been easily forgotten. I was too distracted by my thoughts of Lorenzo to focus on anything but him.

I turned around and walked back over to her. "Here you go," she said as she handed me the stack of gratuity envelopes along with my paystub. "Have a great weekend, Jojo."

"I will," I called out as I stepped through the front door and scanned the parking lot. There, parked next to my car, was Lorenzo's truck. With his feet crossed at the ankles and his arms folded over his chest, my breath stuck in my throat. I'd never seen such a beautiful sight before in my life.

As quickly as I could, I stepped off the small sidewalk in front of me and made my way across the mostly-empty lot toward him. With each step I took, closing the distance between us, I saw the look in his eyes grow more and more intense.

Once I was within touching distance, he reached out for me and pulled me into him. He wasted no time crushing his mouth to mine, keeping my body tight to his, while his arousal pressed into me. Slanting his head, he took the kiss deeper and I moaned into his mouth.

When Lorenzo pulled back, he held the back of my head in his hand and declared, "I've never been more turned on in my entire life than I was in that room with your hands doing what they did to me. Magic isn't even the proper word for your hands, baby."

"I told you I was good."

"Magnificent, Jolie. I'm following you to your place. You alright with that?"

I nodded.

With that, Lorenzo opened my door. Once I was safely inside my car, he got in his truck and followed me home. We wasted no time in getting inside so I could use more than just my hands to make him feel good.

Lorenzo, I learned, was no slouch when it came to showing me just how much he enjoyed his massage.

CHAPTER 11

Jolie

"**O**KAY, I'M READY. NOW WILL YOU TELL ME WHERE WE'RE going?"

After Lorenzo and I had come back to my place following the end of my shift, we made good use of the time we had before we needed to leave for whatever it was that he had planned. I finally finished getting myself ready and hoped he'd now tell me what the plan was.

Lorenzo stood there looking at me and his face softened. Instead of telling me where he planned to take us, he stated, "You look pretty, Jolie."

I walked toward him, wrapped my arms around his waist, and melted into him. "Thank you." A moment later, I added, "But you still didn't answer my question."

"Alright, let's go out to the truck. I've got a present for you in there. That will be your clue."

"A present?" I questioned him as I tipped my head back to look at him. "Boss, we need to have a chat."

He raised his brows and gave me a curious look. "A chat about what?"

I needed to cut right to the chase. "You and your spending."

The curious look was gone and replaced by an incredulous one. "You, Jolie Moore, avid shopper and buyer of everything unnecessary, want to discuss me and my spending?

I nodded.

"You bought pumpkins for Hank and Gracie. They don't even know what pumpkins are and they're too young to even appreciate them."

Now I was getting ticked.

"See, now I've got a few problems with that."

At the mere sight of me working myself up to lose it on him, Lorenzo wasn't the least bit fazed. In fact, I saw him working overtime to fight from breaking out into a full-blown grin.

"First, maybe Hank and Gracie don't know what pumpkins are yet and maybe they're too small to appreciate them now, *but* they will grow up and see the pictures I took of them and with them on their first Halloween and they'll say, 'Our aunt is the shit.' But secondly, and most important to note, big guy, is that *I* didn't buy those pumpkins. If you'll recall correctly, it was *you* who handed the money over."

"I was not the one on a mission to break the bank with frivolous purchases," he shot back. "I could have easily been fine with one pumpkin."

"Oh, what fun would that have been?"

"You've just proven my point that spending money on unnecessary things is like a second job for you. I've seen your closet, baby. You've got more clothes than any woman could ever wear in her lifetime. And don't get me started on the shoes."

If my head could have exploded from shock, it would have. "You did not just tell me that I have too many shoes," I warned him.

"Baby, you do."

"I do not!"

"Eighty-three," he stated.

"What?"

"You have eighty-three pairs of shoes. Or, at least, that's how many boxes I counted lined up in your closet. Considering I counted another twenty pairs of shoes not in boxes, I'm guessing your collection tops a hundred."

I had eighty-three pairs of shoes? He counted my shoes?

"Why did you even count my shoes anyway?" I challenged since I had no other response.

"If this works out long term, I need to prepare myself for the fact that you're a big spender and you buy unnecessary things."

I jerked my head back. "I make my own money. I can spend it on what I want."

"I know that, which is why I haven't said anything to you about it. You work hard, you make your money, you pay your bills. If you aren't drowning in debt and can put food on your table all while being excessive with your spending on things you want, then who am I to tell you what you can spend your money on?"

"Precisely my point," I shot back. *Ha! Score one for Jojo.*

He took a step closer to me, put his forefinger under my chin, and tilted my head back. "No, Jolie, precisely my point."

When my brows pulled together, he explained, "You started this conversation telling me you wanted to talk to me about me and my spending. I'm not sure you're in a position to be telling someone how to spend their money when you aren't exactly being very thrifty yourself."

Score negative one for Jojo, plus one million for Lorenzo.

I was silent so long, Lorenzo went on, "Care to explain

where you were headed with that conversation?"

Swallowing hard, I rasped, "I'm not sure I should."

"I think I'd like to hear it."

"Well, it was the pumpkins," I started. "And then today you came in for a massage. That would have been fine, but before I left, they gave me my tip envelopes. After I finished getting ready, I opened those."

"Yeah? And?"

"You already know you put entirely too much money in there," I answered. "It was unnecessary."

He shook his head and maintained, "It was what I believed you deserved for what you did."

I didn't respond, even though I didn't buy his explanation. He put two hundred dollars in the envelope. That was on top of what he paid for the massage itself.

Since I had no reply, he questioned me further. "So, pumpkins and a massage for myself that I enjoyed more than ninety-nine percent of things I've experienced in my life. Those are your two things that I've spent needlessly on?"

"Well, you just said you had a gift for me in the truck," I pointed out.

He nodded. "I can't buy my girlfriend a gift? I can't get her something I want her to have when I know that once she gets it, she's going to be over the moon? I can't want to make her feel that happy because maybe, just maybe, I get something out of seeing her that happy?"

Suddenly, I couldn't breathe. My lips parted and my breath stuck in my throat, my lungs burning.

Unfortunately, Lorenzo didn't say anything else.

The silence stretched on so long and I knew he'd best me in a battle of patience.

"I'm sorry," I rasped.

"It's okay. I enjoyed it."

"You enjoyed what?"

"Our first real disagreement," he clarified.

My eyes rounded. "You enjoyed having a fight with me?"

He shook his head. "Baby, trust me when I say that what we just did was not even remotely close to having a fight. We had a discussion about something we clearly didn't see eye to eye on. That said, even if you were setting yourself up for failure because that was a battle you weren't going to win, it was fun to watch. You're cute when you're all riled up."

My eyes narrowed at him. "I don't find you very funny."

"Are you ready to go?" he asked, changing the subject.

"I'm not sure I want to go anywhere with you right now," I replied as I looked away, feeling downtrodden and doing my best to sulk.

"Jolie?" he called, his tone serious.

When my eyes came to his again, he obliterated me. "This was a huge moment for me. You were here being sassy and trying to throw your weight around. Instead of realizing that I was right to live in fear that I'd one day become my father by thinking that I had a right to put my hands on you for you even thinking you had a right to your opinion, I found you adorable. Can you give me this victory?"

Never.

Not once in the whole discussion, not before, during, or after, did the thought ever cross my mind that he was worried how he'd react to a disagreement with me. And not once did I ever feel fearful. I knew I had no reason to be, but it was clear he still needed some reassurance. If the way this played out between us gave him some peace about the person he was, then I could certainly stop sulking and give him this victory.

I stepped into him, pressed up on my toes, and touched

my lips to his for a quick kiss. With my lips against his, I murmured, "I'm going to set the DVR for the game just in case we aren't back on time. Then you can take me out to the truck and give me my gift."

"Good idea. We definitely won't be back here before the game starts."

After I got the DVR set and started walking to the door so we could leave, Lorenzo reached out to me and gently tugged me toward him. "Thank you, baby."

This meant a lot to him and it moved me to know that he struggled so much with something that I knew he'd never be capable of. And I knew I wasn't the only one who could see that about him. Instead of telling him this, I gave him his victory by offering a small smile and a nod.

After that, Lorenzo and I locked up and left.

Once we were inside the truck, Lorenzo reached back behind my seat and presented me with a gift bag. Grinning at him, I took the bag and pulled the tissue paper out, tossing it away from the bag and letting it float through the air in the cabin of the truck. I looked down, saw the material and the colors, and my heart began racing.

Reaching inside, I clamped my hand around the material and pulled it out. When I let it fall open and I saw exactly what it was, I nearly broke down into tears. Lorenzo said this was a hint about what we were doing tonight. Realization dawned and I dropped my arms so I could look at him.

"Did you get me Rocco De Luca's hockey jersey because you're taking me to the game tonight?" I asked, my voice indicating I was on the verge of a breakdown.

Lorenzo dipped his chin in response.

I couldn't help myself. I climbed across the center console and threw myself at him, crushing my mouth to his. We kissed a long time, our tongues tasting and teeth nibbling while our hands roamed.

Lorenzo eventually tore his mouth away and rested his forehead against mine. "I love it when you're happy. I love how it makes me feel to see you so happy, especially when I know I'm the one that made you feel that way. And as much as I love how you're expressing your happiness right now, if we don't stop we are going to miss the game."

He needed to say nothing else. I climbed back over to my side of the truck, pulled on the De Luca jersey, and asked, "How do I look?"

"You're the most beautiful woman in the world," he proclaimed.

Then, he started the truck and drove away.

We were fortunate enough to live so close to our home team. Thirty minutes later, Lorenzo and I were walking into the arena and I was bursting with excitement on the inside. We got through the security check-in and Lorenzo held my hand as we worked our way through the crowd of Wyoming Summits fans, who had already started chanting for their team. The atmosphere and vibe was unreal. I'd never experienced anything like it and I was so overjoyed I was having my first live game experience with Lorenzo.

"We're here," he stated over the noise surrounding us.

He ushered me to the side and walked down the corridor. Opening a door, he stepped inside one of the exclusive club boxes.

"What are we doing here?" I wondered.

"This is where we're watching the game from," he replied.

"Are you serious?"

He nodded. "Next time we come to a game, we can get seats behind the goal if you want to be closer to the action."

"Next time?" I asked. "Do you come to the games often?"

"As often as I can," he answered, nonchalantly.

"This is my first live game," I shared. "I'm so excited. Thank you so much for bringing me here."

He wrapped his arm around my shoulders and curled me into his body before he pressed a kiss to the top of my head. "I wanted to bring you to the game because I knew you'd have a good time, but I had another motive," he admitted.

I looked up at him, waiting for another explanation.

"Rocco's looking forward to meeting you."

My jaw dropped. "He knows about me?"

Lorenzo nodded.

I didn't say anything for a long time as I processed the information that he'd spoken to his brother about me already. It wasn't long before I noticed Lorenzo started to worry, so I quickly set his mind at ease.

"Do you think he'll sign my jersey?" I wondered.

At that, my big guy burst out laughing. A couple hours later, we'd watched warm-ups, celebrated two goals, and were nearing the end of the second period.

But we were down by two.

I was pacing.

I was angry.

I was going to be absolutely devastated if my first experience at a live game ended in a loss.

Just then, I watched as Rocco got slashed on a breakaway toward the net. The ref missed it and I couldn't control what came over me.

"Get off your knees ref, you're blowing the game!!" I shouted.

I looked to Lorenzo and found him laughing. "Relax, baby. It's okay."

"What?" I shrieked in horror and disbelief. "Are you kidding me? These guys have missed half a dozen calls."

"I know, but you're so worked up. I don't know how I'm going to be able to wait until we get back to your place to do something about it."

Thankfully, five minutes later, I'd mellowed out a touch because we scored. There was nothing like a Summits' goal celebration. By the beginning of the third period, though, I was right back to feeling frustrated. Lorenzo knew it and came up behind me. His hands squeezed my shoulders, trying to relieve some of my tension. It helped a little having him close, but then the ref made another bad call, put the opposing team on the power play, and I lost it.

With each word I yelled, my voice got louder and louder. "I wonder if this ref's wife knows he's fucking us!" I shouted.

Lorenzo's body shook with laughter behind me. He squeezed my shoulders in response and his mouth came to my ear. "Jolie, you've got a filthy mouth when you're pissed."

A whistle blew and I was shocked to find that a penalty was called on the opposing team. It was about time. We were going to be on our first power play of the game, which was great for us. The Summits were second in the league on the power play, largely due to Rocco's slapshot. He didn't have the fastest one in the league, but he was precise. His accuracy was off the charts.

I couldn't sit, but I couldn't stand still either.

During the last ten seconds of the power play, Rocco got a killer pass from his defenseman and rocketed a shot to the back of the net. I jumped up in celebration and turned toward Lorenzo. Throwing my arms around his neck, we celebrated the goal along with the rest of the fans in the arena.

"He's so good," I gushed. "You've got to be so proud of

him, boss."

Grinning huge, Lorenzo replied, "I am."

The third period ended in a tie, so we went to overtime. Nobody scored during the five-minute overtime, which meant the game ended up going to a shootout. Our goalie was one of the best in the league. He was a seasoned player and had been in his fair share of shootouts.

Two of our guys ended up scoring, one of those guys being Rocco, and we won the game. After a massive celebration in the arena, Lorenzo and I sat down to relax. Rocco was going to need some time before he'd be ready to come out and meet me, and it wasn't like there was anywhere we could go with droves of people filing out. Since we were in the box and had food and refreshments at our disposal, Lorenzo and I ate while we waited.

It was only then that I started feeling some nerves about meeting Lorenzo's brother. Today had proved to be such a wonderful day and I didn't want anything happening to mess with it.

Not quite an hour later, the door to our club room box opened and in walked Rocco. He walked right up to Lorenzo and pulled him in for a hug as Lorenzo congratulated him.

"Rocky, this is my girl, Jolie. Jolie, this is Rocco."

I held my hand out to him. "It's so nice to meet you," I said. "Great game. Congratulations on the win."

"Thanks," he replied. "With the calls being made tonight, it was no easy feat."

Lorenzo's laughter filled the room. "You have no idea. Don't let her ladylike disposition fool you. This woman was livid with the refs throughout the game, shouting obscenities at them."

Rocco's disbelieving eyes came to mine. The corners

of his mouth twitched before he hinted, "Well, it must have worked because we finally got that call at the end."

I offered a goofy grin in return.

"Jolie was hoping you'd sign her new jersey for her."

"Absolutely," he responded. "I'll get you a signed stick before you leave, too."

"Are you serious? I'm going to cry."

For the next ten minutes Lorenzo, Rocco, and I hung out and made small talk. That all changed, though, when Lorenzo excused himself to use the restroom.

The second he walked out of earshot, Rocco leaned in. "I hope you'll take no offense to this, but my brother's put himself through hell for me, so I feel it's my job to do this now. In just the short phone call I had with him a couple weeks ago and seeing the two of you together now, I know where his head is with you. I also know how he's lived his life up until now. I'm thrilled that he's finally opened himself up to love, but I'm worried how he'll cope if this doesn't end well."

I was caught off guard, but I understood Rocco's mindset. "I don't know what to say," I started. "I can't say where this will end up, but I really like your brother. A lot. He makes me happy, happier than I've been in a long time, and I'd like to think I do the same for him. Regardless, I know what he's been through—what you've both been through—and I wouldn't go into this lightly. This isn't just a passing fling for me. I really do care about him."

Rocco dipped his chin. "I can respect that. It just worried me a bit when he told me you weren't ready to tell your family."

"My sister knows," I immediately put in. "I just didn't want to tell the rest of my family yet. My brother's wife just had two babies about a month ago and I don't want to do anything to cause him any stress or worry. I don't believe there's anything for him to worry about, but he's my brother and that's just the way he is."

"I've met Dom. I understand it," he assured me. "To that end, and this is the last I'll say on it, I don't want to see Enzo fall hard for you and then have his heart broken. This was a huge step for him. Please don't make him regret opening his heart to you."

I jerked my head back in surprise. I really hadn't expected this conversation at all. Initially, I understood it, but now I wasn't so sure how I felt about it. I really liked Lorenzo and knew we were well on our way to a much deeper connection. But I couldn't make predictions about the future. I couldn't know for sure that things would turn out the way any one person wanted. As much as I might have wanted to give Rocco that guarantee that his brother and I would go the distance, I couldn't. I did know, though, that I'd never intentionally set out to hurt Lorenzo and that I absolutely hoped we'd go the distance.

I was caught up in my thoughts over what Rocco said that I never saw Lorenzo approach. I also didn't see his face change when he noted the look on my own.

"I was gone not even three minutes," he announced. "Why does my woman look like she's lost inside her own head worrying about something?"

"Enzo—" Rocco started, but I cut him off.

"I'm fine," I insisted. "Rocco and I were just chatting. It's all good."

"Bullshit, Jolie. What did he say to you?"

I didn't want to start trouble between them, but I knew Lorenzo was not going to stand for me staying silent. Thankfully, I didn't have to worry too long about how to share the conversation Rocco and I had because Rocco chimed in.

"I was doing my job and looking out for you, Enzo. I know what we went through and I know how you've handled it. I'm ecstatic you've got her in your life now; I just don't want to see things go south between the two of you and then you end up not living again."

"And you thought it was wise to ambush her when I wasn't here to have her back?" Lorenzo scoffed. "You know I love you, Rocky, but don't ever fucking do that to her again."

Rocco grinned at Lorenzo, which I thought was not a wise move on his part, before he simply stated, "Protector. Always have been, always will be."

Something flashed in Lorenzo's face.

If I understood what happened correctly, Rocco purposely made me uncomfortable to get his brother to see the truth behind the kind of person he was. Rocco knew, as much as I did, that Lorenzo wouldn't stand for anyone 'ambushing' me or hurting me, so he did what he had to do to make sure Lorenzo could see it too. For that reason, Rocco earned a spot on my Christmas card list.

To break up the tension, I wondered, "Alright, so what's a girl got to do to get a signed jersey around here?"

Their eyes came to me. Lorenzo saw that I was no longer distressed, so he relaxed and Rocco knew that I wasn't holding anything against him. Any lingering friction between the brothers vanished and Rocco saw to it that I got my jersey signed.

I also managed to snag a signed stick.

Before we left, Lorenzo and I made plans with Rocco for the next game we wanted to come and watch. After seeing me in action tonight, Lorenzo thought it might be better for us to have the privacy of a box again, but I really wanted to be close to the action. He begrudgingly gave in and Rocco assured us he'd get us great seats.

We said goodbye to him and left.

That night, cuddled up in my bed with him, I found myself falling just a little bit harder for Lorenzo. He'd given me a truly unforgettable day. I thought he should know what it meant to me.

"Boss?" I called, unsure if he had fallen asleep.

"Right here, baby."

"Thank you for today."

His hand, which had been wrapped around mine on top of his chest, lifted mine and brought it to his lips. He kissed my knuckles before placing my hand back over his heart.

"No. Thank you."

I shifted my body a little closer to his and gave him a squeeze.

"Good night, Lorenzo."

"Good night, Jolie."

A few minutes later, we both succumbed to the exhaustion from our fun-filled night.

CHAPTER 12

Jolie

THE MORNING STARTED OUT SIMILAR TO THE ONE I EXPERIENCED the first time Lorenzo and I had gotten together. I had woken up early and snuck out of bed to make some coffee. I figured I'd make the coffee and take an extra cup back upstairs to the bedroom for Lorenzo.

While I waited for the coffee to brew, there was a light tap at the door. It was early and I wasn't expecting anyone, so when I approached the door I asked, "Who is it?"

"It's me, Jojo," the familiar voice answered.

Oh. Crap.

I couldn't pretend to not be home now. I couldn't even pretend to be sleeping.

What was I going to do?

I disabled the alarm, took in a deep breath, and opened the door.

"Morning, Jojo," my brother greeted me as he pressed a kiss to my cheek and walked in.

"Good morning, Dom," I replied, staring at the empty space where he once stood.

After I closed the door, I followed him to the kitchen. He had plopped down onto one of the stools. The moment his eyes came to mine, he pleaded, "I need your help."

Instantly, my body went alert. "What's wrong? Are the babies okay?"

"Yeah, yeah. They're fine," he assured me. "I had to run an errand for Ekko but needed to talk to you about something. Since I was in the area, I figured it was easiest to just stop by. Next week is Ekko's birthday. I want to take her out for a few hours to get her out of the house. She needs a break and I figure her birthday is the perfect excuse. Unfortunately, if I don't have a plan in place, there is no way she'll agree to anything."

"Okay, do you want me to watch Hank and Gracie for you?" I wondered.

His head, which had been looking down at the counter, slowly lifted and he answered, "Yes."

"Sure."

"You really don't mind? It's a lot. With Mom and Dad being away next week, I couldn't ask them. I know Colton and Memphis would never let anything harm them, but I'm not sure how they'd manage on diaper duty. I haven't talked to Kendall, but I'm not sure if she's working at the hospital. I'll reach out to her and see if she's able to stop in then, too."

"Dom, it's fine. I can handle them."

My brother sat there staring at me, relief in his face. I could see how tired he was, but I also knew he loved every minute of being a father.

"What day and what time do you need me?" I asked.

"You tell me what works for you and I'll adjust accordingly. Her birthday is on Thursday, but I can wait until the weekend if that works better for you."

I shook my head. "No, Thursday is fine. I'm working next weekend, so I'll actually be off on Thursday. And you don't need to worry about coming back early because I don't have to be to work on Friday until after lunchtime. Enjoy your time with your wife. The two of you need that time with each other."

"Thanks, Jojo. You're the best."

I grinned at him. "I know."

We sat there grinning at each other, in complete silence, when I suddenly heard the creak from the second to last step on my staircase.

Shit.

I couldn't think fast enough.

Dom's body went alert before he whispered, "Is someone here?"

My eyes rounded, but just as I was about to answer, we heard the voice before the body entered the room, "Jolie, baby, I was thinking—"

Lorenzo stopped speaking. He had walked into the kitchen, in just jeans, and froze. The tension in the air was thick and nobody said anything. The silence stretched on for a long time. I was nervously biting my bottom lip, Lorenzo hadn't moved, and Dom's eyes were narrowed moving back and forth between his friend and me.

When Dom's eyes finally settled, they settled on Lorenzo.

"How long?" he asked.

"A little over a month," Lorenzo replied immediately.

Dom shifted his gaze to me. "Jojo, why didn't you tell me?" His voice was strained, thick with emotion. He was hurt.

I swallowed hard. "Dom, I'm sorry. We got together right after Hank and Gracie were born and you had a lot on your plate. I didn't know how you'd react and the last thing I wanted was for you to have your focus on anything but those babies. It was my choice not to tell you."

Dom looked back to Lorenzo. "You know I love you like a

brother, man, but if she's not different than every other woman you've ever been with, we're going to have a serious problem."

While I really didn't like hearing about Lorenzo with any other woman, a small part of me was amused by the irony of the situation. Last night, Rocco made it clear to me that Lorenzo was his concern. This morning, Dom was making it clear to Lorenzo that his only concern was me.

"She's very different," Lorenzo promised.

My brother stood from the stool and walked around the counter. I held my breath, waiting for the worst possible scenario to break out. Then, I realized I didn't want that to happen, so I moved quickly and put myself between the two of them.

Lorenzo immediately stepped forward, put his hand on my arm, and nudged me to the side so he could position himself in front of me.

"I'm not going to hit my sister," Dom exclaimed.

"I know that," Lorenzo returned. "But if you decide you want to hit me, there's not going to be even a remote possibility that she's going to get caught in the middle of that."

My eyes rounded.

Would Dom hit Lorenzo?

Dom was quick when he lifted his arm and wrapped it around Lorenzo, pulling him in for a man hug. Lorenzo was frozen solid, completely caught off guard.

"I couldn't be any happier for the two of you," Dom shared when he stepped back from Lorenzo. "It should come as no surprise that I want the absolute best for Jojo, but I love this for you," he directed his attention at Lorenzo.

Dom was giving us his blessing. I could have jumped for joy.

"You…" Lorenzo stammered, clearly shocked by Dom's

reaction. "You aren't worried?"

Dom jerked his head back. "Worried about what?"

Lorenzo's voice got quiet and was filled with agony when he answered, "That I could turn out to be just like him and hurt her one day."

"Brother..." Dom trailed off.

I felt myself getting emotional. The lump in my throat was growing by the second and seeing the pain in Lorenzo's face was heartbreaking.

Putting his hand on Lorenzo's shoulder, and with a finality and conviction in his tone that spoke volumes, Dom stated, "Not at all."

Lorenzo dropped his gaze to his feet as the breath left his lungs.

Dom didn't quit. "I'm not sure I could hand pick anyone that I'd trust more than you to do right by her and I don't doubt that you'll do everything in your power to make sure she's always safe. I don't know where things will end up between the two of you, but I know you'd never lay a hand on her."

Lorenzo lifted his head and insisted, "Your blessing means a lot, Dom. Thank you for not making this difficult for us, especially for her."

Dom nodded and looked to me.

"I'm pissed that you didn't tell me, Jojo, but I understand your logic behind keeping it from me."

"I'm sorry and I appreciate you not completely losing your mind this morning."

Dom walked over to me, pulled me in for a hug, and kissed the top of my head.

"Don't hide shit from me," he ordered. "That's not who you are."

"I know. I won't."

"I'm going to get out of here and get back to my wife and kids. Thank you for agreeing to watch them on Thursday," he started as he began walking out of the kitchen. He stopped, looked at Lorenzo, and back at me. "If he's free and wants to join you, I'd feel better knowing you've got an extra set of hands."

"Okay."

I walked Dom to the door and said goodbye. As I walked back toward the kitchen, Lorenzo's back was to me and I noticed he had barely moved.

"I'm so sorry," I lamented from behind him. "He just stopped over to ask me to watch the kids for him this coming week so he could take Ekko out for her birthday. His visit was completely unexpected."

Lorenzo turned slowly toward me. His eyes, so dark and intense, fixed on mine as he brought his hands up to frame my face.

"Why did you do that?"

My body went solid. Did he think I purposely set him up?

"I...Lorenzo, I didn't—" I got out before he cut me off.

"Why did you get between your brother and me?" he snapped.

I didn't understand what he was upset about. I didn't come between them. Dom left on good terms with both of us.

"What? He's fine. Dom's not angry about us being together," I asserted.

Lorenzo shook his head. "No, Jolie. When the situation was tense and he stood a few feet in front of me, you walked over and put yourself in the middle. Why?"

"I didn't want things to get physical. We still didn't know how he'd react and I wanted to try to diffuse the situation before it came to that."

His fingertips pressed in. "If there's ever a situation where there is a threat to me, you *do not ever* get in the middle of it. You do not sacrifice yourself to protect me, Jolie."

I blinked my surprise at him. "My brother would never hit me. I knew that and took advantage to help diffuse the situation."

"No," he clipped. "That is never an option. It's non-negotiable. You do not ever become the target for anyone's unpredictability. And you especially don't do it to protect me."

"Can you?" I asked.

"Can I what?"

"Can you become the target for me? Are you allowed to do what you have to do to protect me?"

"Is that a serious question?"

I raised my brows at him, indicating I was waiting for a reply. He never gave one so, feeling annoyed, I went on, "If you can do it, so can I."

Lorenzo was growing more and more agitated. "If your brother decided to throw a punch at me, I can handle it. If he does that and you get clipped instead, it's going to be a lot worse for you. Why would you ever consider doing that?"

"Because that's what you do when you love someone!" I shouted.

I gasped.

The look in Lorenzo's eyes was intense, but still very guarded.

"What?" he whispered.

"I love you."

I barely got the words out when he crushed his mouth to mine, his hands sliding back into my hair. Lorenzo walked me backward until my back was against the wall. He lifted me up and my legs immediately wrapped around his waist.

"Shirt off," he ordered.

I whipped my sleep shirt over my head and tossed it aside. Lorenzo's mouth went to my jaw. His lips moved down my throat as one hand came up and cupped my breast, his thumb swiping over my nipple.

"Lorenzo," I rasped.

"Baby," he breathed against my skin. "Fuck, Jolie."

He stepped back and lowered me to my feet.

"What's wrong?"

"Need to get a condom," he explained.

I reached my hand out and grabbed his wrist. His eyes came back to mine. "Have you always been safe? Have you been tested?"

"I got myself tested right after we got together," he responded. "I've always worn protection, but I still wanted to be sure for you. Since we've been together, I haven't been with anyone else and I'm clean."

"I am, too. And I'm on birth control," I shared.

His hands went to the fly of his jeans. "Are you sure you want this?"

I nodded, sliding my fingers under the material of my panties at my hips. I began pushing them down and shimmied my legs back and forth until they fell to the floor.

His jeans landed on the ground, his belt buckle clanging against the tiled floor.

Stepping back toward me, he wrapped his arm around my waist and put his other hand on my thigh.

"Guide me in, baby," he encouraged.

I reached my hand between us and guided him in. My back was against the wall as Lorenzo kept himself still, pressed tight against me.

"You feel so good, boss," I moaned.

He pulled back slowly before thrusting back in just as languidly.

The sound of his groan filled the air. "Jolie," he whispered.

My breaths came quick, my chest rising and falling against his. Lorenzo began moving his hips faster, easily finding a steady rhythm.

As he moved, it built. And it built quick on all that I was feeling, on all that I'd just shared. I'd put myself between him and a threat because that was what you did when you loved someone.

I loved him.

I loved Lorenzo.

His mouth took mine. He kissed me hard, wet, and deep. The feeling was beginning to take over me. I disconnected my mouth from his, dropped my head back to the wall, and felt his tongue at my throat.

"Lorenzo," I practically purred, feeling myself close and on the verge.

"Say it," he ordered.

"What?"

He slowed his pace and my eyes shot to his as I whimpered. "Don't stop," I begged.

"Say it, Jolie."

I couldn't focus as I felt my orgasm slip away.

"Tell me how you feel about me," he demanded.

"I love you," I breathed.

He kissed me.

He picked up his pace.

He built me up again in no time at all.

And then I shattered. My body convulsed around his, my limbs clinging tightly to him.

Several thrusts later, Lorenzo buried himself deep and groaned into my neck.

My big guy kept us like that a long time, his strong, powerful body pressed against mine, holding me against the wall. It took a while, but he eventually lifted his chest from mine and began walking with me in his arms.

Lorenzo carried me upstairs, got me steady on my feet outside the bathroom, and instructed, "Go get cleaned up. Meet me in the bedroom."

A few minutes later, I walked into my room and found him lying on his side in the bed underneath the covers. Taking a few strides in his direction, I made it to the bed and climbed in beside him, my back to the bed.

While there were a million thoughts running through my head, I was hoping that he'd say something. I'd just told him I loved him and he hadn't said it back. If I started rambling, I knew I'd end up having a total meltdown.

Thankfully, Lorenzo saved me from my fate. His fingers lightly traced along the top swells of my breasts. "I've never been in love," he stated. "I never gave myself the opportunity to fall in love. For my entire life, I've done everything I can to avoid having that happen. And I've been successful until now. Until you."

I felt the lump forming in my throat again.

"I love you, Jolie. I swear to you that I'm telling you that because it's true and not because you've just said it to me. I didn't want this to happen, but you single-handedly crushed every wall I built. You're the most beautiful woman I've ever seen and your heart is...there's nothing like it. I love the way you live your life and I'm hoping to be part of it for as long as you'll allow me to be in it."

Tears were spilling from my eyes, sliding down into the

hair at the sides of my head. Lorenzo wiped them away.

"It's been a little more than a month since we started this thing between us, baby, and I've got to tell you...it's been the best month of my life. Bar none."

"Lorenzo," I cried quietly.

I turned my body toward his, buried my face in his chest, and held him tight. His free arm curled around me and pulled me close.

"This has been the best day ever," I eventually said.

He gave me a gentle squeeze and agreed quietly, "Yeah, it has."

"It's still early, though," I noted. "How are we going to make sure it doesn't go downhill from here?"

"I can't think of much that could ruin what today has meant to me, but I'd say if we want to continue with the good, we should probably get you donuts for breakfast."

"That sounds fabulous. And then maybe later I can give you a massage with a happy ending."

I felt Lorenzo's body vibrate with laughter. "That'll work for me."

At that, Lorenzo and I got up and got ourselves ready. Then, he took me out for donuts so we could plan the rest of our day. While there wasn't anything that was going to top the morning we had, we still ended up having the best day together.

CHAPTER 13

Jolie

"**H**E WANTS ME TO MEET HIS MOM."

I was at my sister's place, sitting on the opposite end of the couch from her, giving her a life update. It was Wednesday, a few days after Lorenzo took me to my first live hockey game and after we were subsequently discovered by my brother, and I had just given Kendall the details of all that. I also shared that Lorenzo and I had officially fallen in love.

To say my sister was ecstatic was an understatement. I had always been grateful for the fact that I had Kendall there for me. There was nothing like having a person there for you that you knew you could always count on. And while I knew my brothers would move mountains for me, it just didn't compare to having her. No matter how talkative and outgoing a person I was, there were certain things that I'd never share with them that I could always share with her.

One of those things was the fact that two days ago, Lorenzo told me he wanted me to meet his mom.

"That's good news, Jojo. Meeting the parents is huge," she bubbled with excitement for me. "Why does it seem like you're worried about this?"

"This wasn't something I wanted to share, but Lorenzo said it doesn't bother him if I do. I'm not meeting his parents; I'm just meeting his mom."

"Okay, I still don't understand."

"Remember when all of Dom and Ekko's wedding stuff was going on and you and some of the other girls said you could see that Lorenzo was attracted to me? Remember how I tried to do something about it on the day of the wedding and he shot me down?"

"Of course. As much fun as we had at the wedding, you were completely devastated. How could I forget?"

I took in a deep breath and blew it out. "He wasn't turning me down because he wasn't attracted to me. He was doing it because he was afraid of hurting me."

She made a face and said, "Wow, if all men would be that chivalrous."

I shook my head. "No, sissy. He isn't necessarily worried about breaking my heart. He believes that he'll physically hurt me."

Kendall's body tensed and she sat up a little straighter. "What?"

"Lorenzo's father abused his mother through a good chunk of his childhood. It continued until Lorenzo finally took a stand at the age of fifteen. They got out, but he still worries he'll end up being just like his father."

My sister's face was filled with shock and concern. "Wow, Jojo, that's awful. The very few times I've been around him, he always seemed so quiet and focused. I mean, you had to practically jump him to get him distracted at bowling. What about Dom? Does he know about Lorenzo's family?"

I nodded. "Yeah, and that's what came up this weekend when Dom stopped over. I told you Dom found out about us, but I didn't tell you that I thought they were going to throw down right in my kitchen. I stepped right in between them and Lorenzo immediately moved me. After Dom gave us his blessing because he completely trusts Lorenzo and knows the kind of guy he is, he left. Then, Lorenzo got angry with me."

"Wait, what? What did he do to you?"

"He was angry I stepped between him and Dom. He said that it's never an option for me to put myself between him and any potential threat. I told him that that's what you do when you love someone. Then we made love."

Kendall was quiet for a minute while she processed everything I told her. When she spoke, she asked, "So, if this was how he responded and you look at everything that's happened between you since the first time you met him, I don't get why he thinks he'll end up like his father. He helped you out when you had that situation with the guy at Carter's."

"That's just it," I stressed. "It seems that everyone else can see how great of a guy he is, but he can't. He keeps thinking back to the fact that his father wasn't always abusive. His mom fell in love with a man who, at some point, treated her right. Lorenzo said the abuse didn't start until he was eight."

She shook her head in disgust. "I feel so horrible for him. So, let's bring this back to meeting his mom. Are you worried about it?"

Shrugging my shoulders, I answered honestly, "I'm not sure. You know me, I'll talk to anyone. But Lorenzo said that it was fifteen years ago when his father put his hands on his mother for the last time. He said it broke her spirit. I don't know if I know what to say to her."

"Be yourself, Jojo," she insisted. "Look, everything you've told me so far leads me to believe that Lorenzo is a level-headed guy. I don't think he'd put you nor his mom through that if she was fragile. I'm not saying that the abuse she endured didn't affect her life in a big way, but I'm sure she's figured out how to live her life in a way that's peaceful to her now."

"I don't want to disrupt that for her, though," I worried.

"I get what you're saying, but I don't think you'll be doing that. And if this is the man you love, then you've got to trust that he knows what he's doing in this situation."

Kendall was right.

Lorenzo was a very smart man. He didn't do things that didn't make sense and I had to trust him. He knew what his mom could handle, and he knew who I was. I resolved to put my faith in him and trust that he'd do what was best for everyone involved.

I smiled at Kendall and announced, "You're so smart. How is it possible that someone hasn't snatched you up yet?"

She rolled her eyes, "Your guess is as good as mine. I just don't know if it's ever going to happen for me, sis. I'm not getting any younger and it's slim pickings out there."

"He's out there. Before you know it, he'll come crashing into your life and you'll almost forget what it was like to live without him."

"Ha!" she scoffed. "I won't hold my breath."

"Don't be so cynical, Kendall. Trust me, he's out there."

She shot me a small smile and a head tilt.

"Well, I've got to get going. I have to be at work in thirty minutes."

"Yeah, I'm just relaxing today because I'm working all weekend," Kendall shared.

I got up off the couch and started gathering my things. Kendall stood and walked with me to the door. After giving hugs to one another, we said goodbye, and I left.

I walked into work, made sure my room was ready for my

first client, and still had ten minutes to spare. Ava happened to be working the same shift, so we used that time before our clients arrived to catch up.

After I brought her up to speed as quickly as possible on all things between Lorenzo and me, she told me about her plans to go and visit her family for the upcoming Thanksgiving holiday. Ava and her family were originally from Wyoming, but when Ava was going to school to become an aesthetician, her parents decided to move to Colorado and now lived in a smaller town just outside of Denver. Wyoming has always been home to Ava, but she still tries to visit with her parents regularly.

"I bet they're excited you're coming to visit," I said. "How long will you be gone?"

"I have a lot of time saved up and it's been a little while since I've seen them, so I'm going to leave next weekend and stay with them through the Thanksgiving weekend. My mom is ecstatic. Dad is too, but he doesn't vocalize it nearly as much as Mom. But don't worry. I'll be available for you to vent if the meeting of his mom doesn't go well. Are you planning to have him over for Thanksgiving with your family?"

I tilted my head to the side, my ear hovering above my shoulder. "We haven't yet made official plans, but now that Dom knows and he's cool with us, I don't think I'll need to worry about the rest of the family. If they all see he's cool with Lorenzo and me, they'll all be cool too. Besides, with Hank and Gracie in the picture now, nobody can really stay mad for too long anyway."

Trudi walked into the back room and said, "Ava, your client is here."

"Okay, thanks. I'll be right out," she replied before turning her attention back to me. "I've got to get to it, but if I don't catch up with you before you leave, good luck on meeting the mom."

"Say a prayer for me!" I called out to her departing backside.

A few minutes later, my client had arrived, and I got myself focused on my work. The hours passed and, with each massage I gave, I found myself becoming more and more relaxed. Between Kendall's words from earlier that day and the words Lorenzo said to me over the weekend, I had no reason to believe that meeting his mom wouldn't go well.

Since I worked until closing, I didn't get home until a little before eleven o'clock. After locking up and setting my alarm, I climbed the stairs, took a shower, and crawled into bed. Reaching out to grab my phone off the nightstand, I sent a quick text to Lorenzo.

Hey, I didn't want to call so late. Hope you had a good day.

Not quite a minute later, my phone rang.

Smiling into the phone, I answered, "Did I wake you?"

"I can't fall asleep until I hear from you and know that you're home safe, so no, you didn't wake me."

Warmth spread through me.

"How was your day?" I wondered.

"Relatively uneventful, all things considered. Yours?"

I laughed. "The complete opposite. I visited with Kendall for a while this morning. Then, I chatted with Ava for a bit before my first client came in. I had a full schedule tonight, so there wasn't much downtime for me."

"Are you ready for tomorrow?" he asked.

I wasn't going to lie to him. "I'm nervous," I admitted.

"About meeting my mom?" he questioned me.

"Yeah."

"Baby, she's one of the kindest women you'll ever meet. I promise you."

I loved that he was worried about me like that. "It's not necessarily her liking me that I'm worried about, boss. I'm concerned that I'll do or say the wrong thing and make her uncomfortable."

"If I were there right now, I'd kiss you," he stated. "Jolie, if you just be yourself, you've got nothing to worry about. My mom's been through a lot, but she's a strong woman. And she's really excited to meet you."

"Okay," I accepted his promises.

Silence settled between us.

I eventually broke it when I whispered, "I miss you, boss."

"Miss you too, baby."

"I like falling asleep with your arms around me," I divulged. "I'm lonely now."

Lorenzo didn't respond, but I heard him rustling around.

When too much time had passed without a reply from him, I called, "Lorenzo?"

"Right here."

"I didn't know where you were. You didn't say anything," I explained.

"I was getting clothes on. What's your code?"

"My code?"

"For your alarm. I can get in without the key, but I need the code."

I wasn't surprised he could pick my lock, but I didn't expect him to drive to my place at this hour. "You're coming here?"

"Do you miss me?"

"Yeah."

"You said you're lonely, Jolie. I've spent a lot of my life

living in solitude. My woman is in her bed right now feeling sad because she's alone. I know what that's like, so I'm coming over to keep her company."

This was why I loved him. Unfortunately, I wasn't sure it was a good idea that he came over tonight.

"Lorenzo, that's not necessary," I advised. "We both need to get a good night's sleep. Tomorrow is a big day."

"I'm already in my truck. Are you going to give me the code or are you planning to wake your neighbors when your alarm goes off?"

"Zero, two, one, nine," I rattled off.

"Okay, I'm on my way. See you soon, baby."

Just over ten minutes later, I heard his footsteps on the stairs. A few seconds after that, I saw him walk into the bedroom. I heard his shoes thud when they hit the floor followed by his clothes. And a moment later, I felt the bed depress with his weight.

Climbing under the blankets with me, he brought his mouth to my bare shoulder and kissed me there.

"Lorenzo—" I started before he cut me off.

"Shh, let me give you what you need, Jolie. You have a big day tomorrow; let me be here with you tonight."

"Love you, boss."

"Love you too."

Minutes later, tucked tight to Lorenzo's body and no longer feeling lonely, I fell asleep.

"You're a dream come true."

"What?" I gasped.

Soft, kind eyes met mine. "I've prayed for years that he'd find you."

I was sitting next to Lorenzo's mom, Marilena, inside her quaint little home in the suburbs. Lorenzo and Kendall had been right. Apparently, being myself was all that was necessary because Lena, as she asked to be called, wasn't holding anything back.

Lorenzo and I had arrived about two and a half hours ago. After introducing his mom and me, we all fell right into an easy, light-hearted conversation. Lorenzo took the lead, guiding it for all of us and making sure things never got awkward. We had just finished up lunch and Lorenzo left his mom and me there alone while he took her dog out for a walk. Lena was now taking that opportunity to tell me how she really felt about me.

"You prayed he'd find me?" I questioned, not sure I understood.

Her shoulders sank.

"My boys are the lights of my life. I know they're grown now, but they'll always be my babies. Rocco hasn't let anything get him down. He's so resilient, you'd never know what he endured as a child. He owes that to his brother; he was lucky he had Lorenzo there for him."

She paused a moment, composing herself.

"Lorenzo took it all in, shouldering that responsibility, shielding his brother from it. I'm so proud of him, but I saw what it did to him. We all went into therapy as soon as I could make that happen, but so much damage had already been done. And over the years, I saw my boy go inside himself."

My heart was breaking. I wanted to hear everything she had to tell me, but I wasn't sure how much more I could handle.

"When he started working as a private investigator, I knew it was about more than just needing a job. He needed to feel like he was doing something to right wrongs. But he also found a job that would allow him the opportunity to work alone. And that's okay; he's really good at it."

She slowly began shaking her head back and forth, seemingly disappointed. "But as the years went on, he never talked to me about anything personal. His life always seemed to be about work, the guys he worked with who became his closest friends, or his brother. Never a girlfriend, never a female friend. And I knew that was my fault. I should have gotten him out of there sooner. I shouldn't have let it get to the point that it did because it made him seclude himself. Seeing what his father did to me broke something in Lorenzo."

Tears were welling up in my eyes.

"Whatever it was, it was broken until you. He came to see me a couple weeks ago and, the second he walked in the door, I knew. I knew he'd found you. Or maybe it was you who found him. It doesn't matter how it happened; all that matters is that it did. He was so lonely. I knew it and I didn't know how to get him to see that it didn't have to be that way for him. He's got so much love inside him. It would be a shame for him to never share that with someone."

As the tears spilled down my cheeks, I finally spoke. "Lena, he's worried he's going to become his father. He fears that one day down the road he'll hurt me."

"Jolie, he won't. He's such a gentle, protective man who loves so hard he couldn't possibly ever hurt you. I promise you that he would never raise a hand to you."

I smiled at her and assured her, "I know that. I knew that from the moment I met him. I just wish he could see what everyone else sees in him."

"Give him time, dear. You might not see it because you didn't see that change in him over the years, but I do. He's slowly coming back. I saw it a couple weeks ago just barely there. But today, I see it even more. Lorenzo has had a massive weight lifted off his shoulders. He's still working on trusting in who he is deep down, but I know he's going to get there. And seeing him today with you, I feel like I didn't completely fail him as a mother. Now I feel like I'll be able to finish healing."

I don't know what prompted me to do it, but I blurted, "He told me he loves me."

She let out a little laugh. "You don't need to tell me that, Jolie. I can see it. A lot of mothers worry about their sons growing up and finding a good woman, wondering if she'll take care of him the way he needs. I don't have a single doubt in my mind that you are perfect for my son. You've taken that loneliness from him. He smiles more now. And the way he looks at you...I just know he's fallen so hard for you."

Her words were slowly killing me. I had been so worried about how this meeting of his mom would go, but I clearly had no reason to be concerned. She was seeing a positive change in him and that was helping her. I had a feeling that the broken spirit Lorenzo spoke of when he talked about her had little to do with what his father did to his mother and more to do with what Lorenzo witnessing that did to him. Lena had been holding on to guilt that her choice to stay in that home with that man for as long as she did took something away from her child. Now that he was getting that back, I had a feeling it wouldn't be long before Lorenzo started seeing a change in her.

As if on cue, the door opened and Daphne, Lena's Great Dane, came charging in. Lorenzo walked in behind her, took one look at his mom and me, and sighed, "Something told me not to go. I knew I was going to come back and find at least one of you crying."

I stood and walked over to him. Wrapping my arms around his waist, I promised, "It's all good, boss."

His arm came around my shoulders and curled me into his side. We managed to get about two seconds of cuddling in before Daphne was barking at our feet. I immediately gave her my full attention with a few scratches behind the ears. That turned into her rolling to her back, demanding some belly rubs. I obliged her by not only rubbing her belly but also talking to her the entire time.

Thirty minutes later, Lorenzo suggested, "We should get going, Jolie. We have to be at Dom and Ekko's soon and you insist on stopping to buy gifts for the babies."

"Babies?" his mother wondered.

"My niece and nephew," I explained. "Today is my sister-in-law's birthday and my brother wanted to take her out for the first time since she gave birth to twins at the beginning of last month. Lorenzo and I are watching the babies for them tonight."

Lena's eyes began to sparkle. Suddenly, I think she had visions of her son giving her grandchildren one day. It was still way too early in our relationship for something like that, but I knew I wanted children one day. And the thought of having those kids with Lorenzo filled me with warmth.

To get the visions of Lorenzo as a dad out of my mind, I bent back down to Daphne. "Next time I visit you, I'll bring you something fun to play with, girl. I didn't know you were here or I would have brought something this time."

"Jolie, you don't need to bring toys for the dog."

I scowled at Lorenzo. "Yes, I do."

He shook his head and rolled his eyes at me.

After giving one last round of scratches and rubs to Daphne, Lorenzo and I said goodbye to his mom, promising to visit again soon.

Twenty-five minutes later, we'd ended up at the mall so I could buy things to spoil Hank and Gracie. While I was there, I managed to find something for a lovable Great Dane, too.

If he really had a problem with it, Lorenzo never gave me a hard time about it.

CHAPTER 14

Jolie

"**W**HAT DO YOU THINK ABOUT FRENCH BULLDOGS?" I asked Lorenzo as I looked up at him from where I had my head resting on his chest. I was curled up next to him on the couch at Dom and Ekko's place and both babies were asleep. We had a hockey game on the television, but it wasn't Rocco's team. As a result, my mind wandered and my thoughts drifted to a dog.

"I'm sorry?" Lorenzo returned.

"French bulldogs," I repeated. "What do you think of them?"

"Why are you asking?"

I grinned. "I think I want to get a dog. Frenchies are so cute. They've got flat faces, wrinkly heads, and they aren't big."

"You want a dog?" Lorenzo asked.

Nodding my head, I added, "He'd be good company for those nights you can't be there with me."

"What did you do before I was in the picture?"

"I guess I didn't realize just how lonely I was until I had you," I admitted. "When you're not there, I really miss you."

Lorenzo's face softened. He leaned forward and pressed

a kiss to my forehead before running his fingers through my hair.

After the silence stretched on for a while, Lorenzo finally explained, "A Frenchie isn't going to be a very good guard dog. A German Shepherd or a Rottie might be a better choice."

I pushed back from his chest and countered, "But I'm not looking for a guard dog. I want a cuddly dog."

Lorenzo just laughed at me.

I didn't get a chance to discuss a dog with him any further because one of the babies started stirring.

Bolting up off the couch, I said, "I'll be right back."

I took off to the twins' bedroom and found Gracie was staring up at me, happy as a clam. "Hey, baby girl," I whispered as I lifted her up in my arms, not wanting to wake Hank. "Auntie Jojo missed you while you were sleeping."

I looked over at Hank, who was still sound asleep, and decided it was best to take Gracie out into the living room to change her diaper. My niece did not like being naked, so it was a sure thing she'd cry as soon as I changed her. I figured we'd have greater success of keeping Hank sleeping if I moved her out of the room.

Once I changed her diaper, I sat down next to Lorenzo and started talking to Gracie. It wasn't long before she was no longer happy listening to me ramble on and on about my plans for a puppy.

Turning my attention to Lorenzo, I asked, "Would you mind holding her while I go get her bottle?"

He immediately tensed. "What if she cries?"

I giggled. "She's a baby, so that's a strong possibility, especially since she's hungry. Just talk to her or rock her until I get back."

I didn't give him a chance to refuse. I simply settled her in his arms and took off toward the kitchen.

Prior to leaving, Ekko had pumped and left bottles for the babies. Even though they weren't planning to be gone overnight, you wouldn't have known with the amount of milk and instructions she left me. I warmed Gracie's bottle in the bottle warmer, confirmed it wasn't too hot, and walked back toward the living room.

When I stepped into the room, I nearly melted into a puddle on the floor. Lorenzo was holding Gracie in one arm, her whole hand wrapped around one of his fingers, and she was staring up at him like she didn't have a care in the world. What made it even more heart-melting was the fact that when I walked in, Lorenzo didn't even look up at me. He kept his eyes on the precious little girl in his arms.

Moving over toward them, I caught his attention when I declared, "I think she likes you."

He grinned at me and teased, "I tend to have that effect on the ladies."

I rolled my eyes at him and snatched my phone up off the table. After snapping a picture of the two of them, I sent it off in a text to Dom.

Your little girl already has eyes for this guy. Seems like you'll have your work cut out for you in a few years!

Dropping my phone back on the coffee table, I held Gracie's bottle out to Lorenzo.

"Oh, uh, maybe you should feed her," he suggested.

Just then, Hank started crying.

I laughed. "Pick one. Feeding Gracie or getting Hank and changing his diaper," I offered him his options. "Just a warning, boys can be dangerous when having their diapers changed."

Without hesitating, Lorenzo took the bottle from my hand. As I stood to go get Hank, I looked down at my big guy and felt my heart swell. I only gave myself a few seconds to feel that before turning and walking away to get my nephew.

"Perfect timing, little man," I cooed as I lifted him out of the crib. After giving him a bunch of smooches, I set him down on the changing table. "Okay, little guy, here's how this is going to go down. You know that really handsome guy who came here with me? Well, he's out in the living room holding your sister right now. I really like him and he likes me too, but I have a feeling he might not want to get near me tonight if you pee on me. So, can you do your auntie Jojo a solid and not let that happen? I promise to be quick."

Hank squirmed and chewed on his fists.

Even though I worked faster than I ever had before, Hank was not interested in helping me out. The second I took his wet diaper off, he sprayed me.

"Hank! That's not cool, dude. I thought we had an agreement," I playfully scolded him. "Now I've got to change your clothes, too!"

Once Hank was in fresh clothes, I picked him up and carried him out to the living room. "Sorry that took so long," I lamented. "Hank decided not to cooperate with me."

Lorenzo chuckled, "I heard. Grace and I were laughing at you out here."

"What?"

"The monitor was on. We heard it all."

I frowned, bummed that I forgot the monitor was on.

"I have to get Hank's bottle," I announced.

"I'll take him," Lorenzo offered.

I blinked in surprise. "But you have Gracie."

Lorenzo gave me a disbelieving look. "I've got two arms, baby. They aren't crawling around anywhere yet. I think I can manage."

"She's not done eating, though."

Pulling the bottle out of her mouth, he looked down at my niece and claimed, "Grace is a good girl. She'll cooperate for me and hang tight until her aunt gets back. Won't you, princess?"

She smiled at him. She was absolutely in love with him.

I couldn't say I blamed her because not only was I madly in love with him, but I also *adored* that he was talking to her and that he called her princess. My heart couldn't take much more, so I walked Hank over and settled him in Lorenzo's free arm.

Once I had Hank's bottle ready, I sat down next to Lorenzo and scooped up my fussy nephew. While he ate, I asked, "Has she burped yet?"

"She's not done eating," Lorenzo pointed out as he reached for her bottle.

"Yeah, but she's had about half of that bottle. You should try burping her so she doesn't get a belly ache."

Lorenzo frowned and looked down at the little girl in his arm. "Alright, lady, no spitting up on me," he instructed. After a few gentle pats on the back, Gracie burped.

And she didn't spit up on him.

Lorenzo got back to feeding her, and after a few minutes had passed, I looked over and saw she was not even remotely interested in eating.

"She's totally smitten with you," I marveled. "My niece is too busy flirting with my man to finish her bottle."

Lorenzo leaned toward me and promised, "Don't worry, Jolie. She's cute, but she's too young for me. Besides, even though you smell like pee, I couldn't possibly find you more attractive than I do right now."

"Oh, be quiet. I don't smell."

He let out a laugh and said, "I know. I'm just teasing you. Give me a kiss."

I gave him a quick peck on the lips before we both turned our attention to the little faces looking up at each of us. For the next little while, all that existed were the two of them. Grace wanted nothing to do with me, her bottle, or sleeping. Lorenzo was all that mattered to her and he gobbled it up giving her all the attention she wanted. I had to keep telling myself that I was imagining it because she wasn't even a full two months old yet, but I swore the girl had to know exactly what she was doing.

Hank, on the other hand, was all about business first. Food was his number one priority. He ate and he did it quick. Once that was taken care of, he was content to just sit back and relax. He didn't seem to mind one way or the other if I chatted with him, but since I had decisions to make, I figured I'd get his opinion. We chatted about his auntie Jojo getting a puppy and I was certain he smiled at me when I asked him if he thought it was a good idea. There was no way I could deny him the privilege of coming to my place when he was older and having a furry friend to run around and play with.

It wasn't much later when Dom and Ekko walked in the door. They came into the living room and Dom asked, "How were they?"

"Perfect little angels," I sighed.

"I missed them so much," Ekko murmured. "Did they eat?"

"Hank is a champ when it comes to eating," I praised my nephew. "Your daughter, on the other hand, can only manage that if she's not too busy flirting."

Dom's eyes narrowed on Lorenzo, who returned a blinding smile.

"Look at her," I started. "She's been looking at him like that for the last forty-five minutes."

"Aw, she's got good taste. You can't fault her for that," Ekko chimed in.

Dom looked to his wife and scowled.

"It's my birthday," she reminded him. "You can't get mad at me."

"How was your night out?" I changed the subject.

"Magnificent," Dom answered, wrapping his arm around Ekko's shoulders and curling her into his body.

She agreed. "As much as I didn't want to leave them, we really needed this time with each other to reconnect. Thank you so much to the both of you for being here for them and for us."

"Anytime," Lorenzo assured them, as he shifted Gracie and rested her head on his shoulder. Her eyelids were getting heavy. And they should be considering she barely blinked for nearly an hour.

"Yeah, well, my daughter's inflating your ego, so I understand why you're willing to watch them now," Dom joked.

"I'm glad you enjoyed yourself, Ekko. Happy birthday," I said, ignoring the banter between the men.

"Thank you. If you don't mind, I'm going to take a minute to run upstairs and change," she explained.

"Not at all. Go ahead," I encouraged her.

Dom sat down in the chair across from the couch Lorenzo and I were on. "I know we've already said it, but it bears repeating. Thank you so much for being here for the twins today. Life has been all about them since they were born and Ekko and I hadn't realized how much we missed each other. We really do appreciate you both."

"It's not a problem at all, Dom," I insisted. "Lorenzo and I had fun with these two."

When I looked over at Lorenzo, I saw that Gracie had finally fallen asleep again. Her head was resting on his shoulder. She was so tiny in comparison to him, but she looked so peaceful and content.

I continued, "But I'm not kidding. This little girl knows what she likes."

Dom just shook his head in disbelief.

A few minutes later, Ekko joined us again. I stood with Hank in my arms and carried him over to his dad. Ekko walked to Lorenzo and carefully cradled her daughter against her. Gracie did not like being disturbed, especially when that disturbance resulted in her removal from the comfort of Lorenzo's hold.

She cried.

Hard.

Ekko thought it was adorable, the scowl returned to Dom's face, and Lorenzo looked truly pained that Gracie was upset.

"We should get going, so you can get them to settle again," I suggested.

Lorenzo and I said our goodbyes, wishing Ekko a happy birthday one last time before we got in the truck and drove away.

That night, we went back to Lorenzo's place. I had been to his place twice before over the course of the last few weeks, but Lorenzo preferred coming to me, so we typically spent the time at my place.

Before we went to visit his mother, I had packed a small bag since I knew I wouldn't be going home that night. When we arrived, Lorenzo carried my stuff in for me.

In the light of his home, I could see he was preoccupied.

"Hey, what's going on, boss?" I asked.

He shook his head. "It's nothing."

My head dropped to the side. "Something's bothering you," I pressed, knowing there was something on his mind.

His eyes came to mine. "I love that little girl," he told me, his voice soft. "Both of them, obviously, but she's special."

My heart exploded.

"Babe," I began, stepping in toward him and wrapping my arms around his waist.

"She was crying when we left. Do you think she's okay now?"

I giggled. "I'm sure she's fine, Lorenzo."

"How sure?" he worried.

Stepping out of his arms, I pulled my phone out of my purse and sent a text to Dom.

How's my niece? Has she settled down?

Dom replied almost immediately with a picture of Gracie in her crib, sound asleep. I held my phone up and showed it to Lorenzo.

"She's not crying anymore."

His face went soft and he visibly relaxed.

"Are you ready for bed?" I asked.

"Yeah."

With that, the two of us climbed the stairs and got ready for bed.

Once we were under the blankets and my body was tucked tight to his while he spooned me, Lorenzo threw an unexpected question at me.

"Do you want kids one day, Jolie?"

I was so caught off guard, my body tensed. "Yes," I eventually replied. "I mean, not now, but definitely one day I want to have kids."

He didn't reply.

In fact, he was silent so long I began to worry what that might mean. And the feeling I had told me that it was possible he didn't want children.

"Lorenzo?"

"Yeah?"

"What about you? Do you want kids one day?"

I felt him inhale a deep breath behind me. After he let it out, he shared, "I never thought about it before tonight, to be honest. Before you and I became us, I hadn't even considered what we have now. But seeing you tonight with them and holding that little girl in my arms has me thinking about things that never crossed my mind before now."

I leaned back into him and turned myself around to face him. Even though it was dark in the room, my eyes had adjusted enough that I could make out his features.

"Talk to me," I urged him.

"I don't know what to say," he started. "I used to live my life taking each day as it came. But since you've come into my life, things have changed and thoughts have crossed my mind. All of it is my future. A future I really think I want to build with you."

Lorenzo wanted a future with me. I wanted that, too.

I didn't get a chance to respond because he continued, "I know we haven't been together very long, baby. I'm not saying we are at that point yet, not even close, but I want to know it's something that you're looking to work toward with me. Tonight, seeing how you were with those kids, it'd be a shame if you didn't share that love with children of your own. And for me, holding Gracie and Hank tonight did something to me. They are completely helpless and totally reliant on someone to care for them. It made me realize that I want the chance to be a father. I want to be the one that I never had."

I rested my palm against his cheek and assured him, "I think you'll be an amazing daddy one day."

"I'm scared, though," he confessed.

My big guy.

So tough, so strong.

Strong enough to admit and own up to his fears.

My thumb stroked back and forth along his cheekbone. "What scares you?"

"Not being good enough for them. Hurting them. Hurting you. Mostly…becoming my father."

"If Hank and Gracie were ever in danger, if someone was trying to harm them, what would you do?"

Without hesitating, he responded, "I'd risk my own life to protect them and make sure they were safe. I'd never let anyone hurt them."

"Don't you think your need to protect would be that much stronger for your own children?" I asked.

"I'd hope it would be," he returned.

"I know you said you and your brother went into counseling when you were younger. Have you considered talking to someone again now that you've got these new feelings? I have zero doubts about the man you are and I'll listen to you talk about it anytime you want, but if you want to seek the help of a professional, I'd support that, too."

Lorenzo squeezed my hip. "I love your faith in me, baby. I'll think about talking to someone."

After leaning in to kiss his throat, I said softly, "You aren't an abuser, Lorenzo. You've protected me from my own clumsiness, you've defended me when someone tried to get the best of me, you stood up for your mom, you shielded your brother, you rescue people all the time for your job, and you just admitted you'd sacrifice yourself to protect my niece and nephew. Every day you prove that you're a good man and that you're a protector. If I've got to remind you of that, I will."

Lorenzo pressed his lips against my forehead before he whispered, "I love you, Jolie."

I wasted no time in returning the sentiment.

Once I did, Lorenzo's mouth found mine and we ended our day in the most fabulous way possible.

CHAPTER 15

Jolie

"**O**KAY, I'M READY."

"It's about time. I'm starved," Lorenzo grumbled.

Except I remembered something and realized I wasn't ready.

"Wait!" I cried. "I forgot Daphne's gift!"

Lorenzo waited at the front door to my condo while I ran back through and up the stairs to my bedroom where I'd put the squeaky dog toy I'd picked up earlier in the week.

It was Thanksgiving Day, and Lorenzo and I had a full day planned. We were just about to head out the door to go to his mom's house. There, we'd have an early Thanksgiving lunch with her, Rocco, and Daphne.

Sadly, earlier in the week, Lorenzo told me that Rocco and his girlfriend had split. They'd only been together about six months, which is precisely the reason why she didn't know what to expect when hockey season started. Apparently, she thought she would be okay with his schedule during the season, but that quickly changed once Rocco started traveling a lot. With him gone so often and their relationship being so new, she realized it wasn't something she was cut out for. I felt bad for Rocco but had no doubts that he'd soon find a girl that was perfect for him. In fact, when I found out, I was actually a bit bummed that Ava had gone home for the holiday. Even if it wasn't going to be anything long-term, it still would have been nice to have someone with whom to spend the time.

Grabbing the bag with Daphne's toy off the floor, I hurried back down the stairs. I waved the bag in my hand at Lorenzo and exclaimed, "I've got it. Okay, I'm ready now."

"The dog didn't need a gift, Jolie," he muttered.

"Yes, she did. Besides, since I don't have my own dog to spoil yet, it makes me happy to spoil her."

"You are crazy."

I couldn't argue with that. "That may be true, but you still love me."

His face softened. "Yeah, baby, I do." He gave me a quick peck on the lips before he urged, "Come on, let's go."

When we walked into Lena's house, we were greeted first by Daphne.

"Hi, puppy," I said, leaning over and giving her rubs and scratches. She loved it.

"She's not a puppy anymore, Jolie," Lorenzo pointed out.

I frowned. She wasn't and I certainly couldn't even pretend she was considering her massive size.

Lorenzo reached for my hand and led me through the house toward the kitchen where we found both Lena and Rocco.

We all exchanged Thanksgiving wishes and hugs.

"Can I help?" I offered, seeing Lena in the throes of preparing her feast.

"Everything is just about done, except for the potatoes. I've boiled them, but they need to be mashed. If you want to do that while I work on turkey carving, we can get the food on the table a lot sooner."

"Do you have a special recipe for your potatoes?" I wondered.

She shook her head. "No, I usually just put some butter and salt."

"Are you open to me mixing it up?" I asked.

"Of course, dear. Need anything special?" she returned.

I grinned. "Do you have cream cheese?"

She practically jumped for joy. "I do! I picked up a couple so I could make some pumpkin roll, but still have one package left. Will that be enough?"

I looked over at the potatoes in the pot. "It'll be perfect," I declared.

Lena handed me the cream cheese and I got to work on making my world-famous mashed potatoes. They weren't exactly world-famous, but they were certainly a crowd pleaser. As I worked on potatoes and she carved the turkey, Lorenzo and Rocco talked about hockey. I could have easily joined the conversation, but I wanted them to have their time together.

Before we sat down, Lena stated, "Lorenzo, I made my cider punch yesterday so it would be ready today. Would you mind pouring some for me and Jolie if she'd like it?"

I didn't know what cider punch was, but it sounded good. "I'd love some, babe," I chimed in.

He smiled.

Then, he got glasses and poured cider punch.

Rocco grabbed lagers for Lorenzo and himself.

Ten minutes later, the four of us were sitting around the table diving into a delicious meal. When he first told me about everything that happened with his father when he was younger, Lorenzo mentioned that Lena's cooking was almost always the start of an argument. He also said that his mom was a great cook. He wasn't kidding.

"The food is excellent, Lena," I praised her.

She beamed a beautiful smile at me before she replied, "Thank you."

Lorenzo squeezed my thigh under the table. When I looked up at him, I found a warm expression on his face. He was letting me know that he appreciated my kind words to his mother.

I knew Lorenzo and I would be thrown into chaos when we left to visit with my family, so it was nice having a quiet, yet utterly enjoyable afternoon. We weren't starved for conversation either. Lena was so extremely proud of both her boys, so talking about anything happening in their lives made her happy. Of course, since I was a huge hockey fan, I enjoyed that part of the conversation. Given that I loved Lorenzo, any discussion pertaining to him interested me. Even though it was a small, intimate setting, I loved spending my afternoon with Lorenzo, Rocco, and Lena.

By the time we were ready to leave, I was feeling sad, though.

Rocco couldn't stay late because he had a morning skate session since the Summits had a game tomorrow night. Lorenzo and I were leaving to visit with my family and Lena was going to be home alone with just the dog. It wasn't that I thought she couldn't be happy with just Daphne, but it upset me to know she'd be spending the holiday without anyone else to talk to.

Pulling Lorenzo aside, I whispered, "I think I'd like to invite your mom to come with us to my parents' house for dinner. I feel awful that she's going to be here alone. Would you be alright with that?"

Lorenzo engulfed me in his arms and said softly, "I love

you so much, Jolie. Thank you for thinking of her. It really means a lot to me that you care about my mom."

We walked back out to the kitchen where I found her pouring herself another glass of cider punch.

"Lena, I was just talking to Lorenzo and I told him that I'd like to invite you over to my parents' house for dinner. Would you like to join us?"

She shook her head and a bashful look came over her. "Oh, no that's okay. I appreciate the offer, but I'll be fine here."

"It's really no trouble at all. I have a big family and there will be plenty of food."

"Thank you, Jolie. It's really very sweet of you, but I can't go."

My brows pulled together, but before I could ask why, Lorenzo stepped in.

"What's going on, Ma? Rocky's getting ready to head out soon and it's still early. It'd make me feel better knowing you weren't spending the holiday by yourself."

Her eyes filled with tears.

Something was wrong.

"I won't be alone, Lorenzo."

Rocco, having been listening from the living room, walked over to where we were standing.

We waited for her explanation.

She took in a deep breath and blew it out before she blurted, "I've met someone."

Lorenzo and Rocco instantly went on alert.

Lena continued, "His name is Michael and I've been seeing him for about eight months now."

"Last name," Lorenzo clipped.

"What?"

"What's his last name?"

Lena grew visibly uncomfortable.

Yep.

Something was very wrong.

"Lorenzo, darling, I need you to relax and sit down a minute. You don't need to look into this man. He's a good man."

"I realize you might think that and I hope to Christ he is, but I'm still going to look into him," Lorenzo insisted.

"Who is he, Mom? Where did you meet him?" Rocco chimed in.

She looked back and forth between her boys. They were both wound tight, anxiously awaiting her reply. "Well, I decided to go to Windsor State Park one day with Daphne. We'd walked along the lake trail there and I sat for a few minutes on a bench to just clear my head. While I was sitting there, a nice man came up and sat next to me. We started talking, we had a very nice conversation, and before I left, he asked me if I'd like to meet up for coffee sometime."

Lorenzo shook his head and blinked his eyes. Throwing his hands out to the side, he ranted, "You just started talking to some random guy at the park and then agreed to meet him for coffee? You know what I do for a living and all the bad stuff I see and you didn't even think it might not be a smart idea?"

Her eyes narrowed and she scolded him. "You need to watch your tone. You might be all grown up now, but I'm still your mother. I realize I didn't always make the right choices years ago when you two were little. I'm sorry, I can't change that. But I'm still young and I don't want to be alone the rest of my life."

"We don't want to see you alone either," Rocco started, his voice soft. "But you could at least give Enzo his name so he can make sure there's nothing bad about this guy. It would help put our minds at ease."

"I didn't do that because after we met for coffee and had a really great time, we made plans to go out on another date. Between our coffee date and our dinner date, we talked a few times on the phone. I enjoyed having someone to talk to, someone to ask about my day. In fact, he was so interested in me and I had been missing having anyone interested in me that it wasn't until we went out to dinner that I learned I'd never have to have you check up on him."

"What?" Lorenzo asked, very little patience left in his tone.

Lena remained silent a minute, looking back and forth between her boys. She finally settled her eyes on Lorenzo and shared, "His last name is Drake."

Lorenzo's jaw clenched.

Michael Drake.

I knew the name Drake sounded familiar, but I just couldn't place it.

"Fuck," Lorenzo hissed.

"What am I missing here?" Rocco asked.

"Bright side," Lorenzo started as he turned toward Rocco. "We don't have to look into this guy."

"What? How do you know?"

"Downside?"

Rocco nodded.

"He works with me."

Rocco's head jerked back. My mind scrambled trying to think of all the guys that worked at Cunningham Security. I didn't recall a Michael Drake.

"Babe?" I called.

Lorenzo turned toward me.

"Who's Michael?"

"Luke Townsend's father-in-law."

Then it hit me. Luke Townsend was a professional snow-boarder. His wife was Nikki and her maiden name was Drake. I didn't know all the details of the story, but I recalled hearing through the grapevine that her father had been wrongfully imprisoned back in California and lost a lot of years with his daughter.

Lorenzo looked back at his mother and stated, "I've been walking into work for the last eight months and he never let on that he even knew you existed."

"He probably knew I should be the one to share it with you."

"So, why didn't you tell us?"

She shook her head. "I don't know. I didn't want you to worry about me any more than you already do."

"He's coming to see you today?" Rocco asked.

Lena nodded. "Yes. We talked about it and decided to do things this way. He's spending his morning and afternoon with his daughter and her family while I spend mine with my boys. He's coming over here tonight and we're making dinner together."

I started to feel the tension leave Lorenzo's body. He took a step toward his mom. His voice was gentle when he wondered, "Does he make you happy?"

Her eyes got wet as she nodded. "Yes, darling. I'm happier than I've been in a really long time. He's a good man."

"I know he is," Lorenzo returned quietly. He paused a moment before continuing, "I'm happy for you, Ma."

"Thank you, Lorenzo."

"Does he watch hockey?" Rocco asked.

Lena grinned and shared, "I watch every single one of your games and unless he's working late or there is something going on with his daughter, he watches every game with me."

Rocco gave her a nod of approval and tossed out, "It's a home game tomorrow. I can probably still get a box or seats. If you want to invite him to a game and Lorenzo and Jolie want to come, I'll make it happen."

Her eyes widened. "He'd love that. I'll ask him tonight and let you know."

Lorenzo looked at me. "You up for it?"

I made an angry face at him and asked, "What kind of question is that? Of course, I'm up for it!"

At that, Lorenzo gave his mom a hug before Rocco did the same.

The four of us said goodbye to one another before Lena walked us to the door.

We had been driving for about five minutes when Lorenzo sighed, "She's going to get it back."

"What?" I asked.

"Her spirit," he clarified. "My father took it away from her. She's going to get it back. Hope like hell it's Michael that does it for her, but even if it's not, at least I know she wants to fight for it. Now that I think about it, the last few times I've seen her these last two months or so, she's been happier."

"Lorenzo?" I called softly.

"Right here, baby."

"The day I met your mom, and you took Daphne out for a walk, I talked with her about a lot. While I won't deny the fact that what happened to her at the hand of your father was not easy, I don't think that's why she's been so upset or depressed."

"What do you mean?"

"It was you," I started. "She told me that you had done such a good job of shielding Rocco from what was going on that he doesn't seem to suffer from the lasting effects of it that you do. Her biggest worry was you being alone, secluding yourself. Now that we're together, I think it's helping her let go of some of the guilt she's felt for a really long time. You said it yourself. You've noticed the change in her over the last two months. We've been together nearly that long."

Lorenzo kept his eyes forward, focused on the road, but I knew he was hearing everything I was saying to him.

"She just wants you and Rocco to be happy. She knew he was trying to get it. You weren't and that hurt her. It hurt her to know that her choice to stay and endure what she did instead of getting out of there impacted you to the point you wouldn't try to be happy." I paused a moment, but eventually ended, "You're both well on your way to finding happiness, Lorenzo. It's all good now."

Lorenzo remained quiet, but he reached across the center console and wrapped his hand around mine. He held it all the way to my parents' house.

When we arrived, we found that everyone was already there, except for Dom, Ekko, and the kids. We went in and mingled with my parents, Kendall, Colton, and Memphis after I made official introductions. Everyone already knew Lorenzo through his working with Dom and, obviously, the wedding, but this was different. He was no longer just Dom's co-worker and a private investigator. He was dating their sister and, in my parents' case, their daughter.

Colton and Memphis had met Lorenzo a long time ago through work. Even though they worked for the Rising Sun Police Department and Cunningham Security was located in the neighboring town of Windsor, sometimes it was inevitable that cases crossed over the towns. Regardless, working on a case together and finding out that the guy was dating your sister were two different things. Somehow, though, my brothers managed to surprise me and welcomed Lorenzo with open arms.

Kendall loved him. I already knew that, and I was thrilled she had no problem letting him know just how much she loved him for me.

Mom and Dad didn't require a whole lot of convincing either.

"Dom has always spoken highly of the guys he works with," Dad said. "He's had plenty of good things to say about you. The fact he had you stand up for him at his wedding tells me everything I need to know. Take care of my girl."

With a downward jerk of his chin, Lorenzo indicated he would do just that.

No sooner did we make our way through everyone when Dom and Ekko arrived.

"Happy Thanksgiving, everyone," Ekko announced, holding Hank in her arms as they walked in. "Sorry we're late. Getting out of the house to get anywhere on time these days is virtually impossible."

"You brought my little munchkins," Mom acknowledged as she made her way over to Ekko. "Waiting an extra couple minutes is not a problem."

Taking Hank from Ekko, she immediately doused him with kisses. The same happened with my dad and Gracie. While the rest of my family made their way over to kiss and cuddle the babies, I looked at Lorenzo. He had his eyes focused on the scene in front of us, longing in his face.

I reached my hand over and wrapped it around his. After giving him a gentle squeeze, his eyes came to mine. "You want to hold her?" I wondered, even though I already knew the answer.

He hesitated to answer, but eventually said, "It's okay. Let her family have their time with her. I can wait."

"Well, you're much stronger than me. I can't wait any longer," I declared as I walked over to cover my niece and nephew in kisses.

Once Dom and Ekko had a chance to come in and get settled, we started moving the food to the dining room table. The babies had fallen asleep, despite all of the commotion around them.

It was during dinner though when my heart swelled with love for the man sitting beside me. Everyone had started eating and chatting. Lorenzo was about halfway through the food on his plate when the crying started.

Ekko's head dropped forward. "One day," she started. "One day I'll make it through dinner."

Everyone laughed.

That is, everyone but Lorenzo.

As Ekko put her napkin next to her plate and started to stand, Lorenzo pushed his chair back from the table and instructed, "Stay and eat. I've got her."

Ekko was stunned, but she still confirmed, "Are you sure?"

He returned a nod and insisted, "Positive."

As he walked out of the dining room, Gracie's crying only got louder. It was mere seconds later when her crying ceased and I saw Dom and Ekko both fully relax. A few minutes later, Lorenzo walked back in the dining room, with Gracie tucked safely in the crook of his arm. Everyone's gaze went to him, but he didn't seem to mind. It was mostly because he wasn't paying attention to anyone but the little girl in his arms.

He sat back down next to me.

I put my hand on his thigh and asked, "Do you want me to take her so you can finish eating?"

He shook his head. "I'm good," he answered.

Sure enough, it wasn't more than another five minutes, when Hank decided he wanted to be part of the action as well. Colton stood and went to get him.

And it was when he brought my nephew back in and sat with him at the table that I realized just how much I had to be thankful for that year. Looking around the table, I found everyone caught up in their own conversations, but it when I looked at Lorenzo that I stopped searching. Gracie's hand was wrapped around his finger and she was clearly flirting with him. Feeling my gaze on him, he looked up at me and smiled.

"Love you, Jolie," he whispered softly, only for me to hear. "Best Thanksgiving of my life, baby."

I leaned closer and promised, "It only gets better from here."

When I pulled back to look him in the eyes again, I could see that I wasn't the only one appreciating just how blessed I was.

CHAPTER 16

Jolie

"**H**OW WAS COLORADO?" I ASKED AVA.

"It was so nice," she answered. "I enjoyed the time off, my parents loved having me there, and I really had an opportunity to unwind. How were things here?"

It was Monday the week after Thanksgiving and I was just now getting the opportunity to catch up with Ava. She arrived back in Wyoming yesterday afternoon and this was the first chance we were having to talk to each other. We'd texted while she was away, but since I wasn't having any major life incidences that required my best friend's advice, I tried to give her the time to be with her family uninterrupted.

Of course, that now meant that we were making up for the lost time here at work, where my shift had ended and hers was just about to start.

"Great," I sighed. "I mean, you know everything went well with meeting Lorenzo's mom. Things between the two of us have been wonderful. My family loves him, especially my niece. I only have one issue."

Her brows pulled together. "What's going on?"

"I think I love him too much," I worried.

"What? Is that even possible?"

I shrugged my shoulders. "I think so. It's just that every time I'm around him I find myself falling harder and harder for him. He does all these little things that seem insignificant, but they mean the world to me. And considering how hesitant he was to open up to me months ago, I'm thrilled with how freely he shares his thoughts with me now."

"Communication is a good thing, Jojo. It's important in any relationship. Why is it a problem?"

I swallowed hard. "I hate when he's not around. I don't mean when I'm here at work or if he's working. I can do my own thing, but when it's late at night and I'm home in my bed while I know he is home in his, I want him there with me."

"So, why don't you just tell him this?"

"I have," I admitted. "I mean, not to the extent that I feel it, but I've told him. I just don't want to come across as needy."

Lorenzo had been so accustomed to being on his own and we were still very new considering we'd only been together for about two months. I couldn't imagine being in his shoes, going from feeling completely content in solitude to having to adjust to the pressures of a girlfriend who wanted to be with him every night.

"I don't think he'll see it that way," Ava put in.

I shook my head. "I have to think about it. We're still so new. The last thing I want to do is scare him off."

She laughed. "You're crazy. I saw the way he looked at you that night at Carter's. He's way into you. And if everything you've told me that's happened since that first night is true, he's not going to just walk away."

"I hope you're right," I replied. "We should plan a girls' night. Me, you, and Kendall."

"Sounds good to me," she agreed. "Figure out a time that

works for her and I'm up for it as long as I'm not here. If we go out, though, it's going to be your job to return the favor I did for you with Lorenzo."

I shook my head at her. "And you say I'm the crazy one?"

"Hey, a girl has needs."

Just as I was about to walk out of the back room, Susana opened it. "Ava, Samuel said your client just got here."

"I'm coming," she returned as the two of us followed Susana down the hall to the reception area.

After getting my tip envelopes and confirming my schedule for the rest of the week, I announced, "Alright, I'm out of here. See you guys tomorrow."

"Later, Jojo!"

I walked outside and started fishing through my purse for my phone. I wanted to call Lorenzo and let him know I was heading home to make dinner and would be ready once he finished at work. We were planning to eat dinner together before going to look at some French Bulldogs. I'd officially decided I wanted one, a gray one, and he wanted to take me to look at them.

Keeping my head down as I searched my purse, I continued walking. I was moving slow, not paying attention to anything around me. Just as my fingers found my phone, I heard the squealing.

I stopped dead in my tracks and looked up to see where the sound was coming from. I'd already stepped out into the parking lot and there was nothing in front of me.

I looked to my right. It was empty.

By the time I looked to the left, it was too late to react. The car was barreling toward me, and the driver was making no attempt to stop. My hand, still in my purse, tightened around my phone, but my body was frozen.

I couldn't move.

Until I did.

Because the car had plowed into me, the bumper smashing into my legs, hurling me up over the hood and off the side. My eyes were open as I watched the sky move farther away from me.

Then, my body plummeted to the ground and my head smacked the pavement as I landed on my side and everything went black.

Lorenzo

"I'm not in a position to talk to you about hiding it, but I wish I would have known sooner what was going on," I said.

"Trust me, Lorenzo, it was not easy," Michael began. "I didn't think it was a wise idea to hide it. I thought you and your brother should know, but especially you considering our working relationship. Your mom saw things differently, and no matter what my opinion was, I had to respect where she stood with this."

I was standing in the back offices of Cunningham Security, where our surveillance systems, back up storage devices, and additional technology was stored. When I arrived at work today, I knew I wanted to clear the air with Michael. We'd all gone to Rocco's hockey game on Friday, but there wasn't an opportunity for me to speak with him alone, so I was taking the time to do it today. As soon as I walked into the room and locked eyes with him, I knew he knew precisely why I was there.

And like a man, he was prepared to hear me out.

"I appreciate you honoring her wishes. She deserves to have someone who will respect her. I'm hoping you'll continue to do that for her. But I've got to talk about something else. Has she shared with you what she's been through?"

Michael nodded. And when he did, I saw the anger and frustration in his face.

"Good," I began. "I know you're a good guy and I saw the way you were with her on Friday. I know you had some shit happen that was completely out of your control. But I still need to say that I expect you to do right by her. She's endured enough in her life. I want her happy and I don't want her spending her life alone. I'm sure, given the hand you were dealt, you can appreciate what unwanted solitude is like. I can think of nothing better than the both of you finding each other, but I still need your word that she's going to be treated like she's made of porcelain."

"Your mother is stronger than you think, Lorenzo."

"I know that. There's not a lot of women who can suffer through what she has and still come out the other side standing. I'm not saying she's fragile; I just want reassurance that you're going to treat her like she is."

"I always do," he replied without hesitating.

"It's all I can ask."

A moment of silence stretched between us. I was just about to walk out when he called, "Lorenzo?"

"Yeah?"

"Since I met your mom, she's always had something weighing on her. As time went on and we got to know one another, I learned about her past and, incidentally, yours. It finally hit me about four months ago where that cloud hanging over her head was coming from."

I braced for it.

"It was guilt. Guilt over what she could have done differently so that you wouldn't have secluded yourself and kept yourself from experiencing real love. Over the last month, I've seen that storm cloud vanish. Knowing you've finally found a way to let go of whatever was holding you back from finding your happiness has finally given her the chance to let go of her guilt. I've never seen her happier."

Guilt seeped into me.

Jolie had mentioned something like this to me once, but hearing it from Michael, who had spent months with my mom, was different.

He must have realized where my mind was because he went on. "Don't go there, Lorenzo. You had your reasons, valid ones, for living the way you did. Your mom's concerns are expected and normal. I've got a grown daughter and I'll always worry about her. I just wanted you to know that it's a good thing you've both found a way to pick yourselves up from something awful and move on in a healthy way. She's proud of you and she loves you. To that end, I can't tell you how happy she is that you've found Jolie. Having only met her Friday, I've got to say you two are the definition of opposites attract. She's perfect for you. I see it. Your mom sees it. We're both happy for you."

Just then, Dom walked into the room. "Hey, De Luca. You got a minute?"

I gave him a nod and looked back to Michael. "Thanks, Michael."

He smiled.

I turned toward Dom.

Before he could get out a word, my phone rang. I pulled it out of my pocket and saw Jolie's name on the display.

Looking up at Dom, I noted, "It's your sister. Give me a minute."

I put the phone to my ear and answered, "Hey baby. You finished at work?"

Dom started to walk away.

"Oh my God," the voice screamed into the phone. "You have to hurry!"

Dom stopped walking, easily hearing the screaming in the phone.

"Hello?" I called, my body tense and alert.

"Lorenzo, this is Ava."

Ava was frantic, sobbing uncontrollably. I put my phone on speaker.

"Ava, what's wrong? Where's Jolie?"

Dom went alert and closed the distance between us.

"She's...oh my God, it was awful. They came out of no-where and just hit her."

My gut clenched.

"Who, Ava? Is someone with you? What happened? Where are you? Where's Jolie?"

"Jolie was walking to her car after work. Someone just," she paused to breathe through her sobbing. "They just hit her with their car and took off. She went flying, Lorenzo. It was bad."

"Where is she?"

"The ambulance just took her to Rising Sun Medical Center," she cried. "She wouldn't wake up. Oh my God. I saw it happen, so I'm waiting here for the police, but I'm coming as soon as I can."

"Right. Thanks for calling me."

I disconnected the call and heard Michael order, "You two, hospital. I'll take care of the rest and let the boys know."

Wanting to waste no time, Dom and I took off.

"I'm calling Kendall on my way there," Dom called out as he ran toward his truck. "Keep you posted if she knows anything yet."

I got in my truck and squealed out of the lot.

As an adult, I never felt this feeling.

I'd worked so many cases over the years, some very high-risk, and I never felt the fear I was feeling right now. Never on a case.

The last time I felt like this was when I was hiding my brother in one of our bedrooms while nobody was protecting our mother.

I sped to the hospital, Dom pulling in to a spot right next to me. We jumped out and took off running toward the building.

We ran inside. I was prepared to tear down walls to find Jolie, but two seconds after we were in, we saw Kendall. Her horrified, puffy, red-rimmed eyes met ours.

"She's unconscious," she whispered. "At a minimum, she's got a ton of scrapes, cuts, and bruising all along her left side. That would be the best-case scenario."

"She's unconscious, Kendall. This is more than scrapes and cuts," Dom pointed out.

Kendall nodded quickly while she tried to stop herself from breaking down into tears. "I don't know much about the accident, but from what they told me, her head hit the pavement first. This could be very bad."

At that, Kendall completely lost it. Dom pulled his sister toward him, holding her in his arms, and offered her comfort.

"Can we see her?" I pleaded.

Kendall shook her head. "I was a mess," she sobbed. "They...they made me get out. She'll need X-rays and CT scans. It could be a while before we know exactly how bad it is."

We had no choice but to wait.

I thought I was going to crawl out of my skin not knowing if she was alright.

I didn't care what happened as long as she survived.

It didn't matter to me how many cuts or scrapes she had.

I didn't care if she had broken bones.

It wouldn't matter if bruises marred her body.

I just needed to know that she was going to survive.

Kendall managed to bring us to a private area of the hospital where we could wait. An hour passed when my phone rang.

Jolie's name was on the screen.

"Ava?" I answered.

"Hey, Lorenzo. I'm here at the hospital. Where is she?"

"Hang tight. I'll come out to meet you."

I made the short walk from where we were to the front to get Ava. She looked a mess. As I indicated she should follow me, I saw Pierce, Cruz, and Holden walking in, their faces grim.

The guys made their way over to me. "Come back," I urged. "Dom's back here. Kendall is, too."

We made our way back to where Kendall and Dom were waiting, consumed with grief and worry for their sister. Dom saw us, stood, and immediately walked over.

"What do you know?" he asked.

"They're going to pull the footage from the parking lot cameras to see what's on them. It was a hit and run. We don't know if it was random or specific."

The thought never crossed my mind.

Why would someone ever come after Jolie?

"Ava, you said you saw what happened," I remarked. "Can you tell us what you saw?"

She closed her eyes, tears streaming down her cheeks. "We had just been talking to each other in the back. She was getting ready to leave; my first client had arrived. I was out in the front reception area when she walked out. I wasn't paying attention, but then I heard the tires squealing. When I looked up, I saw the car moving toward her. I was frozen. She was, too."

Ava stopped speaking, swiping at the tears on her face. Kendall moved toward her and hugged her.

"I'm so sorry, Kendall. I should have reacted quicker."

"It's not your fault, Ava. What happened next?"

"The car didn't slow down. I couldn't make out if the driver was a man or a woman, but the car just plowed right into her. She flew up onto the hood, up into the air, and off the side. She landed on her side, but her head took the impact."

Fuck.

Fuck.

"What does this mean, Kendall?"

Kendall shook her head, closing her eyes. "She could have anything from a mild concussion to severe head trauma. We won't know until she wakes up."

"She will wake up, though, right?" I confirmed.

Kendall's haunted eyes came to mine. "She better."

I couldn't process anything after that. If Jolie didn't wake up, I wasn't sure I'd survive. Deep down, I knew I'd spend the rest of my life searching again for peace, something I'd managed to do once in my life. Peace I only ever found in solitude. Before she came into my life, I found that place. The eye of the hurricane. Everything outside it was chaos, but I was safe as long as I was there.

Now, I was out in the storm.

And I knew, beyond a shadow of a doubt, that I'd never find serenity again without the sounds of Jolie's voice and laughter surrounding me.

"Is Detective Baines on this?" Dom asked the guys.

"Yeah," Pierce replied. "He knows we're getting involved and, given that family is affected, he understands we're not going to do anything to jeopardize the investigation…not that we ever would anyway."

Dom paced the room. "I'm calling Colton and Memphis after I call Ekko. Kendall, you should call Mom and Dad."

While Kendall and Dom called their family, I sat there silent. I could have called Rocco or my mom, but I couldn't. Calling them and telling them meant it was real. And until I saw her for myself, I didn't want to do anything.

What felt like hours later, even though it hadn't been that long, hospital staff entered the room.

"How is she?" Kendall asked after she'd indicated that it was okay to share the news about Jolie to everyone in the room.

"Stable," the doctor answered. "She's going to be hurting for a while. There's very severe bruising all down her left side. Jolie is one tough cookie, though. She didn't sustain any broken bones, but she does have a severely sprained knee and ankle, which is likely from the initial impact with the front end of the vehicle. The biggest area of concern is her head, specifically the brain. We did a CT scan and didn't find any bleeding, which is a great sign. There's definitely a severe concussion, though, but we won't know the extent of that until she wakes for more than a few minutes."

"She woke up?" I asked.

The doctor nodded. "Yes, but it wasn't for long. She was

scared and disoriented."

"Can we see her?" Dom questioned the doctor.

"Sure. I think she's up on the third floor. Kendall, you can get the exact room number there. I'll be on all night, so I will be checking in on her throughout the evening."

"Thanks, Doc," Kendall replied.

At that, we followed Kendall and made our way to the third floor.

The ride on the elevator felt like it took forever, which was good because I used that time to prepare myself for what I was going to see when I walked into Jolie's room. Something told me that despite having witnessed my father abuse my mother for years and seeing the bruises on her body, this was going to be completely different.

When I walked into Jolie's room, I realized I was right.

CHAPTER 17

Lorenzo

BATTERED.

There was no other way to describe it. Walking into Jolie's hospital room, I found her sleeping in her bed completely battered.

Just as the doctor said, there were cuts, scrapes, and bruises covering her left side. Most of her left arm had been bandaged up. I could tell her face had been cleaned of the blood that had to have come from one of the wounds there. The left side of her face was red and shiny, covered with ointment.

A blanket covered her body from her waist down, but I knew her leg wasn't going to look good at all.

Her eyes were closed.

I moved to the right side of her bed, picked her hand up and kissed it before resting the back of it against my forehead. Kendall and Ava were in tears standing on the left side of the bed.

I felt a hand squeeze my shoulder. When I turned my head to the side, I saw Dom there. He had one hand on me, the other on his sister's uninjured leg.

Pierce, Cruz, and Holden stood against the wall at the foot of the bed. Their faces were littered with concern, anger, and frustration.

We hadn't been there more than five minutes when Colton and Memphis walked in. They had come from the station, seeing as they were still in uniform. The looks on their faces could best be described as agony.

"How did this happen?" Colton seethed.

"Hit and run," Dom replied. "She was walking out of work."

"What's the extent of her injuries?" Memphis wondered.

Kendall answered, "No broken bones. She's got a sprained knee and ankle, scrapes, bruises, cuts, and a severe concussion."

Suddenly, we heard a sharp intake of air. The eyes of everyone in the room shot to Jolie. She was blinking her eyes, staring straight ahead at Colton and Memphis. Her brows pulled together, but she winced as she did it. Then, her eyes went to her sister.

"Am I in trouble?"

"What? No. Why would you be in trouble?"

She looked back to her brothers, confusion taking over her features, before she worried, "The police are here."

My entire body tensed. This could not be happening.

Kendall looked over at Pierce and ordered, "Find her doctor now."

Pierce took off.

"Doctor?" Jolie repeated looking back at Kendall.

"Can you tell me your name?"

"Am I in trouble?" she asked again.

The burning started in my lungs and worked its way up my throat. I glanced around the room and saw that everyone knew just how bad this was.

A minute later, Pierce was back with the doctor.

Ava and Kendall stepped back as the doctor walked right up to her and shined a light in her eyes.

"How are you feeling?" he asked her.

"I have a headache," she answered. "Am I in trouble?"

"No, you're not in trouble."

"Why are the police here?"

"Can you tell me your name?"

She nodded but didn't answer.

"What's your name?"

"Jojo."

I felt only mildly relieved that she knew who she was. She still hadn't looked in my direction and I didn't know if I was prepared for that either. If she didn't recognize her brothers, how would she ever know who I was?

"Great," the doctor praised her. "Can you tell me where you are, Jojo?"

Jojo looked at him, then her sister, back down at her body, nervously to Colton and Memphis, and back to the doctor.

"The hospital."

"Good."

"But am I in trouble?" she asked again, her eyes darting back to her brothers.

"You are not in trouble," the doctor reassured her. "Can you introduce me to all these people in the room with you?"

Her eyes were on Kendall when she answered, "That's my sissy."

The breath left Kendall's lungs fast.

"That's Ava," she continued before she moved her eyes to Pierce, Cruz, and Holden. She struggled with them. "Do I know them?" she whispered.

I knew that Jolie had met them before, but I wasn't sure how well she knew any of them.

"It's okay if you don't," Kendall answered. "Introduce everyone else."

"Those guys are the police," she went on, referring to Colton and Memphis.

Her eyes came to the right side of the bed. She locked gazes with Dom.

"Dom, am I in trouble?"

"No, Jojo, you're not in trouble," he answered, his voice gruff.

She was still worried. "Don't let them arrest me," she begged.

"You're not getting arrested. You're not in trouble."

She turned her head slightly to look at me. She looked at me a long time, saying nothing. I couldn't remember feeling more scared in my entire life than I did at that moment, worried sick that the only woman I'd ever opened my heart to and fallen in love with wouldn't remember me.

"What are you doing here?" she asked, her voice a whisper.

Shit.

Shit.

"Jolie?" I returned, not knowing what else to say.

"He's going to be angry," she said quietly.

My brows pulled together. "Who?"

"Dom. He doesn't know we're seeing each other."

She remembered me.

She remembered me but didn't remember that we told her brother about us.

"He knows, baby," I assured her. "He's not angry."

Her eyes went back to Dom. I didn't look at him, but I assumed she got the reassurance she needed from him because she looked back at me and gave me a small smile.

"What happened?" she asked. "Am I in trouble?"

The doctor jumped in. "Jolie, you were in an accident. Do you remember the accident?"

She looked down at her lap, clearly trying to remember the accident. "No," she finally answered.

"Okay. Well, you were injured in the accident and you hit your head pretty hard. I think you're going to have a headache for a couple of days and it seems you're suffering from a bit of memory loss. This is all common and I expect your symptoms will subside. Some may only take a few hours, but others could take a couple of days. You have a sprained ankle and a sprained knee along with a lot of bruising, scrapes, and cuts. That will all take a lot longer to heal."

"I feel tired."

The doctor assured her, "That's expected. We're going to keep you here overnight for observation. We'll see how you're doing in the morning and decide where to go from there."

At that, the doctor walked out of the room. Kendall followed behind him. No sooner did they walk out when Jolie's parents came running in.

"Jojo, darling. Are you okay?"

"Am I in trouble, Mom? Don't let them arrest me, Dad."

Fear washed over her parents' faces as they came to an abrupt halt.

"She's suffering from some memory loss," Dom explained. "The doctor expects that to go away. It could take a few hours to a few days."

"Dom? Lorenzo?" Colton called, speaking for the first time since Jolie woke up. "A word, please."

I stood to give Jolie's parents some room to see their daughter and to walk out of the room with her brothers, but her hand gripped mine tight.

"What's wrong, Jolie?"

"Don't let them arrest you," she pleaded.

"Nobody is getting arrested," I assured her. "I'm stepping outside the room a minute. I'll be right back."

She loosened her hold on my hand. I leaned down, pressed a kiss to her temple, and walked out of the room.

The minute Dom and I were there with Colton and Memphis and the rest of the guys, Colton all but roared, "What's being done right now to find out who did this to her?"

"Detective Baines and his guys are already working on it," Dom began. "Our team is on it, too. We'll find out whoever did this to her."

"You need to make sure Baines knows he's got a deadline before I get involved," he snapped.

Kendall walked up and wrapped her hand around his bicep. "You've got to keep it together, Colt. She's going to be alright."

"She doesn't fucking know who we are!" he barked.

Kendall closed her eyes. "I know. But I also know what is happening with her. She's really confused right now and she's perseverating. That's why she keeps asking the same question over and over again. You've got to be patient and give her time to heal."

I couldn't even begin to imagine the grief Colton and Memphis were feeling. If Jolie hadn't remembered me, I didn't think I'd be handling it half as well as they were.

"I don't want to leave her right now, but I don't think we're helping either," Memphis chimed in.

"We're definitely not helping here, either," Pierce added. "She's already dealing with enough. I don't want us adding to her confusion, so we'll head out and see what, if anything, the guys have found."

"Keep us posted," I requested.

"You do the same," Cruz demanded.

After Pierce, Holden, and Cruz took off, Memphis explained, "I'm going to say goodbye to her, but I'll come back after she's had some time to gather her bearings. Maybe we'll have better luck then."

We walked back into Jolie's room. As Memphis and Colton moved toward the side of the bed, her eyes widened. Colton put his hand to the back of her head, kissed the top of her head, and said softly, "Love you, kiddo. We'll be back to see you later."

Memphis did the same. "Take it easy, Jojo. Love you."

She watched them leave, her eyes tentative.

"I don't want to leave you right now, Jojo, but Ekko's been home alone with the babies for a long time. I know she's worried about you, too. I'll let her know you're going to be okay, and depending on what the doctors say, maybe she'll stop in tomorrow."

"The babies," Jolie sighed as she closed her eyes. "Kiss them for me."

"I will," he promised before he said goodbye.

It was getting late and Jolie was clearly exhausted. After the rest of us sat with her for a while, nobody really saying much at all, one of the nurses walked in and told us that visiting hours were over.

"I'm not leaving her," I stated.

"Please promise to call us if anything changes with her," Jolie's mom, Angie, pleaded.

"I will," I promised.

"If you don't mind, I'll walk out with you," Ava stated.

After Ava and Jolie's parents kissed her and said goodbye, they left. Kendall was working until eleven, so she was staying for a few more hours. She left the room to get back to work, but not before making sure we had everything we'd need along with letting us know she'd be back in to check on her.

The moment the two of us were alone, I pulled the chair up next to her bed, sat down, and held her hand in mine. Kissing her knuckles, I whispered, "I was so scared today, baby."

"I don't remember what happened. Ava gave me the details when you went out earlier, but I don't remember it."

"I know, but maybe that's better for the time being. Right now, you just need to focus on resting and healing yourself."

"I'm really tired," she murmured.

I stood up, kissed her on the lips, and urged, "Sleep, Jolie. I'll be here with you all night."

It wasn't more than a minute before she had closed her eyes and fallen asleep. On the other hand, I struggled to find any rest.

Millions of thoughts ran through my head.

Just the simple fact that Jolie was the victim of a hit and run was enough to have my mind going crazy. The idea that this could have been something premeditated churned my stomach. Jolie was the sweetest, kindest woman I'd ever met, so I found it hard to believe that this was anything more than a random act. Until I knew what was on that video footage, there was no telling anything for sure.

Beyond that, while I was more than grateful that she was alive, it had still been so heartbreaking to see her struggle when she woke up. Not knowing her brothers, worried that she'd done something wrong, and being simply confused was a tough thing to witness. I didn't care how much time or effort it took to get her body healed, but I wanted her mind healed soon. I wanted my Jolie back, and I hoped it wouldn't take long for her to come back to all the people who loved her.

At some point, with her hand still in mine, I managed to drift off to sleep.

I woke early the next morning when Detective Baines came into the room. Jolie was still sleeping, but I didn't want her waking alone, so we stood on the opposite side of the room and kept our voices quiet.

"What's going on?" I asked. "Please tell me you've got some information on the person that did this to her?"

"We managed to pull the footage from the parking lot security cameras," he started. "All we know right now is the color, make, and model of the vehicle, but we don't know who the owner is. There's an image of the license plate, but the cameras are old, so the footage was grainy. We've got to try to clean it up in order to get a clear plate number. We believe it was a woman driving the vehicle."

"If you need any help on enhancing that footage, get it over to us. You know Trent Michaels is brilliant at that stuff; he should be able to have a plate number in no time. Did you get anything else from the footage?"

A look of regret flashed in his face. "I hate to tell you this, De Luca, but Jolie was specifically targeted. The car sat in the parking lot for more than an hour waiting. When Jolie walked out, she wasn't paying attention to anything around her. In fact, while she was searching for something in her purse, she continued to walk into the parking lot toward her own vehicle. She didn't get very far and you can see the minute she realizes something is going on. Her head snaps up and she looks around. By the time she realizes what's happening, it seems like she's too shocked to move. The car barreled toward her and never once tried to stop."

"And you're certain it wasn't just a distracted driver who got scared and took off after?" I confirmed.

I needed to know how sure he was.

"Of course, it could have been, but experience tells me it wasn't. This car was waiting. The driver didn't move until Jolie started walking away from the building and into the lot. I wholeheartedly believe the driver intended to hit her."

Damn it.

"What's the extent of her injuries?" Detective Baines asked.

"Her entire left side is covered in bruises, scrapes, and cuts. That's the best of it because she's also got a sprained ankle, sprained knee, and a severe concussion. She didn't even recognize two of her brothers. They were in uniform when they were here. She saw them, didn't know who they were, and thought she was going to get arrested for something."

"No shit?"

I shook my head.

"I was hoping to have a chance to talk with her this morning and see what she could tell me about what happened."

"She doesn't remember it," I responded. "We asked her yesterday, but she couldn't tell us anything."

He frowned. "I was afraid that might be the case. Alright, give me a call if anything changes today or if she does recall something. It might not be anything we can use, but I'd rather know than not."

"Absolutely," I agreed. "Thanks for stopping by. And don't hesitate to reach out if you need help with that footage."

He gave me a curt nod, looked over at my sleeping girl, and walked out.

I went back to her.

Ten minutes later, one of the nurses walked in to check Jolie's vitals. While she was there, Jolie woke up.

"Hey, honey, how are you feeling this morning?" the

nurse asked.

"Tired," she answered. "And I still have a headache."

"How about the knee and ankle?"

She shrugged her shoulders. "The pain in my head is worse."

"Okay. Do you think you are up for something to eat this morning? It'd be a good idea to start taking in some foods."

"Yeah, I guess I could eat. Are there donuts?"

I wanted to laugh. Only my girl would be determined to have donuts for breakfast, even when she was in the hospital.

The nurse laughed before she responded, "Sorry, but that's not on your menu. We need to give your brain the best foods it can have to heal itself. Sugary and fried foods aren't part of that. I think the doctor is going to recommend that you stick to a healthy diet for the next two weeks or so. It should consist of fruits, vegetables, protein, whole grains, and a little bit of dairy."

Jolie's shoulders slumped. "Okay."

The nurse handed her a folded pamphlet and explained, "Here's the menu. Just hit the button on the phone for the kitchen and you can order whatever you want. Try not to stare too long at the menu though. It can be stressful on the brain right now."

When the nurse walked out, I took the pamphlet from Jolie. "I can read it to you," I started. "I'd rather have you rest and heal. Do you have a preference?"

"Well, I wanted donuts," she huffed. "Since that's not an option, how about you surprise me?"

"I can do that."

I picked up the phone and called down to the kitchen. I ordered the same thing for the both of us.

After I'd put the phone down on the receiver, Jolie shared,

"I think I need your help."

"Anything. What do you need?"

"They told me I have a sprained ankle and a sprained knee. I'm not sure what I'm supposed to do yet as far as walking goes, but I really need to use the bathroom."

I hadn't yet seen her leg. She'd been covered when I got in her room yesterday and since she was already so confused, I didn't want to bring any more stress on her.

Standing from the chair I'd spent the night in, I walked around to the opposite side of the bed, where I unplugged her IV machine and pulled back her blankets. Even though her knee was bandaged up, a large portion of her leg was exposed. I felt sick seeing just how beat up she was.

Carefully, I lifted her out of the bed and carried her to the bathroom. Setting her down in front of the toilet I instructed, "Put the weight on your right leg."

She did but still wobbled. "I feel a little dizzy."

"It's okay," I assured her. "I'll stay with you. Lower yourself and hold on to me."

"I can't pee with you in here."

"Why not?"

"I have a shy bladder," she reasoned.

I shot her a disbelieving look. "You're the most outgoing woman I've ever met and you're telling me your bladder is the part of you that's shy?"

She nodded.

Keeping one hand on her, I reached over and turned on the sink.

"What are you doing?" she asked.

"Trust me. Just carefully sit down and go."

"You have to turn around," she insisted.

I shook my head. "I'm not doing that, Jolie. If you get

dizzy and fall, I can't react quick enough if my back is to you. Sit, keep one hand on me so you stay steady, and I'll turn my head."

Thankfully, she did as I suggested and managed to take care of business. After she washed her hands, I carried her back to the bed, got her settled, and went back to the bathroom to take care of business of my own. By the time I walked back into the room, I saw the food had been delivered.

I made sure she was settled and eating before I started. I'd ordered both of us egg white omelets with peppers, onions, mushrooms, and cheddar cheese. We both had a side of wheat toast and fruit as well.

She was still eating when the door to her room opened. Her brothers walked in.

Jolie looked up from her plate, finished chewing her bite of toast, swallowed, and said, "Good morning, guys."

I wasn't sure if she was just being friendly or if she knew who they were.

"Jolie?" Colton called.

"Colton?" she returned.

"You remember me?"

Clearly caught off guard by his question, her eyes darted back and forth. "Um…you've been my brother since I was born. Why would I not remember you?"

Colton walked right over to her, sat on the edge of the bed, and pulled her in for a hug. Jolie was completely caught off guard.

When he pulled back, she asked, "Why do I feel like I've missed something?"

Memphis answered, "We were here yesterday, and you had no idea who we were."

"What?"

They both nodded at her.

I explained, "They were in their uniforms and you kept asking if you were in trouble and if they were going to arrest you."

She blinked her eyes at me. "Are you serious?"

"Yeah."

"Oh my God," she whispered. "I'm so sorry."

Memphis shook his head and maintained, "Don't worry about it. You didn't forget us on purpose."

She grinned at both of them. "Never."

We spent the next half hour keeping the conversation light while Jolie finished her breakfast. Over those thirty minutes, I felt myself begin to relax a little bit. My conversation with Detective Baines that morning had left me feeling unsettled, but seeing a little bit of Jolie's spunk back and the confusion gone helped. I knew my girl was going to recover and that's all that mattered to me.

CHAPTER 18

Jolie

"**D**AMN IT!" I SNAPPED.

I was sitting on the edge of my bed in my room. It was morning and I needed to use the bathroom. Unfortunately, when I reached out for my crutches, I accidentally knocked them over and they slid along the wall to the floor away from me.

There was still a lot of swelling in my knee and ankle and no matter how tough I was, I knew there was no way I'd be able to put any weight on them.

Lorenzo stayed with me last night, but it seemed he got up before I did and had gone downstairs already. It was likely he was making breakfast for us since he'd been doting on me since before I even left the hospital.

Since I had no idea how quickly he'd be back and my bladder felt about ready to burst, I had to improvise. I scooted my body to the edge of the bed and shifted so my right leg was hanging off the bed. Thankfully, the dizziness that I'd felt Monday evening and Tuesday morning started to subside by the late afternoon yesterday. If it hadn't, I wouldn't have been able to even consider what I was about to do.

As carefully as I could, I put all my weight on my right leg and slowly hopped toward the crutches. Every time I jumped, I thought I was going to wet myself. Once I made it around my nightstand, I put my hands against the wall to steady myself. It was as I was squatting down with my left leg outstretched in front of me that I realized how lucky I was that I did one-legged squats from time to time.

No sooner did I lower myself to just a few inches above the ground when I heard, "Jolie?"

I was so startled, I fell to my behind and threw my right arm back to catch my fall. As I did that, my hand hit the nightstand and I cried, "Ouch!"

"Christ, Jolie," Lorenzo muttered. "What are you doing?"

"The IV fluids they gave me have done a number on me. I need to use the bathroom," I answered, my frustration beginning to take over. I hated this.

He came around, put his hands under my arms, and lifted me before he bent down and grabbed my crutches. As soon as I had them positioned properly under my arms, I made my way to the bathroom.

"Thank you," I murmured when I came back into the room.

"Why wouldn't you just call me if you needed help?" he wondered.

I shrugged my shoulders. "I don't like feeling helpless. And I wasn't sure you'd hear me anyway."

Lorenzo moved closer to me, stopping only when he was close enough to wrap an arm around my waist.

"Baby, you were hit by a car two days ago," he reminded me. "You're hardly helpless. Cut yourself some slack."

I didn't have it in me to argue with him, so I gave him a gentle nod.

"I made you breakfast," he shared. "I thought you might

want a change of scenery, so I left it downstairs."

"Downstairs would be nice," I answered.

"Can I help you downstairs or do you need to prove your independence to me?" he teased.

My shoulders fell. "I'll be honest," I began. "In the very short time I've been awake, I've already worn myself out."

Lorenzo took a step back, kept one arm around my back as he put both of my crutches in that hand, while he bent down to put his other arm under my legs. He was careful not to squeeze too tight as he held me against his body and carried me and my crutches down the stairs.

After getting me settled on the couch, Lorenzo brought me a plate of scrambled eggs, breakfast potatoes, and fruit. Unfortunately, as much as I could have used a cup of coffee, the doctor had suggested I stay away from the caffeine for as long as possible while I gave my brain the time to heal from what I'd been through. Lorenzo was adamant about sticking to the doctor's orders because he set a glass of water down on the coffee table.

"I can't wait to have a cup of coffee," I sighed.

He leaned over and kissed me on the lips. "I know, but I want you to heal. Just a few more days, please?"

Since he was going out of his way to take care of me and wasn't allowing me to go through this alone by joining me in the caffeine ban, I gave in.

We ate for a while in silence before I said, "Thank you."

"For what?"

"This. Everything. Thank you for being here for me through this. I know I'm getting frustrated easily. You're being amazing even when I'm irritable."

His face softened. "You've been through a serious trauma. I don't know what it feels like to be in your shoes right now, but

I can understand your frustration. Even if none of that happened, I'd still be here dealing with your irritability over just about anything. And I'd be doing that because I love you, baby."

"I'm so lucky to have you," I breathed.

Having finished his food, he set his empty plate on the coffee table. "I love that you feel that way, Jolie, but I'm the lucky one. You know I was living quietly before you came along. I went to work, focused on my job, was there for my friends, supported my brother, and made sure my mom was safe, but that was it. You said it yourself; I was living in solitude. I found comfort in hiding because it was the only real peace I managed to find after everything happened with my father. But then you came along and, no matter how hard I fought giving in to it, you were a miracle in my solitude. You, being the woman you are, brought me a peace I didn't even know could exist without silence."

I swallowed hard, my lips parted, and tears welled in my eyes.

My voice was rough when I spoke. "You can't say things like that. I'm not supposed to be working my brain too hard."

"Nothing I said should be making your brain work, Jolie. I've been silent for a long time and I'm finding, especially after what just happened, I don't want to be like that anymore. I'm not going to hide anymore, particularly not how much you mean to me."

Unable to speak, I held my nearly empty plate out to him. "My head...I think I need to rest," I murmured.

Lorenzo took the plate from me and chuckled. "I'll let you play that card right now, but from now on you need to be prepared. I won't stop myself from telling you everything I think you deserve to hear."

With that, he got up from the couch, handed me my water,

and took the plates to the kitchen. I sat there with the glass of water to my lips, trying not to think too much about anything he'd just said because I was certain my brain was working harder than it ever had before in my life.

When Lorenzo came back in the room, he grabbed the remote and shifted me on the couch so I was settled between his legs, my back to his chest, with my leg elevated on a pillow.

"What are you doing?" I asked.

"Relaxing with you."

"Don't you need to work?" I wondered.

I felt his body vibrating with laughter behind me. "Do you think I'm just going to leave you here alone to fend for yourself?"

"I'm just going to lie around," I noted. "It's not like I'm planning to do anything crazy."

"Baby, you nearly injured yourself again just trying to get to the bathroom this morning. The boys are working with the WPD to figure out what they can on your hit-and-run case. They'll contact me if and when they find something. In the meantime, I'm staying here with you for the next few days and taking care of you. Deal with it."

"No need to be so bossy," I shot back.

"Jolie?"

"Yes, boss?"

"Close your eyes and rest."

If I hadn't been so exhausted, I would have gone toe-to-toe with him. Unfortunately, I didn't have the stamina.

Lorenzo turned on the television and I watched for about three minutes before my eyes drifted shut.

Two days later

"I'm not, by any means, complaining, but I feel so bad you did this."

"You're family, Jojo," Ekko announced. "That's what you do for family. Besides, we knew the kids missed their auntie, so there really was no choice. I think that's why they cooperated so well today."

Dom and Ekko came over and brought Hank and Gracie with them to visit me. They also brought dinner. Lorenzo had been doing a phenomenal job taking care of me, making sure I was getting fed regularly and resting all the time, so I was very grateful to my brother and sister-in-law for giving him a break tonight.

Over the last couple of days, the swelling in my knee and ankle had gone down considerably. I still had quite a way to go before I could really start any sort of therapy. I knew enough about the body to know I wasn't ready to start finding the range of motion I had prior to the accident.

The bruising was still very prominent down the side of my body, but my face had been healing nicely, only a bit of redness remaining from some of the scrapes I'd gotten. The worst of the bruising was on my shoulder, my hip, and my outer thigh.

Despite all my injuries, now that I'd had a few days of sitting around doing nothing, I had time to reflect on the accident itself. I didn't know much at this point other than I was a victim of a hit-and-run and that the Windsor Police Department and the Cunningham Security team were working together to locate the suspect. Most important of all, I realized just how lucky I was. I still didn't remember the accident itself, but I'd been given a full account of what happened. Based on what I'd been told, I knew things could have been much worse for me.

Lucky for me, I was still alive and well enough to do things like sit on the couch and give kisses to my cuddly niece while she and her family visited me. We'd finished having dinner a little while ago and now I was getting in my cuddle time with her.

Yes, for the first time in a very long time, I was in the same room as Lorenzo and Gracie and I was holding her. Lorenzo was holding Hank. I had gotten my cuddles with Hank before dinner.

"Well, I really appreciate it. I've been going a bit stir-crazy here. Mom and Dad stopped by on Wednesday, but I wasn't great company."

"How are you feeling?" Ekko asked.

"Rested, that's for sure," I joked. "In all seriousness, I'm doing a bit better now on the sleep front. I don't take as many naps throughout the day, which is a good sign. It's just been hard because I'm trying to limit my television time since I know I shouldn't be watching too much of it. I was a bit bummed since Rocco had a hockey game the other day. Not only could I not stay awake to watch the whole thing, but when I was awake, I didn't look at the television. I just kept my head in Lorenzo's lap, closed my eyes, and listened to the game."

"It was the most relaxed I've ever seen her during a game," Lorenzo added.

"I made an appointment for a follow up with my doctor next week, so I'm hoping I'll be cleared for some activities."

Ekko shook her head in frustration. "I'm still just so shocked that someone actually did this to you."

"It could have happened to anyone. I just happened to be at the wrong place at the wrong time."

A look of confusion washed over Ekko's face. As quickly as it was there, it was gone.

"What was that?" I asked.

"What? Nothing."

"Bullshit," I shot back. I looked between Lorenzo and Dom. "Why do I feel like there's something you're not telling me?"

Dom's jaw clenched as Lorenzo put his free hand on my good ankle to give me a squeeze. "Let's not worry about it right now," he urged. "You just need to focus on healing and getting yourself better."

I studied him a minute and thought about what I'd just said.

Wrong place. Wrong time.

Unless it wasn't.

"Did someone do this on purpose? Was I targeted?" I asked, feeling myself grow anxious.

"You need to stay calm, Jojo," Dom reminded me.

"Calm?" I repeated. "Bro, someone purposely hit me with a car. I could have died! How many people do you know that can remain calm when someone tries to kill them?!"

He had no reply.

I closed my eyes.

"I'm so sorry," Ekko lamented.

I turned my head toward her and opened my eyes. "It's not your fault," I replied.

Slowly shaking my head in disbelief, I looked down at my niece. I ran the backs of my fingers down her soft, chubby cheek. I didn't even know how to begin processing what I was feeling in that moment and a single tear rolled down my cheek.

Suddenly, I felt movement at my side. Lorenzo had given

Hank back to his Dad and come over to me. He sat down on the edge of the couch next to me and wrapped an arm around my shoulders.

"Nobody is going to touch you, Jolie," he promised. "Until we find out what's happening and find whoever is behind this, you aren't going to be left alone."

I leaned into him and whispered, "I have a headache."

He put his hand in my hair, kissed the top of my head, and suggested, "Okay, how about you give me Gracie and we get you up to bed?"

I nodded in response.

As Lorenzo took my niece from my arms, he spoke, "Hi, Princess. I know you probably want to cuddle, but I've got to take care of your aunt right now. Can you be a good girl for your mom and dad so I can do that?"

God, I loved him.

Before Lorenzo handed Gracie over to Ekko, she came over and hugged me. "They'll keep you safe," she whispered in my ear. "You just have to put your faith in them to do their job while you rest and let yourself heal. Okay?"

I nodded again. "Thanks, Ekko."

Dom walked over to me, lowered his body with Hank in his arms so he was eye level with me, and vowed, "Nothing is going to happen to you. We're doing everything we can to get to the bottom of this."

"I know."

Wrapping a hand behind my head, Dom gently tugged me forward and pressed a kiss to my forehead. "Love you, Jojo."

"Love you."

After he walked them to the door and locked up, Lorenzo came over to me, lifted me in his arms, and carried me upstairs.

I'd been trying to reclaim my independence over the last

few days, refusing to allow him to carry me everywhere, but tonight was different. Learning what I did tonight coupled with the headache I now had, it just wasn't in me to prove anything.

"Do you need the bathroom before I take you to bed?" he asked.

"Yeah, I need to brush my teeth, too."

Lorenzo carefully carried me to the bathroom. Once he set me down, he kept his hands on me to make sure I was steady and asked, "Are you good?"

"Please don't leave me," I pleaded.

"You're not feeling good, I'm not leaving you alone. I'll leave the water on and brush my teeth while you take care of business."

Relief swept through me. After I took care of business, washed my hands, and brushed my teeth, Lorenzo took me to my bed.

I was tucked close to Lorenzo, his hand behind my head as his fingers massaged my scalp and stroked through my strands, and his lips were at my forehead.

"There isn't anything I won't do to protect you, Jolie. I promise you."

"I'm scared," I admitted.

"I know you are, but I won't let anything happen to you, baby."

I wanted to believe that and I knew that he would do everything he could to see that I was safe. It still did little to help me come to terms with the fact that it was even necessary.

Why was someone after me?

"You've got to calm yourself," he said softly.

"I know. I'm trying."

With his hand still putting gentle pressure at my scalp,

he maintained, "Relax, Jolie. Your whole body is still wound tight. That's not good for your head. I need you to heal, baby. To do that, you've got to trust me to keep you safe and stop worrying."

I didn't respond because there was nothing for me to say. Everything he said was the truth. Of course, that didn't change the fact that I was still going to worry.

"I understand it," he went on. "I get where you're coming from, but I really want you to get better. Just try your best to think about good things, like Hank and Gracie, and let me worry about everything else."

"Then I'll be worrying about you."

My face had been planted against his throat when his hand stopped moving in my hair. He opened the space between my face and his throat by pulling back. He looked down at me and asserted, "Trust me. I've always been good at what I do. Do you think now when I've got someone I want to spend my life with, that I'm going to let anything happen to me?"

"No," I replied softly.

Lorenzo moved close again and held me. We were in silence a bit before something new replaced the thoughts in my head. "Why did you lie to me?"

"I'm sorry?"

"You didn't tell me the truth about the accident. I just don't understand why you'd hide something like that from me?"

"Jolie." He sounded a bit irritated.

"What?"

He was silent a moment.

"Baby, go to sleep."

"It was just a question," I said softly.

"Yeah, but it's a ridiculous one. One that I shouldn't even

have to explain to you," he retorted.

"I'm just saying that for someone who says they want to spend their life with me, lying doesn't seem to be a good way to do it."

"Jolie, I didn't lie to you."

"You kept the truth from me. That feels a lot like the same thing," I explained.

Lorenzo rolled away from me, sat up in the bed, and turned on the light. "So you think I'm a liar? You don't think I've had any justifiable reason to keep the truth of what happened from you for the time being? The thoughts that ran through my mind when I heard you'd been hit by a car...fuck, I can't even describe it. It was like being stuck with a knife in my gut. My goal in not telling you had nothing to do with lying to you. I haven't said anything because I don't want you overworking your mind right now. I want you to heal, baby." He paused, taking in a deep breath, trying to regain his control. When he continued, he completely shattered my heart. "This is fucking why I kept myself secluded. Because the second I think I figure it out—the second I finally believe in myself enough to know I've got what it takes to go the distance with you and not become the man I despise—you prove to me that I was right to be alone since I've obviously hurt you. You sat there and called me a liar, Jolie. How is it even possible that you don't know how much you matter to me that I'd do anything I could to protect you?"

The sound of his voice held more than an edge of hurt. Pain sliced through me knowing I'd made him feel that way. He'd spent years secluding himself from the possibility of finding love and when he opened his heart up to me, I proved that living in solitude would have been safer. Because, in that moment, no matter how much my head hurt or how many bruises covered my body, I knew it paled in comparison to the hurt I'd just unloaded on Lorenzo.

"I'm sorry," I whispered, realizing just how big of a mistake I'd made.

He sighed. "It's fine, Jolie. Just go to sleep."

On that, I didn't say anything else. Sadly, it wasn't easy to fall asleep because I knew, despite what he said, that it wasn't fine. So, while my mind was no longer on the hit-and-run ordeal, which was a huge plus, this was worse.

With the pain in my head not subsiding, I did my best to try to relax. Eventually, still unsure if the pain I felt in my heart was worse than that throughout my body, I drifted.

CHAPTER 19

Jolie

A week & a half later

"**H**EY," I SAID INTO THE PHONE, TRYING TO BE CHIPPER.

"I'm heading there now. I should be there in about ten minutes," Lorenzo replied.

"Okay, that's perfect timing. Kendall was just about to head out."

"See you in a few," he returned, disconnecting the call before giving me an opportunity to say anything.

I pulled the phone from my ear and looked at my sister. I'm sure my expression told her everything I was feeling.

"Something is definitely wrong," I shared. "He didn't tell me he loved me. He didn't even say goodbye. He just hung up."

Her face changed, but the words she spoke next didn't match the dread I saw there. "I'm sure everything is fine. Maybe he didn't want to be driving and talking on the phone," she suggested, attempting to brush it off.

My eyes welled with tears. "I miss him, sissy," I croaked.

Kendall pulled me close. "He's here with you every night," she reasoned.

I shook my head as I held on tight to her. "He's here, but

he's not. His mind is somewhere else."

"Tell him, Jojo," she urged me. "Tell him what's upsetting you. You're the outspoken one. Maybe he's feeling things, too, and he doesn't know how to talk about it. You've got to open up and talk to him about what's on your mind."

I nodded. "I will. Tonight, I will."

"I have to go," she began. "If you need me, though, you call. You know I'm always here for you."

"I know, Kendall, thank you. Love you."

"Love you, Jo."

After my sister left, I thought about everything that was going on in my head.

It had been more than two weeks since my accident. A lot had happened in that time.

From a physical standpoint, things were much better for me. My face had no remaining scrapes or redness. The cuts and scrapes on my arm had completely healed. The severe bruising on my shoulder and hip was nearly gone and I was finally walking on my own again without crutches. Even though I was getting around better, I hadn't yet returned to work because of my knee and ankle injuries. I was still dealing with quite a bit of soreness and fatigued easily if I stood for too long, so I continued to do some exercises to help strengthen the muscles and regain my range of motion.

The dizziness I experienced not long after the accident hadn't returned, which was great, but the same couldn't be said about the headaches. I was still occasionally having them, though not nearly with the same frequency I had within the days following the accident.

So, physically I was on the mend, but emotionally I wasn't doing well at all.

Lorenzo had been wonderful with me. Whether it was

making meals or driving me to my doctor's appointments, there wasn't anything he hadn't done for me. And while I appreciated all of it, there was still something lingering. Ever since the night I learned the truth about the hit-and-run not being an accident, but rather something intentional, I'd been feeling all sorts of emotions. Sure, I was frightened about what they would find and it made me nervous to think that someone had targeted me, but what bothered me the most was the fact that Lorenzo and I never spoke again about the conversation we had later that night after Dom and Ekko left with the kids.

I never thought he'd explode the way he did, but I guess it never really dawned on me why he had kept the truth from me. Now that I'd had time to think about it, I realized that his reasons for keeping it from me were justified.

And I hated what I'd done to him.

Despite me calling him a liar that night, he never faltered in showing me just how much I mattered to him, doing anything he could to help my recovery.

I wanted to talk about it with him. No. I needed to talk with him about what happened. He deserved to know that I understood why he'd done what he'd done, and most importantly, he deserved an apology from me. I needed to do that now because it would be impossible to build the life that I wanted to build with him otherwise. There were just too many things about him that told me he was the kind of man I'd been searching for all these years. I wasn't prepared to give him up.

So I had to do something about it.

Because what was happening between us right now was not working. At least, not for me. And I hoped it wasn't something he was okay with either.

Lorenzo ended up going back to work a week and a half ago. For the first few days, he did that from my place since I was having trouble getting around. He spent time on his phone, making calls, or working on his computer. I didn't want to interrupt him while he worked, obviously. And when he finished working, he didn't seem to be in any mood to discuss much of anything.

While we weren't arguing with each other, there was a definite shift in our moods. I'd been particularly quiet, which was completely out of character. Lorenzo was quieter than was typical for him. We'd fallen into a routine.

Work for him.

Lounge and rest or therapy for me.

Eat.

Watch TV.

Sleep.

I couldn't handle it any longer and decided that I was going to be doing something about it today.

My sister had come over this afternoon to hang with me while Lorenzo ran out. I assumed he had a few things to take care of at work, but didn't know for sure since he hadn't said exactly where he was going. I had shared with Kendall everything that I'd been dealing with over the last couple of weeks and she'd insisted that Lorenzo and I were just being stubborn. If we simply communicated what we were feeling all would be right between us.

I wasn't a total fool and knew this made complete sense. But something about the way he'd been lately was keeping me from doing it. That and the fact that I was embarrassed I'd been so foolish. Embarrassed that I called the man I loved a liar when he was anything but.

But today it had to change.

Because I just couldn't allow things to continue like this between us.

I loved him and I needed to make things right.

So, I was going to make dinner for us tonight and I was going to apologize. Hopefully, from there, things could be worked out.

I was out in the kitchen, looking in the refrigerator for something to make for dinner when I heard Lorenzo come in and call, "Jolie?"

"In the kitchen," I yelled back.

I had closed the refrigerator door and opened the freezer door when I heard him walk into the kitchen. As I thumbed through the contents of the freezer, I started speaking, "Hey, so, I was thinking I could make dinner for us tonight. I don't know how you feel about it, but I have some things I need to say."

I heard a small cry from behind me and froze.

"Jolie, turn around," Lorenzo instructed.

I closed the freezer door and turned around. My jaw dropped.

Oh.

My.

God.

Lorenzo was standing there, smiling brightly at me, as he held a pure blue French Bulldog puppy in his hands.

"You got a puppy?"

He shook his head and grinned at me. "No, baby, you got a puppy."

My mouth still hadn't closed as I walked toward him and the pup.

I reached my hand out and ran it over the puppy's soft, wrinkly body. "She's so cute," I marveled.

"He."

"What?"

"He's so cute. It's a boy," he clarified.

My heart squeezed. He was the most adorable little thing I'd ever seen. "How old is he?"

"Seven weeks," Lorenzo answered. "Would you like to hold him?"

I bit my lip and nodded.

Lorenzo passed the little guy over to me and I instantly fell in love. He was the cutest and squishiest pup I'd ever laid my eyes on.

And he was mine.

I cuddled him close, gave him kisses, and told him just how much I already loved him.

I looked up at Lorenzo, feeling the happiest I'd been since my accident, and asked, "Why did you do this?"

"That look on your face right now," he stated. "I've missed seeing you smile all the time, so I wanted to do something that would cheer you up. I wanted that dimple back."

"Lorenzo," I whispered as I leaned into him, my emotions getting the best of me.

My big guy wrapped his arm around my shoulder and offered gently, "I know, baby. I had originally planned on getting him for you for Christmas, but it's been rough these last few weeks and I couldn't handle going another day without seeing a smile on your face. I miss you, Jolie."

I sagged in relief against him. "I just told Kendall the same thing about you."

He gave me a squeeze and ushered me into the living room.

We sat on the couch and I put our puppy on my lap. He stood up, looked at me curiously with his big, blue eyes, and walked over to Lorenzo's lap.

"You've got to be kidding me," I muttered. "He prefers you over me."

Lorenzo laughed. "I have a bigger lap, that's all. Give him some time; you'll be his favorite soon enough."

"You think so?" I asked, looking up at him.

His face softened and he assured me, "I know so. You're my favorite, too."

Dropping my head to his chest, I sighed, "I'm so sorry, Lorenzo. I was wrong. So wrong to say what I did to you."

"It's okay, Jolie."

I pushed back from his chest and sat up to look at him. "No," I insisted. "It wasn't okay. I was hurt that you kept it from me, but I should have approached the situation differently. I never should have called you a liar or made you feel the way that I did."

"I appreciate the apology. I need you to know that I never planned to keep that information from you indefinitely, though. You were still having headaches, you were still napping regularly, and the doctor hadn't yet cleared you to resume the most basic of activities like watching television for prolonged periods of time. My biggest concern was making sure your head was in a place to heal, not to be filled with worry over who caused the accident. I would have told you what was going on, but I wanted to give you some time to recover physically. Bottom line, I knew you were here, I was with you, and you weren't in any danger as long as that was the case, so I made a judgment call to not dump something on you that would have hindered your recovery."

I had been such a fool.

"So, I screw up, make you feel like crap, and you buy me a puppy?"

He shrugged his shoulders. "Let it go, baby. We talked, you're smiling, and I'm happy. It's done."

I reached over and scratched my puppy behind his ears. While I admired the little guy, I called, "Lorenzo?"

"Remember when I told you that I felt lonely when you weren't here at night?"

"Yeah."

"I know you've been here with me every night since the accident, but I've been so lonely."

"Jolie..." he trailed off.

"It's okay," I assured him. "I just wanted you to know that I'm happy we worked it out and you're here with me now."

He brought his hand to the top of our puppy's head and gave him a good rub. Then, he took in a deep breath and declared, "No, it's not okay. You went through some serious trauma, you were trying to heal, and when stuff happened, I didn't help you. I let you live feeling sad and hurt. That's not what I want for you or for us. So this doesn't all fall on you. I'm not sorry for not telling you everything I knew about the accident, but I am sorry for letting too much time pass before working it out with you."

Dropping my head back to his shoulder, I sat there next to him thinking about everything.

Eventually, I declared, "He needs a name."

"You choose," Lorenzo urged. "Whatever you want to name him."

Lifting him from Lorenzo's lap, I held him up in front of my face. After giving him kisses, I set him down on the floor. Secretly, I was hoping he'd do something that would give me an indication of what his name should be.

He offered no help.

The little pup scurried around, his tiny body bouncing, as

he sniffed everything and explored. I couldn't help but laugh. He was so adorable.

"We should probably go and get him a bed and food for tonight," I suggested.

"I already took care of it," Lorenzo started. "I figured it would be fine for now and if it's ultimately something you don't like, I'll take it to the office. I'll use it for when he's there with me."

I raised my brows in question. "You're going to take him to work?"

"Not now, but when you go back to work. There's always someone there, so even if I needed to run out for a case and couldn't take him with me, he'd be taken care of."

My heart melted. He didn't want the little guy being left alone. "Oliver's the luckiest pup in the world," I proclaimed.

Lorenzo's eyes came to mine. He cocked an eyebrow and repeated, "Oliver?"

Nodding, I added, "We can call him Ollie for short."

Lorenzo grinned, pulled me close, and kissed me on the forehead. I tipped my head back a bit and gave him my mouth. Lorenzo didn't hesitate to take what I was offering. It was clear he had missed this part of us at least as much as I did.

With my head being cradled in his hand, Lorenzo slanted his and took our kiss deeper. We hadn't had sex with each other since before the accident. And with the way things had been between us since I'd called him a liar a week and a half ago, this kind of affection had been lacking. Finally feeling his mouth on mine, having that intimacy between us again, I was quickly turned on. I moaned into his mouth, as his free hand traveled up my thigh, squeezed, and continued moving up along my side. His thumb had landed at the underside of my breast and had just swiped over my nipple when we heard the yapping.

Breaking the kiss, I pulled away and looked at Ollie. He was barking at us, clearly upset we weren't paying him enough attention, and he wanted to make sure we knew just how he felt.

"He's not very happy with us," I pointed out.

Lorenzo made a sound and huffed, "Well, the feeling is mutual. I haven't kissed my woman like that in a long time and I missed it. He just put an end to that."

I looked at Lorenzo and smiled. "That felt nice to have again," I said softly.

"Yeah," he returned.

"I should make us some dinner."

He gave me a nod and explained, "While you get that started, I'll take Ollie out. We'll get his things out of the truck and I'll let him walk around out there for a little so he can relieve himself. When I come back in, I'll help you with dinner."

"Okay, boss."

It was only when we stood from the couch that Ollie stopped barking. Evidently, he realized he was getting his way.

My eyes went to Lorenzo's. "Apparently, he takes after you."

Lorenzo's brows pulled together. "What is that supposed to mean?"

"He's bossy," I clarified.

Lorenzo laughed. "He's only bossy if he's successful. That means you can't give in to him. If you do, you'll create a monster."

"He's too cute, babe. I'm not sure I can say no to him."

"You'll regret it, Jolie. Don't let him think he's in charge."

I cocked an eyebrow and asked, "So, if in a year or two when Hank or Gracie have already had a cupcake and one of them walks up to you asking to have another cupcake when you know that Dom and Ekko would not agree to a second one, what are you going to do?"

Lorenzo's eyes narrowed. "You're not fighting fair."

"It's the same thing!"

He shook his head. "No, it's not. Dom and Ekko are supposed to set rules and boundaries for Hank and Gracie the same way we need to set them for Ollie. As Hank and Gracie's uncle, it is my job to help them break the rules that are silly."

I couldn't argue with him. He'd called himself their uncle. I liked the way that sounded and I really liked the way it made me feel.

"I love you," I breathed.

Lorenzo brought his mouth to mine, kissed me, and returned, "I love you, too."

Ollie started barking again.

Lorenzo and I laughed. Then, I walked to the kitchen to start dinner while Ollie and his dad went outside. By the time they came back, I already had dinner in the oven. While we waited for it to cook, Lorenzo and I got down on the floor and played with our pup.

Ollie had the best time.

When the timer for the oven went off indicating dinner was ready, my perfect puppy was all worn out. He curled up in his bed his daddy bought him and took a nap.

Lorenzo and I ate and cleaned up from dinner. Then, we made our way to the couch to get reacquainted with one another. Just as things started heating up between us, a bossy little Frenchie started barking.

Feeling sexually frustrated, I sighed, "Maybe I'll have to reconsider giving in to all his demands."

At that, Lorenzo burst out laughing and buried his face in my neck.

A minute later, he lifted Ollie off the floor and brought him up on the couch with us so we could watch Rocco's hockey game together.

And for the first time since my accident, I went a full day without having a single headache.

CHAPTER 20

Jolie

BARK.
Bark.
Bark.

While I couldn't fully understand exactly what Dom and Ekko went through with the newborns, I certainly had an appreciation for their ability to function with little to no sleep. Ollie woke us up a few times throughout the night with his whimpers.

About twenty-five minutes ago, Lorenzo leaned over, gave me a kiss on the cheek, and declared, "Morning, Jolie. I'm going to go let him out."

"I can do it," I suggested.

Lorenzo gave me a look that told me I shouldn't even consider doing such a thing since he was there. "I've got it."

"Okay," I acquiesced.

He looked down at Ollie and instructed, "Let's go, boy."

Our excited puppy followed behind Lorenzo as he walked out of the bedroom. Exhausted, I stayed in bed, hoping Lorenzo would come back and join me.

But when more than enough time had passed and they still hadn't returned, I began to worry that something bad happened. Just as I sat up in the bed, preparing to go down to make sure everything was alright, I heard Lorenzo's footsteps climbing the stairs.

When they walked in, Ollie went right to his bed, curled up, and fell asleep. I looked to Lorenzo for an explanation.

"I took him out. He relieved himself and then I played with him. He's worn out now."

Having missed him so much, I asked, "Any idea how long he'll stay sleeping?"

Giving me a sly grin, Lorenzo sauntered back over to the bed. "At this age, he'll need an average of twenty hours of sleep a day. I think he's going to be out for a while."

Lorenzo dropped his jeans, put a knee to the bed, moved toward me, and settled himself over half my body.

"I missed you, boss," I said softly.

"I'm right here, baby."

I shook my head. "No, I mean I've missed you. I've missed being with you."

Lorenzo brushed his knuckles down my cheek.

"Will you make love to me, Lorenzo?"

He didn't answer with words. Instead, he lowered his mouth to mine and kissed me soft, slow. My arms wrapped around his shoulders as his hand that had been at my face dropped to my hip. He gave me a squeeze there and deepened the kiss when his tongue dipped into my mouth. His hand trailed up my side until he reached my breast.

Palming my breast in his hand, Lorenzo forced a moan to escape. He'd held me so many times over the last few weeks, but it was nothing like this. Nothing at all like this.

This was sweet relief.

This was finally, finally having him back.

"Lorenzo," I breathed when his mouth started traveling

down along my throat.

His lips were featherlight on the skin of my chest, hovering there, when he returned, "Missed you too, baby. Missed you so much."

"Please," I pleaded with him. "I need you."

Lorenzo lifted, shifted, and removed his boxer briefs while I whipped my camisole over my head. Before I had a chance to think, Lorenzo's hands were at my hips, yanking my panties down my legs.

"So beautiful, Jolie," he rasped.

Then, he disappeared between my legs. His mouth was on me, gentle at first, then deliciously hard. Claiming. He devoured me, his tongue swiping through my wetness before plunging inside me.

It had been too long, way too long, so it took very little effort for Lorenzo to bring me to the brink of an orgasm. He knew I was there, ready to fall, and pulled his mouth from me.

I whimpered, ready to burst into tears at the loss of him.

"It's been too long without you. First time after all that's happened, I want you coming with me inside you, baby."

"Hurry," I begged.

Lorenzo hurried.

In one swift movement, he positioned himself and slid inside.

I gasped.

"Babe," I breathed, the air leaving my lungs.

"Way too long, Jolie," he croaked.

"Take it home, Lorenzo."

He did.

And it was beautiful.

Our bodies connected, hands roaming, and mouths tasting left us panting, breathless, and building to something extraordinary. Lorenzo took us there and he did it effortlessly.

Slow.

Gentle.

Tender.

"Take it, baby," he encouraged me.

I took it. Pleasure shot through me and Lorenzo worked me through it.

Two thrusts after I started to come down, he found his and took it, his groan low, deep, and very, very sexy.

Lorenzo collapsed on top of me, only briefly, before rolling to his back and taking me with him. With my body draped across his, my big guy held me while we took some time to catch our breath.

After some time had passed, I lifted my head and declared, "I really didn't enjoy the way I've felt since the accident, but if what just happened is the result, I don't mind that I had to take one for the team."

Lorenzo's body vibrated with laughter underneath mine.

"I'm not real keen on going through what we just went through ever again, but I'm more than willing to give you what I just did whenever you need it as long as you give back just as good as you just gave me," he said.

"That works for me," I agreed.

After a few minutes of silence passed, he asked, "How do you feel? Is anything hurting you? I wasn't too rough with you, was I?"

I shook my head. "I'm perfect. You were perfect and you didn't hurt me."

He returned a gentle smile. "Love you, Jolie."

"I love you, too."

I glanced over at Ollie and found him still sleeping, looking absolutely adorable. Feeling so much love for him and for the man holding me in his arms, I looked back at Lorenzo and spoke. "Thank you for Ollie."

Giving me a gentle squeeze, he returned, "You're welcome."

Putting my cheek back to his chest while I had all the emotions I did running through me, I started talking about the accident. Or, more accurately, I started talking about the person behind it.

"I trust you, Lorenzo," I began. "I trust you and the rest of the guys to do what you need to do to keep me safe from whoever did this to me."

"It means a lot to me that you feel that way," he replied. "But we're stuck."

My body tightened. "Stuck?"

"I don't want you to worry, but I'm not going to hide this from you. That didn't lead us anywhere good last time."

I lifted my head to look at him. "I think I should go get cleaned up before we get into this discussion."

He dipped his chin and left me to it.

When I returned, I pulled on a clean pair of panties and a camisole before I climbed back into the bed.

"Okay, boss. Give it to me," I demanded.

"After Trent put in a bit of work to clean up the image on the video, we were able to get a clear shot of the plate number from the vehicle that hit you. We found the owner. It was a woman; her name is Melinda Starnes. Dom and I talked about it. He doesn't know her, so there's certainly no family connection. You don't know anyone by that name from your job, do you? Maybe a client?"

I took a minute to think, but the name didn't ring a bell. "No. I don't recognize that name. Has she been found?"

"Not yet, but Detective Baines is personally looking into

locating her. We are, too. The house where the car is registered to has been vacant since we learned who she was. I'm guessing that after the hit-and-run, she never went home."

"Well, that's disappointing," I huffed. "What now?"

"We're still working on it. Right now, I think the issue is that we're searching for someone that isn't our real suspect."

My brows pulled together. "What do you mean?"

"Don't get me wrong," he started. "It was definitely a woman that hit you. We could see that on the footage, which, by the way, was not easy to watch. So, she definitely needs to be caught and justice served for what she did. What I'm saying, though, is that I don't think she acted alone. I think someone else is involved. That's the bigger reason we need to find her. If we can, we'll hopefully be able to figure out who she's working with."

"So what happens now?" I wondered.

He shook his head. "Nothing's going to be different for you. I don't want you alone until we solve this case. I don't know when you're planning to go back to work, but if that time comes and this is still unresolved, I'll take you to work and pick you up."

"I was planning to call them later today," I began. "I feel awful about it, but I don't want to rush myself through my recovery. My clients are important to me and I want to give them the same service they've come to expect from me. If I'm in pain, I won't be able to do that, so I've decided to wait until January. I'll call today and have the girls there reschedule my clients."

Lorenzo took a moment to process what I'd said and gave me a sad smile. "I'm so sorry this happened to you, Jolie. I know how much your work means to you."

I nodded. "Yeah, I'm bummed, but I've got a cute little

pup that's going to need some training, so I'll have plenty to keep me busy for the next few weeks."

He wrapped his arm around my shoulders and pulled me toward him for a hug. "I'm going to keep you safe," he promised.

"I know you will. I never doubted that for one second," I replied.

Putting his hand behind my head, he dropped his mouth to mine. His lips barely had a chance to touch mine when the barking started. I laughed against his lips and stated, "We have to be grateful that he stayed sleeping a little while ago."

"You ready for breakfast?" he asked.

"Yeah."

After giving me one more peck, he urged, "You take care of Ollie, I'll make you food."

"Okay."

With that, we got out of bed. I gave Ollie cuddles and kisses before taking him downstairs to give him his breakfast while Lorenzo took care of getting our breakfast ready.

"You have everything," Lorenzo groaned.

"I just want to run through it all in my mind one more time," I explained. "I don't want to forget anything."

Lorenzo walked toward me, put his arm around my shoulders, and insisted, "If you forget anything, my mom is going to have it. Did you forget she's got Daphne?"

"I know, but Ollie is used to his things. I want him to be comfortable. We've got a busy day planned with your mom and I want to make sure he's got all of his toys he loves."

I finished rummaging through the bag of filled with Ollie's things and confirmed I had everything he needed.

"Okay, it's all here. We're good."

Lorenzo picked up the bag while I snatched my pup off the ground. We locked up and were nearly to Lorenzo's truck when I remembered, "His leash. I forgot his leash on the coffee table!"

"Mom has extra leads," Lorenzo assured me. "You've got his collar. That's all that matters."

I frowned.

Opening the passenger's side door for me, Lorenzo sighed, "Get in, start the truck, lock the doors, and I'll go get it for you."

I grinned at him.

"You're lucky I love you so much," he said in response.

"And Ollie," I added, holding the cuddly boy up in front of me.

"And Ollie," Lorenzo repeated.

He closed my door and I did as he asked, starting the truck and locking the doors, while he went back to get Ollie's leash.

It was two days before Christmas. Lorenzo was taking me to his mom's house. She and I had made plans to do some holiday baking. Unfortunately, Lorenzo wouldn't be able to stay with us because he had to go to work.

Apparently, they'd finally found Melinda Starnes. Her car was found in a hotel parking lot in Rising Sun. Colton and Memphis were all over the case, unofficially, because of their connection to me. When Melinda was brought in, she was questioned but wasn't talking. They were able to hold her because of the hit-and-run charges; however, it did little to advance the investigation. While I was still uneasy over the fact that there was someone out there who had set this up, I found

242 | **A.K. EVANS**

comfort in the fact that Lorenzo, Dom, their team, the WPD, Colton, Memphis, and now the RSPD were all working on this case. And knowing that Lorenzo's intuition was right helped to ease my mind. Considering they knew she didn't act alone before she was even caught was a testament to their abilities.

I sat there, scratching behind Ollie's ear, watching as Lorenzo walked back to the truck with the leash. When he got in the truck, I smiled as leaned over the center console and offered, "A kiss for your troubles."

Lorenzo accepted my kiss and held the leash out to me. After I took it from him and set it on the floor by my feet, we took off.

When we arrived at Lorenzo's mom's house, we found her outside with Daphne. Ollie had slept in my lap on the drive over and didn't even budge after the truck had stopped and Lorenzo opened my door. While I got out and carried him over to Lena so I could greet her, Lorenzo grabbed Ollie's bag from the back seat.

"How are you doing, dear?" she asked.

Smiling at her, I replied, "I'm doing so much better now. I've been working on strength and endurance for my leg. At the pace I've been improving, I'm certain I'll be more than prepared to get back to work by the time I'm set to go back in January."

"That's wonderful news. I'm so happy you're doing better."

"Thanks," I responded.

"Let's head inside and get to work on our cookies!"

Once we were inside, Lorenzo pet Daphne, said hello to his mom, gave scratches to Ollie, and kissed me.

"I don't know how long I'll be," he started. "If everything goes well, I should be back in a few hours. If not, I have no idea. Either way, I'll keep you posted."

"Don't worry," his mom chimed in. "Jolie and I will be up to our elbows in Christmas treats, we won't even know you're gone."

My eyes shot to Lorenzo's. He cocked an eyebrow, silently requesting me to confirm or, more specifically, deny what his mom had just said.

I leaned in toward him and whispered, "I'll know you're gone. Ollie and I are both going to miss you bunches."

"Good answer," he returned, bringing his mouth to mine and kissing me again. "Alright, I'm going to go so I can get back. Maybe I'll get lucky and can be back here when you're pulling everything out of the oven."

"Not everything will be coming out of the oven at the same time, Lorenzo," his mother informed him. "With the amount of treats we're planning to make, there's going to be several batches going in and out."

"Are you making oatmeal cinnamon cookies?" he asked.

"Yes, of course," she replied. "I know they're your favorite. And we're going to make snickerdoodles for Rocco, too."

"Make the oatmeal cinnamon cookies last," he requested. "That'll increase my chances for getting them warm out of the oven."

"Why don't you just call when you're on your way back?" I suggested. "This way, we can put them in the oven then and they should be ready to come out when you get back."

He grinned at me, gave me another kiss, and said goodbye.

"Love you both," he called out as he walked from the kitchen to the front door.

Lena and I both returned the sentiment.

Ten minutes later, just as she said we would be, Lena and I were elbows deep in Christmas treats.

Five minutes after that, there was a knock at the door.

"Would you mind getting that, Jolie? I need to rinse my hands."

"Sure," I answered.

"Thank you," she responded as I left the kitchen.

When I opened the door, I found an older man on the other side.

"Hi," I greeted him.

"Is Lena here?" he asked.

"Yes, I'm sorry. She's out in the kitchen washing her hands. We're in the middle of baking. I'm Jolie," I introduced myself and held my hand out to him.

He took my hand and shook it. "Vinny."

"Come on in, Vinny," I urged. "It's freezing out there."

After he stepped inside, I closed the door behind him and turned to move past him back toward the kitchen, but looked up and saw Lena standing there.

That's when I knew something was very, very wrong.

CHAPTER 21

Lorenzo

I WALKED OUT OF MY MOM'S HOUSE, LEAVING THE TWO MOST important women in my life inside. I hated having to leave them, especially considering it was only two days before Christmas. Baking wasn't exactly my thing and I wouldn't have been involved in those activities, but I still would have preferred to stay with them.

For me, it would have been fulfilling to be able to see Jolie bonding with my mom. To hear Jolie's laughter and excitement filling the room all while knowing that her presence was giving Mom a peace she'd been searching for for years would have made my year.

But I had things to do.

Because the driver of the car that hit Jolie had been apprehended.

And while she wasn't talking, giving any indication of who she was working for, I knew I needed to dig deeper. There was a connection between Melinda and Jolie somehow; I just had to figure out what it was.

So, that was my plan today. Leave my girl with my mom, baking cookies and bonding with each other and the dogs, while I did what I had to do to make sure she stayed safe.

I pulled up to a red stop light and glanced out the passenger's side window when something caught my eye. On the passenger's side floor was the leash.

The leash Jolie insisted I run back into her place to get.

The leash that if she didn't have would ruin her day today.

I sighed.

It looked like my day was going to be starting even later now since I knew I had to turn around and take Ollie's leash to her.

The light changed and I turned my truck around. I started the drive back to my mom's house and did it thinking of the girl who frowned at me this morning just to get what she wanted.

Surprisingly, I loved it.

After spending a good portion of my childhood and my entire adult life never expecting to get close to a woman, I sometimes found myself in shock over just how much I enjoyed being around Jolie. And it wasn't just enjoying. I craved it.

Craved her.

Needed the light, laughter, and noise she brought into my life.

Having her now, I often wondered how I ever functioned in silence for so long. Something told me it had little to do with being with another person and everything to do with that person being her.

I pulled up outside my mom's house and noticed another car in the driveway. She hadn't mentioned anyone else joining them today, not that there was anyone else I knew my mom hung around with that she'd have here while she was spending time with Jolie. Then again, I couldn't make any assumptions because my mom had done a good job of keeping her relationship with Michael a secret for a long time. It was entirely possible that she had friends I didn't know about as well.

I turned off the truck, leaned over the center console, and grabbed Ollie's leash. As I walked up the stairs, it happened.

Ice ran through my veins.

Blood-curdling screams came from inside the house.

I moved to the door, turned the handle, and found it was locked. As quickly as possible, I slipped the key I had for my mom's house into the lock and opened the door. When I swung the door open, I went from feeling ice-cold fear to burning-hot rage.

My mother was knocked out on the ground, unconscious, and my girl was struggling. Kicking her legs, flailing her arms, bucking her hips, and fighting to breathe all against the man I hated more than anyone else in the world.

My father.

Nobody knew I was there.

I wasted no time. His back was to me, so I strode over, grabbed the motherfucker from behind, and lifted him clean off her before throwing him to the ground.

Then, I delivered a full-fledged assault. There was nothing I wasn't going to do to him.

My foot reared back before flying forward forcefully and landing right in his gut. I did this several times, not letting up, never giving him the opportunity to catch his breath. When I'd had enough of that, I lowered my body over his. My fist connected with his jaw. And it didn't stop.

"Lorenzo!" I heard Jolie shout.

I kept pummeling his face in.

"Lorenzo! You're going to kill him!"

With my elbow pulled back, ready to strike again, I turned and looked at Jolie. She was terrified, but something else had taken over inside me.

My voice deadpanned, I ordered, "Then you better call someone before it's too late."

Jolie turned and ran. I landed another blow to his face.

"You son of a bitch," I seethed, lowering my face to within inches of his, my grip on his throat tightening. "You better hope someone else gets here to save your ass because I have no desire to let you live to see the light of another day."

Blood was pouring down his face.

He was groaning in pain.

And it still wasn't enough for me.

It still didn't feel like retribution.

I pulled back and hit him again.

It still wasn't enough.

I stood and kicked him again.

He was still alive. Justice hadn't been served.

The feel of my fist against his face offered some satisfaction, so I set to strike again. Lowering myself to one knee, I pulled my arm back and my elbow connected with something behind me.

An awful sound combined with a thud caused me to loosen my grip on my father and turn around.

Jolie was on the ground, her hand covering her cheek.

Fuck.

Seeing that snapped me out of it.

"Baby," I gasped, moving toward her.

She was sitting up, but her head was down. I curled one arm around her back and brought the other up to her hand covering her face.

Peeling her hand away, I felt sick to my stomach.

I'd been so focused on seeking revenge on my father that I ended up accidentally striking Jolie.

"Jolie, I'm so sorry," I struggled to get out, my voice ragged.

She looked up at me and her eyes were terrified. I never hated myself more than I did in that moment.

I stood up, wrapped a hand under her arm and around her waist before I helped her up to her feet.

"Are you okay?" I asked her.

Just as she was about to answer, I saw her eyes move to the ground behind me and go wide. When I turned around, a gun was pointed right at us or, more specifically, her.

"Lorenzo," she cried.

A shot was fired and in one swift movement, I cradled Jolie behind her head and around her waist while I used my body as a shield to protect hers.

Searing pain splintered through my shoulder as I heard a loud crash and a second shot rang out. I waited for the hit, but I never felt it.

"Enzo," I heard my mom's fragile voice call.

I turned my head to look at her and saw a sight I never expected to see in a million years. My mother was standing over my father—a gun in her hands pointed at him   and she was trembling.

He wasn't moving.

Just as I was about to lift myself off Jolie, the front door swung open.

Colton and Memphis rushed inside. They instantly took in the scene.

"Jojo?" Colton called.

She didn't respond.

"She's here," I said as I started to lift myself off her, wincing with each movement. Redirecting my attention to her, I confirmed, "Baby, are you alright?"

Jolie had a look of shock and terror all over her face. Her eyes moved to my shoulder and more shock registered on her face.

"He shot you," she declared.

"I'm fine," I assured her.

Her breathing grew shallow. "He shot you," she repeated on a whisper.

"He won't ever do it again," my mom said from behind me. "He can't hurt anyone ever again."

Jolie and I both directed our attention to my mom. Memphis was approaching her slowly, but I was worried about her mental state considering her hands were still shaking.

"Mom?" I called.

As she turned her head toward me, Dom, Pierce, and Michael all came running in.

"Jojo?" Dom called out as he began walking toward her.

"Lena?" Michael gasped, realization dawning as he took in the scene in front of him.

She stopped shaking, but only because the sound of his voice caught her completely off guard. Mom's head turned toward Michael and the second she saw him, she broke down. Just before her legs buckled, Michael moved in, curled an arm around her back and took the gun out of her hand. He passed it off to Memphis and engulfed my mom in his arms.

I couldn't have been more relieved that Mom found him.

My good arm was still wrapped around Jolie's back as Michael and I made eye contact. He was horrified. I tried giving him a sympathetic look but turned my attention away from him when Dom walked up beside us.

"Jojo, are you okay?"

"Lorenzo needs an ambulance," she worried. "He was shot."

Dom looked at me, searched, and found the wound. "Colt, we need an ambulance," Dom ordered as he began pulling at my jacket in an attempt to take it off to inspect the wound further.

"I'm fine," I insisted, shrugging the jacket off.

"You're not fine," Jolie continued to panic. "You're bleeding. You're bleeding because you were shot. And you were shot because you put yourself in front of that bullet to protect me!!"

She started shaking and breathing heavy again as she dropped her head to my chest.

"Jolie?" I called softly, using my good arm to rub her back.

When she tipped her head back to look at me, I asked, "What happened here?"

Her bottom lip quivered, but she didn't answer. Her forehead hit my chest again and she cried.

I looked to Dom, both of us clearly frustrated.

His gaze dropped to my shoulder where he'd lifted the sleeve of my t-shirt. "Just a graze," he confirmed my suspicion.

I gave him a nod.

"Jolie? Lorenzo?" my mom's voice came from beside us. "Are you kids alright?"

Jolie stepped out of my embrace, moved to my mom, and wrapped her arms around her. "Oh, Lena, I'm so sorry," she lamented. "I never should have let him in the house. It was so stupid of me."

"You didn't know who he was," Mom tried reassuring her.

"Why don't we move out of the foyer here and into another room?" Colton suggested. "The boys are going to need to take statements and figure out what exactly happened."

We shuffled out of the foyer and into the living room. Once my mom and Jolie were seated, me between them,

Michael on the opposite side of my mom, Dom flanking Jolie, the officers who had arrived on the scene after Colton and Memphis started with their line of questioning.

Jolie started the explanation. "We were supposed to be baking today," she began, the disbelief in her tone evident. "It's Christmastime. This is supposed to be a joyous time of year. I can't believe I was so stupid."

Using my good arm, I gave her a squeeze and tried to settle her. "Jolie, baby, just take a few deep breaths and try to calm down. They need to know what happened."

She took a few deep breaths, attempting to get everything she was feeling under control.

"Medics are here, De Luca," Pierce interrupted as he walked into the room.

"Send them in here. I'm not leaving her," I returned.

"You've got it."

A minute later, the paramedics walked in. My mom and Michael moved to another seat while they got to work on patching me up. "You're going to need to see a doctor," one of them informed me.

"I'll take care of it after, but right now, I'm not leaving."

The medic got back to work, and the officer prompted Jolie, "So, you were baking?"

She nodded. "Yes, not long after Lorenzo left, there was a knock at the door and since Lena's hands were in the dough, she asked me if I'd answer it. I never knew it was him. I mean, he asked if Lena was here, but I never thought he was who he was. I invited him inside out of the cold and when she came out of the kitchen to the foyer, I saw the look on her face and knew something wasn't right."

"So he saw you," the officer confirmed, directing his attention to my mom. "What happened then?"

"I told him to get out," Mom answered. "But he didn't listen. He took a couple steps toward me, so I told him again to get out before I called the police. That's when he attacked. He lunged forward, toward me, but Jolie stepped in. She tried to get between us."

My eyes shot to Jolie. She put herself between my animal of a father and my mother, and all I could do was recall the conversation I'd had with her weeks ago.

That's what you do when you love someone.

"Jolie," I whispered.

"It worked," Jolie chimed in, proud of herself, as she addressed me and the officer. "He came after me instead."

"I'm not sure any man attacking any woman is something to be excited about, darling," the officer advised.

Her shoulders slumped. "I know. I just," she paused. "I just didn't want Lena getting hurt."

The officer nodded and assured her, "I understand your reasoning, I'm just pointing out that what he did is never okay. What happened next?"

"Vinny slammed her up against the wall," Mom explained, and I felt my blood begin to boil. "Just as he pulled his arm back preparing to hit her, I ran over and jumped on him from behind. He didn't get the chance to strike her because I threw him off balance. But then he turned and tossed me to the ground."

My eyes went to Michael. His focus and attention was on my mother, and I could see that he was struggling to keep it together at what he'd just heard.

Mom continued, "I got back to my feet and went after him again."

"You went after him again after he threw you to the floor?" Dom asked.

"I did it for Lorenzo," she stated.

"Me?" I called. "What does that mean?"

Her eyes came to mine. "I love Jolie. You know that. But the only thought running through my mind when I saw him getting ready to hurt her was that my son finally found happiness in his life. I wasn't going to let that man do anything to Jolie that would jeopardize my son's happiness again. All those years ago, I didn't stand up to him. Tonight, I did what I should have done then."

The burning I felt in my gut had moved up to my lungs and clogged my throat. Jolie had told me, Michael had told me, but now my mom was admitting it to me. Everything my father did to her all those years had affected her in the obvious ways, but she'd clearly healed from that. What she hadn't healed from was the knowledge of what his abuse of her did to me.

"Is that how he ended up with a fatal gunshot wound to the chest?"

Mom shook her head and went on, "When I went back after him, he pushed me away. I kept fighting, clawing my way to him, just to make sure Jolie didn't get hurt. I was so worried she'd get hit in the head. And when I came back after him the third time, he knocked me out. I don't remember anything after that. I only remember being behind him and seeing him pull out a gun and lift his hand. I saw him aim it at Jolie. Then, I watched him pull the trigger while my son put himself in front of that bullet to protect the woman he loves. I wasn't going to let anything happen to either one of them, so I did something about it. Thankfully, one of my guns was close. I got it, stood over him, and used one bullet before he had the chance to pull the trigger again."

Silence filled the room.

Reality was beginning to settle in.

My father was dead.

My mother had killed him.

"What made you come back here?" Dom asked.

I looked to him before looking to Jolie. "Ollie's leash. You left it on the floor of the truck. With how badly you insisted we bring it with us, I knew I had to turn around and bring it back. Where is he?"

"We didn't want them at our toes while we were baking, so we put them in the sunroom and closed the door. That's why Daphne never came in here. Can we bring them in here now?"

Memphis stepped in and explained, "This is technically a crime scene, Jojo. We can't have the dogs wandering around right now."

"He's just a pup, Memphis," she worried. "He's probably terrified."

"I'll go check on him while you finish up in here," Colton volunteered. "Do either of them need to go out?"

Jolie shook her head.

Colton turned and left the room

"I've got to call Rocco," I announced. "He's supposed to be here in a couple hours. I don't want him walking into this."

"Maybe you shouldn't tell him over the phone either, Lorenzo. This isn't the kind of thing you want to find out that way," Jolie suggested.

She was right. Rocco despised our father as much as I did, but that didn't mean it would have been easy to hear over the phone that he was dead.

"My place," Michael suggested. "Why don't you call him and tell him there was a change of plans and that we'll be at my place? This way, he's not walking into this, but he'll also have the opportunity to learn about it when his family's around him."

"Thank you," my mom said, leaning into him. "I'll call Rocco. Lorenzo, please go get your shoulder taken care of now so that you can be there when we tell him."

"Mom?"

"What darling?"

"Are you okay?"

Her brows pulled together, but she nodded.

"You killed someone," I reminded her, not that I believed she forgot. "I know he was a bad man, but you're not a killer."

My mom moved from her spot on the couch and walked over to me. I stood in front of her. She lifted a hand to my cheek and held it there while she reasoned, "I had a choice to make. Kill him or watch him kill my child. I'm okay with the decision I've made because you're still standing here, living and breathing."

I looked to Memphis. "She doesn't have anything to worry about, right?"

"I can't say anything officially, but my guess is that this is a very clear-cut case of self-defense. She did what she had to do to protect herself, you, and my sister. Again, I don't get to make that call, but I'm guessing that's the one that's going to be made."

"It's Christmas in two days," I put in.

I didn't want my mom in a jail cell over the holiday or at all, for that matter, and wanted to make sure that didn't happen.

"She's not a flight risk, De Luca. Her kids are here, her life is here. She's not going to take off and leave that behind when her actions were completely justified. We'll do what we've got to do to see to it that she's with her family for the holiday. The sooner we can get you all down to the station and get through questioning, the sooner we'll know where things stand."

I gave him a nod and turned back to my mom.

"Stop worrying about me, Lorenzo. I'm the parent here and I did what I had to do. If given the chance, I'd do it again because there was no choice."

"Love you, Mom."

She wrapped her arms around me and hugged me tightly. "I love you too."

When she pulled away, she repeated, "I'm going to call Rocco now. You see to your shoulder and Jolie. We'll do whatever we need to do here, meet you at the station, and then I'd like you both over to Michael's house tonight when we break the news to your brother."

"Okay."

At that, my mom turned and moved to Michael. I looked back at Jolie. "I know you need ice for your face, baby. Did you get hurt anywhere else?"

She shook her head. "I'll be fine. We should really go get your shoulder looked at now."

"I'm asking about you," I maintained. "Were you hurt?"

She shrugged. "My head hit the wall, but I didn't black out. My neck hurts a little from when he was choking me. Everything else is just fatigue, honestly. I think the adrenaline has worn off."

"I'm getting you ice for your cheek and then we're going to the hospital to get your head checked."

"Okay. Can I go see Ollie first?"

Dom stood and looked to Memphis. "Can you take her out to the sunroom? I want to talk with Lorenzo."

Memphis took his sister and walked out of the room while Dom followed me to the kitchen. After I pulled the ice out of the freezer, I turned to find his eyes trained on me.

"Took a bullet to protect her," he stated.

"It was just a graze, Dom," I pointed out, not wanting him to make a big deal about it.

"Doesn't matter. You would have taken that hit even if you knew it was going to go right through your heart," he maintained.

I couldn't deny it, so I didn't.

Dom wasn't finished, "I told you before I couldn't have hand-picked anyone else better for her than you. I knew it was the truth then; hopefully you see it now."

I held up the ice. "See this?"

His brows furrowed. "Yeah."

She got my elbow in her cheek because I was beating the shit out of him and she was worried I'd kill him.

"I'm not happy this happened at all. I'm not even remotely excited about the fact that she was involved and hurt. But you did not intentionally hurt her. You're seeing to it that she gets ice and gets seen by a doctor. Her head, her neck, her muscles, and her cheek will all heal from this. But the one thing you've got to realize is that she never needs to worry whether the man she loves would do anything to protect her. She'll go to sleep every night from here on out knowing that she's safe with you."

I didn't respond.

"You protected her and you'd do it again."

"In a heartbeat."

At that, Dom put a hand to my good shoulder, squeezed, and ordered, "Go get that ice on her face and get your shoulder checked. We'll work on things here and see what we can figure out. You've not had contact with him for years, so it's concerning why he suddenly showed up. Let's hope our hit-and-run driver has something else to say now."

"I expect I'm going to be unavailable for the next few days," I began. "You'll keep me in the loop?"

"Without a doubt."

I gave him a nod and walked out of the kitchen toward the sunroom. When I walked in, I found my girl sitting on the floor with her puppy while her brothers watched from behind her. They saw me enter, walked toward me, and gave me chin lifts before exiting the room. Jolie looked up and saw me moving toward her. I sat down next to her, gave Ollie a few scratches on the head, and kissed Jolie's temple. She turned toward me, kissed me once on the lips, and leaned into me.

I put the ice to her cheek and held it there. We stayed like that a long time in silence, neither of us needing to say anything. When the ice turned to water, we finally got up off the floor.

Then, Jolie and I left my mom's house to get ourselves bandaged up.

The silence still hung between us while we did.

CHAPTER 22

Jolie

I SWALLOWED HARD AS I WATCHED LORENZO GETTING BANDAGED up by the doctor, still unable to fully process the reality of the situation.

After confirming Michael and Lena would take care of Ollie for us until we got back, Lorenzo and I made our way to the hospital. Memphis came with us since we technically still needed to go to the police station afterward. They knew we weren't going to take off but needed to play by the rules.

We arrived quite a while ago, and before he'd even consider having a doctor check out his shoulder, Lorenzo insisted that they make sure I was alright. After running a few tests, they gave me a clean bill of health. Or, at least, for my head they did. My neck had some bruising from where Lorenzo's father had choked me, and I had a pretty sizeable knot on my cheek where Lorenzo had accidentally elbowed me. Other than that, my muscles mostly just felt fatigued. Thankfully, I didn't have any pain in my knee or ankle.

Once I was completely cleared by the doctor, Lorenzo finally gave in to getting himself checked out. The entire time his shoulder was being taken care of, I watched him. I could see his mind working. He barely made eye contact with me, but when he did, he looked at me as though it was painful for him.

Between those looks and the silence that had been present from the moment Lorenzo came out and sat with me and Ollie in the sunroom, I was feeling uneasy.

Even though I'd been attacked by Lorenzo's father and felt fear like never before, I still believed that what I felt paled in comparison to what Lorenzo was currently dealing with.

When we had been at Lena's house, he was taking charge of the situation and confirming everyone else was handling it alright. Now, I had a feeling it was all sinking in. Lorenzo's father was not a nice man, but he was still his father. And now that man was dead. I couldn't imagine that was easy to come to terms with.

"I'll be right back with your discharge instructions," the nurse who'd been assisting the doctor said.

Lorenzo gave her a nod.

While we waited for her to return, I thought we'd have a chance to talk.

"Lorenzo," I called softly.

He turned his gaze toward me, but before I had the chance to say anything the curtain flew open and Kendall charged in. "Oh my God, I just heard what happened! Are you guys alright?"

Neither of us answered her as her eyes darted back and forth between us. Eventually, they settled on me and she repeated, "Are you alright?"

I gave her a slight nod and replied, "Yeah, we're okay. Dom called you?"

"Yes," she answered. "He told me what happened and thought I should come down to check on the two of you." Her eyes shifted to Lorenzo and she moved toward him.

Stopping next to him, she put her arms around him and said, "I'm sorry."

"Thank you, Kendall," he responded. "But if you're apologizing to me over the death of my father, it's not necessary. He tried to kill your sister, twice. From where I stand, he finally got what he deserved."

Kendall gave him a look of understanding before she diverted her attention to me. "Are you sure you feel alright?"

"Yes, they checked me out already. I'm all set. We're just waiting for Lorenzo's discharge instructions and then we've got to get out of here. Lorenzo and his mom are breaking the news to Rocco tonight."

She gasped. "I can't imagine that's going to be easy. If there's anything either of you needs, you know you can call me. I'll do what I can for you…the both of you."

"Appreciate it," Lorenzo thanked her before I had the chance to respond.

A few minutes later, the nurse returned with Lorenzo's discharge instructions. After she left the room, I told Kendall that I'd talk to her at our parents' house on Christmas Day and we'd plan a girls' night with Ava sometime soon. At that, Lorenzo and I said goodbye to my sister and took off.

Hours later, the ride to Michael's house was, just like the ride to the hospital and the police station, quiet. When we pulled up outside, I looked at the clock on the dash and realized we still had time before Rocco was set to arrive. I needed to take a few minutes to talk with Lorenzo before we went inside.

He parked the truck, but before he could hop out, I reached across the center console and put my hand on his bicep. "Lorenzo?"

His eyes went to my hand before traveling up to my face.

"Right here," he replied.

I held his eyes quietly for several moments before I practically pleaded, my voice soft, "Talk to me."

Pain slashed through his features and his body tensed up. "I'm sorry, Jolie," he paused to collect himself and control his breathing. "I'm so sorry he was able to get to you. I never expected him. It's been more than eighteen years since I've seen him and I'm not sure why he came back."

"Why are you apologizing to me? You didn't attack me," I attempted to reason with him.

He shook his head in frustration and explained, "My father attacked you. I knew the kind of man he was and I never thought it was him. It's hard not to shoulder the responsibility of what happened to you a few weeks ago and what happened earlier today."

My head jerked back in surprise. "Wait, you don't think he was behind the hit-and-run, do you?"

"Yes."

Lorenzo's single-word answer had not a trace of doubt in it. I trusted him with everything, but I wasn't sure I could get on board with this.

"Boss, I'm not sure about that," I cautioned. "I mean, he came into that house today and specifically asked about your mom. Then, he tried going after her first. That doesn't indicate to me that he wanted anything to do with me. He didn't even know who I was."

Disappointment registered in his face, and while I hoped it was because he believed what I was saying and realized there was still someone out there who tried to have me killed, something told me that wasn't it. I had a suspicion that he was wrestling with the fact that he was certain his father was behind this and, soon enough, he'd be able to confirm that fact.

Since he hadn't said anything, I went on, "How are you feeling?"

"I'm fine," he insisted.

I shook my head and clarified, "No, I'm not referring to your shoulder. I want to know about you. Your heart and your mind. Are you okay?"

"Baby…you're sitting here next to me. And Mom is safe, too. That's all that matters."

"I know," I assured him. "But a man is dead, and that man was your father. I want to know how you're handling that."

He turned his head and looked out the front windshield. I waited patiently while he took the time he needed to gather his thoughts on the whole situation. I adored my parents and knew that if one of them died, I'd be an emotional wreck. Lorenzo's situation was different and wasn't something I could relate to. Regardless of what I thought of his father, I loved Lorenzo and I wanted to make sure he knew he had a place to unload his feelings.

"Vincent Mancini was a bad man, Jolie," Lorenzo began as he continued to look out the windshield. "Maybe he wasn't always that way, but at some point, he changed and never tried to redeem himself. He never sought help. All I feel right now is relief."

"Relief?" I wondered, surprised.

He nodded slowly and repeated, "Relief." When he turned his attention back to me, he explained, "I mourned the loss of my father a long time ago. For a long time, I was conflicted because I hadn't always known him as an abuser. It was hard back then, especially as a kid, to have something good and see it turn into what it did. But there's no love lost there. It's done. It's over. It's *finally*, completely over. The bottom line is that he can't do anything else now. He can't hurt me, Rocco, my mom, or you. He can't hurt anyone else again."

I offered a sympathetic smile as I gave him a gentle squeeze on the arm. "I'm sorry you lost something good, Lorenzo."

"I appreciate that, baby, but I'm really okay. I haven't missed him since before we got out of that situation years ago. Maybe I should feel guilt, but I don't. I have no regrets. While I missed the man he used to be and missed having that for all my life, I don't miss the man he became. As I said before, many years ago, I mourned the loss of the good guy he was. The man he was tonight, the one he became when I was eight years old, is not someone I'm going to feel the loss of. That's a man that I'm going to feel relieved is no longer here."

Understanding washed over me as I processed everything Lorenzo said. It made complete sense. While I never experienced something so horrific in my life, I had what Lorenzo had for the first eight years of his life. A good father. And I knew if my father had become a man like Lorenzo's had, I probably would have mourned him long before he actually died.

"Are you worried about how Rocco's going to take the news?" I asked.

He shook his head. "No. He'll be upset, for sure, but not about our father. He's going to be angry hearing what he did to Mom and you. He'll also be pissed about what he attempted, and thankfully failed, to do to you with that gun. Rocco will feel for my mom and the fact that she had to put a bullet in a man she once loved, but the truth is that Rocco doesn't ever remember our father as a good man. He has no memories of him being anything but an angry, bitter, abusive man."

Silence fell between us again. I felt comforted by the fact that neither Lorenzo nor Rocco would be suffering over the coming days, weeks, and months. It was clear that Lena wasn't going to be mourning either. She did what she had to do to protect her son. I didn't think she'd be feeling regretful any-time soon...or at all.

"Mancini?" I asked, curious about the last name Lorenzo mentioned when he first started speaking about his father.

"That was his last name," Lorenzo said. "After we left him and Mom got officially divorced, she went back to her maiden name. Rocco and I asked if we could change our names from Mancini to hers, which is De Luca. She understood our need to not have any affiliation to him beyond the blood that runs in our veins and didn't hesitate to get our names changed for us."

I smiled at him, happy he and his brother found a way to turn their parents' divorce into something positive for them. Obviously, no longer living in fear of their father and what he'd do to their mother could have been enough, but the name change was something they had a choice over, and I loved that for them.

"Thank you," I eventually expressed.

His brows pulled together as his head tilted. "For what?" he wondered.

My eyes welled with tears as it all came back to me. The magnitude of the situation had settled in me when Lorenzo and I sat in the sunroom with Ollie earlier in the evening. I re-alized then just how differently the day could have turned out, but I couldn't bring myself to talk about it then.

Now, several hours had passed and Lorenzo had shared a lot with me. I was ready to talk about it with him.

Apparently, I'd taken too long to answer because I felt Lorenzo's hand cup my cheek. I blinked my eyes and cleared the tears from them. As they spilled down my cheeks, his thumb stroked along my cheek and he urged, "Baby, talk to me."

"You saved my life today," I whispered, my bottom lip quivering.

Lorenzo's hand moved to curl around the back of my neck, where he squeezed me gently. "Jolie…" He trailed off.

I took in a deep breath and reminded him, "You put yourself in front of a bullet for me."

"I love you."

"I know. But I love you, boss. If it hadn't been your shoulder," I worried, needing to pause because I wasn't sure I could admit the rest of it.

Thankfully, Lorenzo knew what I was trying to say. He gently tugged me toward him and kissed my forehead. I tipped my head back and looked up at him. His mouth lowered to mine. With his lips brushing up against mine, he reassured me, "I'm still here."

"If he'd aimed differently," I started before Lorenzo cut me off.

"He didn't. I'm here with you thanking my lucky stars that you insisted on having Ollie's leash today, grateful you forgot it in the truck, instead of sitting beside you while you're in a hospital bed or worse. You're safe; I'm safe. I gave him space in my head earlier today thinking of how he could have taken you away from me. He wasn't successful and he doesn't deserve to have that power over me. So, don't think about what could have happened, Jolie. You'll tear yourself apart and I can't bear to see that. I don't want him having any space in your head or your heart either."

"He doesn't, big guy," I promised. "You do."

At that, Lorenzo captured my mouth and kissed me. It was a hard, closed-mouth kiss, but I was close to declaring that there was more passion and feeling in this kiss than any other kiss we'd shared before it.

After what we'd experienced that day, knowing what Lorenzo had lived through as a child, and the kiss we just shared, I needed to tell him something. We had just barely separated our mouths when I stressed, "You should know that the person I saw today...you could never be him. That's not you; it never will be."

He touched his mouth to mine in response and returned, "I'm beginning to believe that's the truth, Jolie. Thank you for pushing me to see that."

I smiled and felt my body warm. My man was finally, *finally* starting to see what everyone else saw in him. I couldn't have been more proud of him for believing the truth about himself.

"Wait there," he instructed, pulling back from me. "I'll come around to help you out."

"Okay."

Lorenzo turned off the truck, came around to help me out, and walked beside me into Michael's house, where we found our puppy waiting for us.

Michael and Lena confirmed that Lorenzo and I were both alright and the four of us spent the time together, trying to find ways to focus on anything but what had happened earlier in the day. Luckily, Ollie's playful demeanor helped to lighten the mood and cut the tension.

An hour later, Rocco arrived.

The moment he walked in, he knew something was wrong.

"What happened?" he asked immediately.

Silence filled the room briefly before Lena spoke up, "Rocky, darling, something bad happened today."

"Did he die?" Rocco returned.

I froze and felt Lorenzo's body go solid beside me.

Nobody replied.

Rocco searched our faces and came to his own conclusion. "He's dead."

"Rocky," Lorenzo finally said.

Rocco shook his head and wondered, "Why did you say something bad happened, Mom?"

"Rocky," Lorenzo said again, firmly this time.

When Rocco's eyes came to him, Lorenzo explained, "He showed up at Mom's house and attacked her and Jolie today."

Lorenzo then went on to explain to his brother everything that had happened. Lena chimed in every so often with tidbits of what occurred. When they'd given him the full story, he looked at me and asked, "Were you hurt?"

I shook my head, "I was a little roughed up, but I'm alright."

Rocco didn't like hearing that because his face turned scary angry. Somehow, though, he quickly pushed past whatever he was feeling and turned his attention to his mother. "Did he hurt you?"

"Only when I saw him try to take away the one thing that brought my boy back to life," she replied.

A lump formed in my throat hearing her admission.

"You killed him?" Rocco asked, even though he already knew that she had.

Suddenly, I was worried that he didn't feel so good about how things had turned out. Lena seemed to be a little concerned as well because she answered cautiously, "It was either that or watch him kill Lorenzo. That wasn't an option for me."

Rocco remained silent. His eyes moved over everyone in the room. We stayed quiet, allowing him to have the time to process everything he'd just been told. Then, he moved to his mother and held his hand out to her. When she placed her hand in his, he pulled her toward him, wrapped his arms tight around her, and declared, "I'm so fucking proud of you for standing up to him and protecting my brother."

A sob escaped her as her knees buckled. Rocco held on tight to his mom as the rest of us watched. Tears were pouring down my face, Michael seemed relieved that Rocco was handling the news well, and Lorenzo was clenching his jaw. I figured that breaking down wasn't really his thing, but I knew he was feeling deeply moved by the scene unfolding in front of him.

When Rocco and Lena had separated, Lorenzo spoke up. His voice was thick as he asked, "Are you sure you're alright, Rocky? It's not easy stuff to swallow."

Rocco turned to his brother and stressed, "Enzo, he's gone. You don't have to keep trying to protect me. I'm good."

"He wasn't nice, but he was still your father," Lorenzo noted.

"No, he wasn't. I've got his DNA, but that's it. He wasn't anything to me other than that. I don't miss him. I haven't ever missed him and I don't feel sorry that he's gone. Right now, I pity him. I pity him for everything he missed out on and everything he'll miss out on down the road. The two of us growing up, making something of ourselves, that's on us and Mom. He didn't do that. My hockey? That's on me. And you and Mom pushing and supporting me. He missed out on everything I've accomplished in my life. He's going to miss out on what you'll accomplish in your life. The careers we have, the wives we'll eventually have, the babies we'll ultimately make. I pity him for that. In all of this, all I miss is the idea of a father I never had, but definitely not the one that I did."

And those words did it.

At least for me.

I was pretty sure everyone else felt it, too. It was clear that despite a rough childhood, Rocco hadn't been so negatively impacted by who his father was, not anymore anyway. He had been through what he had and, in the end, could see the bigger picture.

For whatever reason, Vincent Mancini did what he did to his wife and his children, but he ultimately did it to himself. He took away his own happiness and the right to a good life. It seemed Rocco had learned that a long time ago. I had a feeling it completely hit Lorenzo tonight. Lena, I believe, found it somewhere in between the time Rocco got there and Lorenzo did.

Oblivious to the heaviness in the air, Ollie bounced right over to Rocco's feet and distracted everyone. Rocco looked down and asked, "Who's this?"

I stood and moved toward Ollie. Bending down, I picked him up and introduced him. "Rocco, this is your nephew, Oliver. Ollie, meet your uncle Rocco."

Rocco's eyes came to mine and his face softened. Putting one arm around my shoulder and a hand on Ollie's head, he marveled, "I'm an uncle."

I grinned.

Rocco looked to Lorenzo, who was now standing next to us. His hand left Ollie's head, wrapped around his brother, and pulled him close. "Love you, Enzo."

Lorenzo hugged him back and replied, "Love you too, Rocky."

Just then, Ollie started barking. I laughed inwardly and watched as Rocco and Lorenzo separated. They gave each other a look of approval before Rocco turned his attention to

Ollie and took him out of my arms.

"What's the problem, little guy?" he wondered, holding Ollie up in front of him.

I didn't get to see Ollie's response, though, because Lorenzo had pulled me into his arms and squeezed me tight. It was a little while before he let me go.

CHAPTER 23

Jolie
One month later

"**B**oss," I moaned.

I was on a downward glide, my body positioned over Lorenzo's with my hands planted on his chest, and I was seconds away from coming. Lorenzo knew it and reached up to curl his hand behind my head. He tugged me toward him and I went, my body powerless to fight him.

My mouth hit his, our tongues instantly colliding, while he kept one hand behind my head and the other arm wrapped tight around my waist.

Then, he powered into me. Lorenzo didn't relent. He continued to thrust into me, one stroke after another until my body tensed, pleasure shot through me, and I moaned into his mouth.

He slowly worked me through my orgasm before flipping me to my back and somehow managing to bring it home for me again at the same time his orgasm tore through him.

After we'd come down and our breathing had mostly returned to normal, I teased, "You always take over."

"What?" he asked.

"I get myself so close and then you suddenly take over," I explained.

"Baby, there's only so much torture a man can take," he reasoned.

My head jerked back. "Torture?"

He gave me an incredulous look before he returned, "You were on top of me moaning with your hands everywhere on you and then everywhere on me. It was all good until you got close. It's always all good until you get close. Then, you stop moving your hips. I needed the movement and knew you'd get off on me taking over, so I did what I had to do."

I sighed, "I'm just saying it would be nice for you to let me bring it home occasionally."

"Jolie, you have brought it home many times, but this wasn't one of them. For crying out loud, you came once on top, I flipped you over and you came again a second time, right on the heels of the first. Are you really complaining right now?"

I rolled my eyes at him because I had no other rebuttal.

"Right, we'll let that go," Lorenzo started. "So, confirming the game plan for today, you're working and then you've got girls' night, right?"

I nodded. "Yep. I've got to do my part to help out Kendall and Ava."

"Help them out?"

"They're still single," I stated, expecting this would give him all the explanation he needed. When he didn't respond, I went on, "There's nothing wrong with being single if that's what you want. Ava is on the prowl, though I'm not sure she's currently looking for something long-term. Kendall, on the other hand, is actively looking for something permanent. She wants to fall in love."

"She will," he began. "When the time is right, it'll happen for her."

I sighed. "I want her to be happy. Now that I've found you and know just how wonderful and fulfilling it is to fall in love, I want her to have the same thing."

Lorenzo's face softened as he gave my hip a gentle squeeze. "Love you, Jolie," he said softly.

Cuddling deeper into him, pressing my face to his throat, I returned, "Love you too, big guy." I kissed his neck and confirmed, "Ollie's going with you today, right?"

"Yeah."

"You're sure they won't mind that he's there while you're out working in the field?" I wondered.

Lorenzo laughed. "Baby, they love him there. I swear, it's like he's become the official Cunningham Security mascot."

Now it was my turn to laugh. "He's hardly intimidating," I scoffed. "He doesn't exactly fit the profile of a security dog."

His voice went soft and he assured me, "He's got the heart. That's all the matters."

I loved that he saw Ollie that way.

And it was as though the little pup knew we were talking about him because he started barking at us.

"Looks like it's time to get up and get the day started. I'll take him out; you can hit the shower first," Lorenzo instructed as he sat up in the bed.

I got up with him, bent down to scratch behind Ollie's ears, and moved to the bathroom to shower.

While I was there, I thought about how much had happened over the last month. Miraculously, the days following the incident at Lena's house with Vinny weren't as bad as I had originally thought they'd be given everything that had happened.

We made it through the holidays and they were still filled with lots of love and laughter. Lorenzo and I spent a lot of time with his mom, Rocco, and Michael at Michael's house. He'd been wonderful with her, and I knew Lorenzo approved of how well Michael was taking care of her.

Even now, weeks later, he hadn't faltered and still made her well-being his top priority. Lena had experienced some anxiety about returning to her house, as was expected, and he insisted she stay with him. Just a few days ago, Lena shared with Lorenzo and me that Michael had asked her to officially move in with him. She was relieved, knowing that going back to the place where she killed her ex-husband wouldn't have been easy, and she and Michael decided to take steps to get her place cleaned out and put on the market. Lorenzo and I offered to help in any way that we could, so a week ago, the four of us went back into the house for the first time since that night and helped her pack her things. We got it all done within two and a half days. Lorenzo and Michael did the heavy-lifting of furniture, while Lena and I packed up her clothing, kitchen, dining room, and decorative items.

On the legal front, things worked out for Lena just as everyone had assumed they would. No charges were brought against her given she'd acted out of self-defense. While it had been suggested this would be the case, it had taken its toll on Lorenzo. It wasn't until they'd officially made a statement that she wouldn't be charged that I saw some of the tension leave him. My heart hurt to see him so worried, and I was overjoyed when he was finally able to let go of the anxiety.

Then, there was my situation.

Lorenzo had assumed that the hit-and-run was connected to his father. He believed that the woman they apprehended was working for his father. Prior to Vinny showing up at Lena's house two days before Christmas, that woman wasn't talking. She'd kept quiet.

Several days after the incident occurred, Lorenzo got a call from Detective Jackson Baines. The hit-and-run suspect was informed of Vinny's death. Now that they had a link, they brought this information to her and gave her one last chance to come out with the truth. Realizing her time was running out before they'd put it all together, she came clean.

Apparently, Vinny had continued to keep tabs on Lena and his children after they'd left him years ago. Since Lorenzo was still a kid at the time, he never would have known that there was someone following them. He didn't possess the skills he had now to know what to look for.

Over the years, Vinny watched as his sons grew up to be successful men. He'd been following Rocco's hockey career and knew that Lorenzo was working for a private investigation and security company.

Lorenzo asked Detective Baines if the woman had told them why Vinny suddenly decided to make a move after all these years. She didn't know the whole story, but evidently, the woman told them Vinny had shared something about seeing Lorenzo on television with a woman.

That woman was me.

We only figured this out after it was explained that it was at a recent hockey game where we were seen on television. I hadn't known about it, but once we learned the truth, I remembered that I'd set the DVR to record the game that night. We went back and watched the game and, sure enough, after one of Rocco's goals that night, the camera had landed on Lorenzo and me celebrating. The announcers had identified Lorenzo as Rocco's brother and, based on how friendly we were, it was evident to them that Lorenzo and I were together. Anyone watching would have been able to see that.

Unfortunately, even though we now knew that Vinny

had been the one behind the hit-and-run, we had no other answers. Melinda didn't know what his motivation was, or if she did, she wasn't telling anyone. Sadly, it was one of those things we'd likely never have an answer for. It left Lorenzo unsettled and a bit angry initially, but he eventually began to accept what he couldn't do anything about.

On those thoughts, realizing that we were finally at a place where we'd likely not see any more craziness, I finished up in the shower and got out. Once I was ready, I made my way downstairs to start breakfast while Lorenzo hopped in the shower.

He had already taken care of giving Ollie his breakfast, so I dove in and made ours. After we finished breakfast, I kissed Lorenzo and Ollie goodbye and we both went our separate ways.

I was finally back at Serenity. It felt so good to be working again. When I called and told them to start booking my schedule in January, I also told them to keep it light for the first couple weeks. I didn't want to overdo it and set myself back. I'd been feeling really good and thought it would be better to ease myself back to work. I was no longer in any pain, hadn't experienced any headaches, and with each day that passed, I was feeling stronger.

Today was the first day I was going to be working a longer shift and I was looking forward to it. Two hours after I'd made love with Lorenzo that morning, I walked into work.

"Hey, Jojo," Amy greeted me. She was standing behind Niki at the reception desk, reviewing her schedule for the day.

"Morning, Amy," I replied before directing my attention to Niki. "Hey, Niki!"

Niki offered me a smile in return.

I opened the door leading from the reception area deeper

into the spa. When I entered the employee lounge, I found Ava, Ethan, and Trudi there. I barely got through the door when Ethan walked over and engulfed me in a hug.

"It's so good to see you back here, Jojo," he sighed.

"Thanks, Ethan. It feels great to be back," I admitted.

While I'd been back at work for a couple weeks now, with the shorter shifts, I hadn't managed to see all of my co-workers since the accident. Ethan was one of them.

Eventually, he stopped squeezing me so tight, dropped his arms, and stepped back.

"I'm thinking we need to have another group bonding session real soon," Trudi declared.

"Totally," Ava agreed. "It's been a few months and since the last one, so I'd say we're overdue at this point."

"What are we overdue for?" Jenny asked as she entered the room.

Turning toward her, Ava replied, "A group bonding session."

Putting her things down, she offered, "I'll get the girls out front to get it set up."

"Just make sure they choose somewhere other than Carter's for this one," I pleaded.

"So noted."

At that, Jenny walked out followed by Trudi and Ethan leaving me standing there with my best friend.

"Ready for tonight?" I wondered.

"Try and stop me," she returned.

I laughed. "I promise to do my best to get you taken care of tonight. Both you and Kendall. I think you'll be the easy one to get squared away. It's Kendall that's going to be a problem."

"Why's that?"

"She isn't just looking for a break from her vibrator," I

began. "She wants to get rid of it permanently."

"Jojo, your first appointment is here."

I turned around and saw Michaela had popped her head in so she could alert me to my client's arrival.

"Thanks, Michaela. I'll be right out."

I looked back at Ava and stated, "Well, I better get to it. Do you have a full schedule today?"

"Yep," she answered. "This day is going to fly by and then I'm going to get laid. I cannot wait!"

"Me too," I returned giggling.

Ava laughed as the two of us walked out of the lounge and got to work. Hours later, I left work and went home to get myself ready for girls' night with Kendall and Ava.

"This is hopeless," Kendall declared.

She was sitting across from me at the table we'd gotten ourselves at Big Lou's Restaurant and Saloon in Rising Sun. Kendall, Ava, and I had just finished dinner down in the restaurant and made our way up to the saloon searching for a good time.

Much to my surprise, Elle was going to be performing. Elle was married to Lorenzo's boss, Levi Cunningham.

We hadn't been sitting for more than ten minutes when Kendall made her frustration known.

"Nothing is hopeless, Kendall. You just need to be patient," I assured her.

"I don't have any left," she muttered.

"That's why you need to just do what you've got to do to take care of your needs. You don't think you could handle a one-night stand?" Ava asked.

Kendall shook her head. "No judgment, but I personally can't do it. He's got to mean something to me."

"Don't give up hope yet. It's still early," I maintained.

Kendall let out a sigh and looked around the room. It made me sad to see my sister so upset. I understood her frustration because it wasn't that long ago that I was in the same exact position, wondering where I'd gone wrong and why I hadn't fallen in love.

But I knew Kendall was a treasure. And I knew there was a guy out there who would be perfect for her. She really just needed to be patient and stay positive.

"Jolie?" a female voice called from beside our table.

I glanced up and saw a beautiful woman, who looked vaguely familiar, standing there. It took me a few seconds, but I suddenly placed her the moment I glanced to the guy standing next to her.

Luke Townsend.

Professional snowboarder and one of Rising Sun's hometown heroes. He'd won the gold in the last Winter Olympics.

The woman standing next to him was his wife, Nikki. She was Michael's daughter.

"Nikki?"

A smile spread across her face and she replied, "Yes. I thought that was you, but I wasn't sure. I've only seen one picture of you, so I was hoping I wasn't mistaken."

"A picture of me?"

She nodded. "Yeah. At my dad's house. Your man's mom is living there now and she's got a picture of the two of you from Christmas up on the fireplace hearth. It's so nice to finally meet you. Sorry we didn't get to catch up with you guys over the holiday."

"It's great to meet you too. We should try to plan something soon," I suggested.

"That works for me. I'll talk to my Dad and Lena and set it up."

"Sounds great."

"This is my husband, Luke, by the way," she stated, curling her body into his.

"Nice to meet you, Luke," I replied. "This is my sister, Kendall, and my best friend, Ava."

"The pleasure is mine," he said, before turning his attention back to Nikki. "We should get up there before Elle starts."

She nodded and exclaimed, "Hey, why don't you ladies join us? We always come to watch Elle perform, but it's also Logan's birthday today, so we've added another celebration to the mix."

"Logan?" Kendall wondered.

Nikki's eyes went to Kendall and raked over her before she smiled and replied, "Yes. Luke's single, slightly older brother."

Kendall's eyes lit up.

Luke was a good-looking man, so it was a safe bet that Logan was just as handsome.

"Does Logan have any other single friends?" Ava asked.

"Most of the guys from the shop came out tonight," Luke informed her. "Most of them are single."

Ava perked right up in her seat.

I looked at Nikki and declared, "I guess we're joining you."

Not even thirty minutes later, Ava was sitting comfortably next to one of the guys from Logan's shop while Kendall was enthralled with Logan himself. I wasn't sure I'd ever seen my sister so happy.

For the next hour and a half, I hung out with the massive group of people who were there celebrating Logan's birthday and watching Elle perform. Levi's brother, Cruz, even happened to be there because he was with Lexi, Logan's sister. I had a great time, but ultimately, I wasn't where I wanted to be.

After Elle had finished her set, I sought out Kendall and Ava and confirmed they were both comfortable with me leaving. Neither one of them could have sent me away fast enough. Girls' night was officially over.

But I'd done my job.

Satisfied that I'd successfully seen to it that my girls were taken care of, I made my way to the front door. I loved being with Kendall and Ava, but this was really not my scene, not anymore.

I wanted to go home and see my man.

Moving toward the door, I heard a deep voice call, "Jolie."

I turned and saw Pierce Reynolds. He worked with Lorenzo and Dom at Cunningham Security as well.

"Hey, Pierce," I greeted him.

"Heading out?" he wondered.

Nodding, I explained, "It was girls' night. But the ladies have found men to spend the night with, so I'm heading home to mine. Are you just arriving?"

He shook his head, "No, I've been here a little while. Unfortunately, I haven't found any women in the middle of girls' night who are looking to turn it into anything but that just yet."

"Sorry," I replied.

He chuckled. "Don't worry about it."

I returned a smile and said, "I should get going."

"Let me walk you out."

"Oh, that's okay. You don't have to do that," I insisted.

He gave me a look. "It was bad enough when Ekko thought I was going to let her walk in the snow to the bus stop when her car wouldn't start and she and Dom were going through their thing. I would have had just a pissed-off Dom on my hands if I had allowed that to happen. Sending you out there alone now, I'll not only have a pissed-off Dom, but a really pissed-off De Luca on my hands. I'm not fired up about either one of those, so I'm sorry, but you've got no choice. I'm walking you out to your car."

"Okay," I agreed, realizing he felt obligated. Enough bad things had happened lately that I didn't think it was a bad idea.

After Pierce saw me safely to my car, I got in but looked up at him before I closed the door. "Thanks for walking with me to my car. Go find yourself a lucky lady tonight, Pierce."

He laughed. "I'm glad you think she'll be the lucky one. I'm going to need that mindset heading back in there."

I grinned at him. "There's not a doubt in my mind that the lady that ends up with you will be a lucky one."

He gave me a smile and a nod before he ordered, "Drive safe."

"Always."

At that, he closed my door. I turned on my car, shot a quick text to Lorenzo letting him know I was on my way and pulled out of the lot. Twelve minutes later, my big guy saw my car pull up outside his place. I knew this because the second I turned off the car and got out, I saw him standing in the doorway.

Even though I was in my dress and heels, I ran toward him. He took a step toward me out of the doorway and, the second I leaped into his arms, caught me around the waist. My mouth went to his as he carried me inside and closed the door behind us.

"Missed you, boss," I breathed after I'd kissed him.

"Same here, baby," he returned. "Thought about you in

this dress all night."

"This is the dress that started it all," I reminded him.

He grinned. "And I fucking love it."

"I'm thinking you love it more when you take it off me, though," I teased. "Take me upstairs and make love to me, Lorenzo."

He touched his mouth to mine before he moved to the stairs.

Then, he proved just how much he loved that dress.

EPILOGUE

Lorenzo

Three years nine months later

"**U**NCLE ENZO!" GRACIE WHISPERED EXCITEDLY AS SHE RAN over to me, where I was sitting on the couch. "Did you get them?"

I nodded at my niece and asked, "You bet, Princess. But where's Hank? Isn't he coming, too?"

She rolled her eyes and put her hand on her hip as she huffed, "He's too busy playing with the boys from school and his new trucks."

I couldn't help but laugh. Gracie was only four years old and she already had way too much sass. I had no doubts she was going to be a handful the older she got. I didn't envy Dom in the least; though, I knew I'd always be there for her no matter what.

Today was Hank and Gracie's fourth birthday party. Dom and Ekko had invited not only their friends and family but the twins' whole preschool class. There were entirely too many kids running around to keep track of, but I had one of the two most important hidden inside with me.

"It's okay that he's playing with his friends," I assured her.

"We'll save one for him."

"I don't even know why he likes to play with them. Hank is the only boy I like. All of the other boys at school are yucky."

I sighed as I lifted her up and set her down on my lap. "Gracie, honey, you have no idea how much I wish that you'll always feel that way. One day, though, you're going to change your mind about boys and I have no idea what your dad or any of your uncles will do then."

A look of disgust came over her face. "No way. Boys are mean, too," she said sadly.

My protective instincts kicked in and I asked, "What do you mean?"

She frowned. "Today, one of the boys told me he didn't like my princess dress."

I didn't know it was possible to have my heart broken by a four-year-old little girl, but leave it to Grace Moore to make that happen with her sad face and wounded voice. "I'm going to tell you a secret, Gracie," I whispered. "But you have to promise not to tell anyone, okay?"

She grew curiously excited and held her hand out to me. It was balled into a fist with her pinky sticking up. "I can pinky promise," she beamed.

Wrapping my pinky around her tiny one, I shared, "Sometimes, boys pick on girls because they like them."

"That's not nice."

"You're right. It's not. But, trust me, boys love when girls wear dresses that make them look like princesses."

She thought for a moment and asked, "Did you think Auntie Jojo was a princess when she was wearing her white dress so you could get married?"

My mind flashed back to the beginning of last year when Jolie became my wife. I'd always thought she was the most beautiful woman I'd ever seen, but that day she was some-thing else. I knew I'd never forget just how breathtaking she looked as she walked down the aisle toward me. Gracie was too young to really remember the day, but she and Hank were at our house frequently. She'd seen the wedding pictures hung all over our home.

"I did," I answered.

"I don't think I want to marry any of the boys from school. I want to get married to you or Daddy," she announced.

I laughed inwardly. Instead of crushing her little heart, I just redirected the conversation. "Alright, Princess, you ready to have your extra cupcake that I snuck for you?"

Her eyes lit up and she bobbed her head up and down.

Leaning over the side of the couch to the end table, I lifted the plate and held it in front of her. "I got four cupcakes. Two with pink frosting, two with blue."

"I want pink!"

I took one of the pink cupcakes off the plate, removed the wrapper, and handed it to her. She held it in her hand as she looked at me and demanded, "You get to have a blue one."

"You're the birthday girl," I said as I picked up a cupcake with blue frosting and unwrapped it. I looked at her, smiled, and wished, "Happy Birthday, Gracie."

I watched as she took a huge bite. With her mouth full of cake and frosting, she mumbled, "Fanks, Uncle Enzo."

Chuckling, I kissed the top of her head and promised, "You're welcome, Princess. Every birthday you can count on me to sneak you an extra cupcake."

She grinned and took another bite at the same time as me. Just as I was about to take a second bite, I heard an exasperat-ed, "You didn't!"

Looking up from my niece, I saw my gorgeous wife

walking toward us.

"Auntie Jojo!!" Gracie squealed. "Uncle Enzo snuck cupcakes. You can have a pink one!"

Jolie may have acted tough when she walked in, but I knew how easily her heart melted for her niece and nephew. She came over and sat down next to us on the couch.

"If I keep eating cupcakes, I'm going to need to go shopping again," she declared.

"Baby, you're beautiful. Eat a cupcake with us."

"I just had one with Hank!"

My eyes narrowed at her. "Are you telling me that you just walked in here, ready to scold me for sneaking extra cupcakes for Gracie when you did the same thing for Hank?"

She bit her lip and shrugged her shoulders.

"Eat the pink one for the baby," Gracie reasoned.

"Okay," Jolie agreed. "The cupcake with Hank was for me, but this one is for the baby. After that, no more cake for me."

In just nine more weeks, I was going to be a father. Jolie was thirty-one weeks pregnant with our first child.

I never expected that this was what my life would become, but now that I was here, I couldn't imagine things being any different. For so long, I'd never allowed myself to dream of a life with a woman I'd eventually make my wife, let alone having children.

Of course, I had valid reasons for living my life the way I did, but now I realized how foolish I'd been. I no longer worried about turning out to be like my father. With Jolie's love and the love of my mom, my brother, and the rest of our friends and family, I finally saw just who I really was. I now knew that I wasn't that man and I knew I never could be. I'd always do whatever I could to protect Jolie and our children.

Sometimes if I thought about it, which wasn't very often,

I'd think back to the words Rocco said the day everything happened. I'd feel pity for our father and everything he missed out on. Beyond that, I didn't think about him and I certainly didn't feel anything else for him. He made his choices; those choices had consequences.

But his choices would not be mine.

I knew that with everything inside me.

I was a lover.

A protector.

I loved Jolie.

I'd protect her with everything in me.

As I looked over at her smiling at Gracie while they ate their pink cupcakes, my heart felt like it would beat right out of my chest at the sheer beauty that was Jolie and the knowledge that she was mine.

I put my hand on her round belly, still amazed that I had been given such a remarkable gift. She leaned over and kissed me.

When she pulled back and I saw the look in her eyes, I fell even deeper in love with her. That was something I'd always treasure, realizing I could fall harder for her with each day that passed because she was truly a miracle.

And I'd be thankful every day for that miracle.

The miracle that came in my solitude.

Nine weeks later, Jolie gave me another gift.

My beautiful baby girl, Daniela Mae De Luca.

ACKNOWLEDGEMENTS

As always, to my husband: Jeff, without you these books wouldn't be possible. Everyone needs someone, and I'm so lucky that you're mine.

To my boys, J&J: Thank you for finding a way to always make me laugh, even when my books make me cry. I love you both.

To my loyal readers: I write because I love it. I would continue to write even if you weren't there. But it's so much better doing it knowing that someone will be there to appreciate it. From the bottom of my heart...thank you.

To S.H. - You're a talented gem. Thank you for making Lorenzo and Jolie's cover gorgeous.

To S.B. - Thank you for making my babies look pretty. Your dependability is utterly refreshing.

To E.M. - Thank you for polishing my words and always wanting more. I'll never fire you.

CONNECT WITH
A.K. EVANS

To stay connected with A.K. Evans and receive all the first looks at upcoming releases, latest news, or to simply follow along on her journey, be sure to add or follow her on social media. You can also get the scoop by signing up for the monthly newsletter, which includes a giveaway every month.

OTHER BOOKS BY A.K. EVANS

The Everything Series

Everything I Need

Everything I Have

Everything I Want

Everything I Love

The Cunningham Security Series

Obsessed

Overcome

Desperate

Solitude

Burned

Unworthy

Surrender (Coming November 2019)

Betrayed (Coming February 2020)

Revived (Coming June 2020)

Road Trip Romance Series

Tip the Scales (Coming October 2019)

Play the Part (Coming December 2019)

ABOUT A.K. EVANS

A.K. Evans is a married mother of two boys residing in a small town in northeastern Pennsylvania. After graduating from Lafayette College in 2004 with two degrees (one in English and one in Economics & Business), she pursued a career in the insurance and financial services industry. Not long after, Evans realized the career was not for her. She went on to manage her husband's performance automotive business and drive the shop race cars for the next thirteen years. While the business afforded her the freedom she wouldn't necessarily have had in a typical 9-5 job, after eleven years she was no longer receiving personal fulfillment from her chosen career path. Following many discussions, lots of thought, and tons of encouragement, Andrea decided to pursue her dream of becoming a writer.

Between her day job, writing, and homeschooling her two boys, Evans is left with very little free time. When she finds scraps of spare time, Evans enjoys reading, doing yoga, watching NY Rangers hockey, dancing, and vacationing with her family. Andrea, her husband, and her children are currently working on taking road trips to visit all 50 states (though, Alaska and Hawaii might require flights).

Printed in the USA
CPSIA information can be obtained
at www.ICGtesting.com
CBHW021924111223
2574CB00005B/54

9 781732 885875